CW00448954

MURDER FOR BUSY PEOPLE

Also by Tony Parsons

MURDER FOR BUSY PEOPLE

TONY PARSONS

CENTURY

1 3 5 7 9 10 8 6 4 2

Century
Penguin Random House UK
One Embassy Gardens
8 Viaduct Gardens
London SW11 7BW

Century is part of the Penguin Random House group of companies
whose addresses can be found at global.penguinrandomhouse.com.

www.penguin.co.uk

A CIP catalogue record for this book is available from the British Library.

ISBN 9781529197334 (hardback)
ISBN 9781529197341 (trade paperback)

Typeset in 14/17pt Fournier MT Std by Jouve (UK), Milton Keynes
Printed and bound in Great Britain by Clays Ltd, Elcograf S.p.A.

The authorised representative in the EEA is Penguin Random House Ireland,
Morrison Chambers, 32 Nassau Street, Dublin D02 YH68

www.greenpenguin.co.uk

Penguin Random House is committed to a
sustainable future for our business, our readers
and our planet. This book is made from Forest
Stewardship Council® certified paper.

Yuriko

&

Jasmine

&

Stan

Born 27 November 2011, died 11 May 2024.
Nothing loved is ever lost.

PART ONE

Tea and biscuits at the Black Museum

1

Old dogs rise early, as if to make the most of the time that remains.

And so it was that Stan and I were already wandering Hampstead Heath when the sun came up and turned the string of ponds to molten gold.

It felt like the first day of spring. Light early, but the cold of the winter months clinging on. A day that could go either way, weather-wise. Once upon a time there would have been three of us on these walks, but somewhere along the line my daughter Scout, busy with the tricky business of growing up, had lost the habit. So now there was just us two, me and Stan, and as I watched him the old dog paused in the sparkling new daylight, as if remembering.

Or maybe not. Possibly Stan was just staring blankly into space, with not a single thought between his extravagant Cavalier ears.

Now that he was knocking on a bit, our old boy sometimes got distracted, and lost all sense of time and sight of me, even when I was standing next to him. But lifting that button nose – once as shiny and moist as a black olive, now as parched and dry as a date – could also mean that he had picked up the scent of a rabbit or fox that had been late going home to its burrow. A dog's sense of smell is the last thing to go. And it was still so early that the night was not fully over yet on Hampstead Heath.

Then I saw the dog – the dog Stan had smelled – and I paused too. Because he was the kind of dog that would stop anyone, two or four-legged, dead in their tracks.

A big dog, a very big dog, unmoving in the treeline. A giant head of black and tan. And more than very big – massive. Even from this distance, he could only be one breed. Rottweiler.

He watched us without expression. A Rottweiler who is brought up well can be as calm as a Buddhist monk. There was no aggression in him, because there didn't need to be. He could summon all the aggression he would ever need, and more than you could ever handle, at will. For now he was as calm as the water on those golden ponds.

Stan, always a socially active dog, rashly trotted off to say hello.

I cursed, calling his name even though I knew he would not hear. A decline in his hearing was another of Stan's growing list of ailments.

So I slowly followed, looking around for the Rottweiler's owner. A lone runner in the distance was the only other sign of life. So I stopped to listen for someone calling out the name of their lost dog. But there was only birdsong.

And then, as Stan and I got closer to the Rottweiler, I saw why the owner was not calling for his dog.

There was a man on his back, unmoving, almost buried in the long grass, directly in front of the dog.

I edged closer, and closer still, then slowly knelt by his side.

The Rottweiler watched me all the way.

A green-and-gold Kennel Club tag glinted under his face. MY NAME IS BUDDY, it said.

'Good boy, Buddy,' I said. Buddy was unimpressed.

I watched Buddy and Buddy watched me as I leaned closer to his master and placed two fingers to the carotid pulse point on the side of his neck, just under the jaw and beside the windpipe. Nothing. Then I placed the same two fingers on his radial pulse, where his thumb met his wrist. Again nothing. His chest was not rising and falling. I listened for his breath for the standard ten seconds, but I already knew by now that I was never going to hear him draw breath.

This was not a young man. On his wrist was what looked like a no-brand smartphone with a white strap.

A heart-rate monitor.

I stood up, deciding it was his dodgy ticker that had killed him.

There was no sign of violence.

Murder was the last thing on my mind.

I stared at him, that pause that comes when the living contemplate the dead, and I tried hard to see the man he had been.

His thinning, silvery hair was shaved very short in what they once called a number one crop and he wore a green MA1 flying jacket with a vivid orange lining. There were Dr. Martens boots, muddy from the Heath, and his jeans were faded Levi 501s. The skin on his hands was so dry it resembled paper. He was a former Jack the Lad, a skinhead or a Mod back in the day, a tasty geezer who had lived long enough to collect his Freedom Pass.

And then I saw that he had a prison tattoo.

It was one of the classics: five dots, arranged like the face of a dice – a quincunx, they call it.

I have heard a dozen different interpretations of what the quincunx means but the one I always believed was that it represents one lonely human soul, surrounded by four high walls.

But whatever else it stood for, the tattoo meant that the dead man had done time. And what was unusual about this particular quincunx was that it was not on the dead man's hand between his thumb and index finger, which is where alumni of His Majesty's Prisons usually get their five-dots body art.

This one was engraved just below his right eye, staining his pale skin like five inky teardrops.

And it is possible that there are multiple old jailbirds out there who have made the rash decision to have the quincunx tattooed on their face. Perhaps there were prisons where having the five-dice inked on your face was once all the rage. But I had only ever known of one old con with a quincunx tattooed under his right eye.

'I know you,' I said to the dead man. 'Don't I?'

And finally the Rottweiler lifted his handsome head and growled soft and low at me, as if to give me a warning.

2

When I got back that evening after work and gym, there were strange noises coming from my home.

Music. And things being broken. And more things being broken. And laughter.

And the funny thing – the thing that shook me up most of all – was that I didn't recognise the music.

That's a scary moment, when you realise the music is no longer being made for you. That's the moment you grow old. It is an even scarier moment when you realise that this strange music is coming from your home, and someone is breaking stuff in there.

I stood on the street four storeys below our flat as behind me Smithfield meat market stirred itself for the night shift ahead. And I suddenly understood what was waiting for me up there in my home.

You hear about these parties. Every parent hears about these parties.

When your child is growing up, these parties are a part of parental mythology. You can even understand how they happen: the happy absence of the old folk for a week, or a weekend, or a long day when the old man is off to work and gym. An invitation to a few close friends that goes viral, and gets shared far too widely and recklessly in this hideously connected age. And then it's all fun and games and smashed heirlooms until the wrinklies come home or the neighbours call the cops.

Scout, my daughter, was not quite thirteen, and it felt a bit early for one of these parties.

But perhaps these kind of parties were starting earlier these days? Because here we undeniably were, and I could hear voices being raised to be heard above the unknown and unknowable music. There were shrieks, the sound of broken glass, and a pain right at the base of the spine that I thought I had stretched away at Fred's, my gym. The pain began pulsing like a toothache as I went up to the flat, still hot and clammy from Fred's, steeling myself for all those stoned and drunken teenage kids being sick in the sink and fighting among themselves and sexually experimenting.

But it wasn't that kind of party.

3

Our home – an open-plan loft that could do with a lick of paint, and a new boiler, and a fresh couple of sofas – was full of the homeless.

I recognised them from the neighbourhood. Most of them. There was the huge bearded man in camouflage kit who slept in the doorway of a boarded-up shop on the far side of the market, and who never asked for money and who never met your eye, his meagre belongings stored behind him with impeccable neatness. Some old soldier, I assumed.

And there were the two crack addicts, an improbable couple who were always together – a young man and a much older woman, a mother and son age gap – now huddled in a far corner of our loft, their heads bent together, conferring as they snacked on Lily's Kitchen Turkey & White Fish Bites for Senior Dogs as though they were a packet of cheese and onion crisps.

And the overweight kid who needed urgent psychiatric intervention who slept with his supermarket trolley in the doorway of the bookshop. And the elderly tramp forever lost in his own thoughts, his eyes staring out at the streets of Smithfield but seeing somewhere else in some other time.

And then there was Suzanne. I knew Suzanne. In fact, Suzanne was the only one of them I actually knew, and the only one I had ever spoken to, and the only one I ever gave money to. Because how can you ever help all of them?

I knew my twelve-year-old daughter would have an answer.

But Scout was nowhere to be seen.

Suzanne was a young woman who sat on the pavement outside the supermarket and minded dogs. She was one of those people who – in my mind, at least – had everything go wrong in her life that could possibly go wrong. Wayward parents. Rotten boyfriend. Horrible drugs. And then in the end, or close to the end – nowhere to live. She was perhaps ten years older than my daughter – young, so young, with the pallor of advanced addiction, and the teeth of someone who had most of their life behind them. Yet there was a sweetness about her, a light in her eye, and a smile that came slowly, and there was a gentle quality about her.

She liked looking after dogs.

Suzanne habitually clutched a child's stuffed toy – a ragged rabbit she had told me was called Mr Flopsy. When I first saw her sitting on the pavement outside the supermarket minding a couple of Labradoodles and holding her stuffed rabbit, I had assumed it was some begging technique designed to elicit sympathy and tug at the heartstrings. But I didn't believe that anymore. She seemed to genuinely find comfort in her pet stuffed rabbit. And I gave Suzanne money every time I saw her because I always thought there was a good chance it was going to be the last time I ever saw her. She looked that far gone. Suzanne was not built for a life on the streets. But then who is?

Suzanne was sitting cross-legged on the sofa by the TV with the remote in her hand. That's where the deafening music was coming from. One of those stations that lurk at the far end of the guide. Suzanne and I watched it together for a few moments. Young women in bathing suits were dancing on yachts while young men glared and gloated and contemptuously flicked banknotes at the camera.

And I wondered – *How can anyone enjoy this shit?*
You're getting old, Max.
No – already old.
You got old tonight.

I looked around the great wide-open expanse of our loft, desperately seeking Scout, my sigh of frustration coming like a punctured balloon. The boiler was wheezing like a geezer with emphysema. Our home was full of things that needed fixing.

Our guests were not all as sweet as Suzanne. My heart went out to her and to the neat old soldier and the kid who slept in the bookshop doorway. But I didn't care for the crack addicts, the odd couple who I would see late at night, leaning over their tin foil, sucking up the fumes, and trying the handles of parked cars, and I had seen the tramp with the faraway stare projectile vomiting often enough to not relish him sitting at my kitchen island.

I looked around the room. I didn't doubt they all had their stories of hard luck and bad choices. But now I just wanted my daughter.

Scout was in the kitchen, making toast for her guests. She was small for her age, bright-eyed, and to her father's gaze, impossibly pretty. Physically quite fragile but with a fire in her eyes. She was ready for a flaming row if I thought I could handle it.

She looked at me with a kind of fierce-eyed defiance and I felt the base of my spine pulse with pain. Tonight had not come out of nowhere. There were precedents.

Over the last year Scout had taken to buying a meal for the homeless and I had felt mixed emotions. A parental pride at my caring daughter, and a worry that her kindness would be used against her in ways I could not imagine.

I didn't want to argue. I just wanted the party to be over. I just wanted everybody out and my home back.

'Shall we call it a night, Scout?'

Quitting while she was ahead, Scout began herding her guests to the door.

Only Suzanne said goodnight, Mr Flopsy clutched tight to her chest.

After everyone had gone, Scout and I looked at each other.

Then we looked at the flat.

The mess wasn't as bad as it might have been. Discarded plates of buttered toast were scattered everywhere. Stan, our ruby-coloured Cavalier King Charles Spaniel, was ignoring the senior dog treats that the crack addicts had left on the floor and was busy licking the butter from the chewed crusts of a rogue slice of toast. His priorities were impeccable. Buddy the Rottweiler, our house guest, watched him impassively. But of course clearing up the mess was the easy bit.

Talking to each other – that was the hard part.

Scout and I looked at each other again. She cleared her throat.

'Do you know how many homeless people there are in this country?'

Ooh, I knew this one.

'About three hundred thousand?'

'That's a *town*. That's a *city*. And they never sleep on side streets. They always sleep on main streets. Because it's too dangerous. And we all have so much. And they have so little.'

I nodded. Couldn't argue with any of that.

And I was proud of her for caring. But I would have preferred that she didn't do the caring inside my home. Is that hypocrisy or human nature, I wondered. Possibly a bit of both.

'You want to help me clear up, Scout? It's a bit of a mess. The flat, I mean – not the world!'

I attempted a smile.

It fell on stony ground.

Scout expertly loaded the dishwasher.

She had the brisk independence of a child raised in a single-parent household. We didn't look at each other. And we didn't say much. Because we didn't need to.

She thought the homeless were all sweethearts. And I knew they were not all sweethearts. And she would have told me – *It's not about anyone being a sweetheart.* So – no need to argue then. No need to say a bloody word. Agree to differ. These days I was aware that entire conversations seemed to go by with just a dishwasher door shut just a touch too firmly, and plates put away in eerie careful silence, and toast deftly dumped in with the food waste as the dishwasher hummed across our silence.

There was so much we could have said, but it was already bloody obvious, and so we didn't bother with chatter about school nights and the unfairness of the world.

It was all there in our silence, and our polite, practical exchanges, an understanding honed under the weight of our twelve years together, and all the things we never spoke about.

'Goodnight then,' Scout said when we had finally finished and she headed for her room.

'Night, Scout.'

She touched Stan on his head and she was gone. I could hear her brushing her teeth.

I went to the window and stared out at the bustle and lights of the meat market, where the night had hours still to go. And although I had tried to comfort myself with the thought that my daughter's attempts to heal the world had precedents, I could not deny that tonight felt new.

Because having a child who is on the edge of thirteen changes everything.

You still love them, and just as much.

But they are emphatically their own person by now, and there is this bitter-sweet edge, as you realise this little nest where they have grown up will not hold them for-ever, or even much longer, because now you understand that time is running out.

You still love them when they are on the edge of thirteen.

You just don't recognise them anymore.

4

'There's not a lot on your dead man,' said Sergeant John Caine, keeper of the Black Museum. 'His name was Ray "Butch" Lewis. A bit player in one of the biggest robberies of the last fifty years. That's Butch's one and only claim to fame. And that's where you know him from, Max. Come and see.'

The Black Museum is where the Metropolitan Police remembers. The Black Museum remembers the Met's past, and the Met's dead, and two centuries of convicted criminals. It is cold, and it is dark, and the massed ranks of glass display cases make it feel like a car boot sale for long-dead villains and the police who pursued them. The Black Museum is history, and it is a bit of a mess, and although it serves as a teaching aid for young coppers about to make their way in the world, it is almost always totally silent and empty in there.

I followed John Caine to a distant corner, my gaze flicking over the glass cases.

Over the last 150 years or so, the museum has had multiple names and locations. It started out as the Central Prisoners Property Store a bit before the Jack the Ripper case was an active murder investigation. When I first came here, it was called the Crime Museum but we knew it as the Black Museum and it was in Room 101 of New Scotland Yard, up on the first floor, when the Yard was across the street from Westminster Abbey in Horseferry Road. Today the Black Museum is in the basement of the Curtis Green Building, in the new New Scotland Yard, facing Waterloo across the river. But it felt unchanged from the first day I saw it. And Sergeant John Caine remained, older but also unchanged in all the ways that matter. John was a fit and hard old-school copper, his hair still thick and cut short, his build as lean as a butcher's dog.

We walked between the glass cases.

Many of the exhibits on display were used to kill, or to attempt to kill, members of the public or the police. There are bombs, knives, umbrellas that had doubled as swords, and firearms of every description, from derringers hidden in Victorian walking sticks to submachine guns.

There were the notebooks of the detectives who hunted Jack the Ripper, and the terrorists who tried to assassinate Queen Victoria, and the death masks of men and women who were hung before the huge cheering crowds at Newgate, and a glass case containing the portrait of every serving Met police officer killed in the line of duty over the last 150 years.

There were people I had served with among those smiling portraits of the dead, and there was a woman I had loved, and would always love. But I did not linger.

Today I was here to kickstart my memory of a man with a five-dot prison tattoo under his right eye.

'I know you remember the Hole in the Wall Gang,' John said.

'It's coming back to me. Two brothers were the top boys.'

'Terry and Mick Gatti. Anglo-Italian heritage, but as South London as – what's very South London? Pie and mash. The Elephant and Castle. Millwall FC. As South London as all of that. Terry was the brains and the bollocks, Mick the muscle and bone. They both grew fabulously rich on the proceeds of their sins and yet they never did a day inside. The dead man on the Heath – Ray "Butch" Lewis – was their driver.'

In a quiet corner, we stopped in front of a large upright glass case. Inside there was a rusting safe the size of a coffin. The safe door was ajar, hanging on strangely pristine hinges. The safe was empty. There was a framed front page of a long-defunct newspaper next to it, showing a fading photograph of a young uniformed policeman, hardly out of his teens, escorting a slim blonde woman whose hands were cuffed behind her back.

The young uniformed policeman was me.

HISTORY'S BIGGEST HEIST? said the dead newspaper's banner headline.

'They didn't blow the safe,' I said. 'I forgot they never blew the safe.'

Most stolen safes were opened with gelignite or some other form of explosive.

'They didn't need to blow it,' John said. 'They took it away to a nice quiet farm in the Cotswolds and the top Peterman in the country opened it. Without key, combination or any of the stuff that goes bang.'

'Peterman?'

'Safecracker. Peterman is the old-school term for a safecracker. The etymology is unclear. *Péter* is the French verb for to burst, to break, to crack – and to pass wind. And the Peterhead prison in Aberdeenshire was famous for housing a lot of safecrackers. The Peterman who opened this safe without blowing the door off was a safecracking superstar called Ian Doherty. And Butch Lewis was a top-of-the-range getaway driver back in the day, too.'

'A bunch of criminal masterminds, eh?'

'Not quite,' John said. 'Mick Gatti, Terry's older brother, was always as thick as mince. And they had some wild young kid along with them for the heavy lifting. His name escapes me but I remember they called him The Nutjob. So criminal masterminds is probably a bit of a stretch.'

'They didn't do time, did they?'

'None of them did.' John indicated the front page. 'Not for this job. Only her. Only the woman in the picture. Only Emma Moon.'

'Emma Moon,' I repeated, staring at the front page inside its glass case. 'I remember her.'

'Of course you do.'

'And I remember the house. I had never been inside

20

anywhere like it. This mansion in Belgrave Square. You could see the queen's back garden from the top floor. It was rented by some foreign billionaire looking to launder his loot in the London property market. As they do. The safe was gone by the time I got there. And nobody ever knew what was in it, did they?'

'There were rumours. Blood diamonds. Gold bars. Rolex galore. The purest cocaine this side of Bogotá. Stacks of new notes in a dozen different currencies. But there was also meant to be some prize they were not expecting.'

I waited.

John Caine stared thoughtfully at the rusting safe.

'I don't know what that was, Max. Nobody knows. But whatever was in that safe, it was enough to bankroll the good life for the top boys in the Hole in the Wall Gang. Which was not the guy who drove the car or the guy who cracked the safe. The Gatti brothers have dined out on the contents of that safe for nearly twenty years. I imagine that those further down the food chain – the driver, the Peterman – were on a flat fee.'

I looked at the safe, remembering.

'Men died that night,' I said. 'Two of them. I saw their bodies.'

'Yes – the chief of security. Stabbed multiple times. And a gardener who turned up later to deliver some plants, the poor bastard. Killed with a single blow to the head, as I recall.'

'And Butch Lewis was the wheel man. That's where I know him from.'

'He was arrested during the big round-up after the job – they all were – but it never even went to trial. Butch did time later – but not for this one, not for the big job, his greatest hit. Butch did time later for petty drug deals that went south. That's where the lovely tattoo came from.'

'And the Hole in the Wall Gang got away with their heist.'

'Not all of them,' John said. 'Not Emma Moon.'

I leaned in closer to look at the fading front page.

Emma Moon was tall, lean and blonde in the picture. I recalled that she had been a dancer of some sort. She was in her late twenties in the photograph, which put her in her forties now. The face of the young police officer who had her in handcuffs – my face – was white with tension.

John chuckled. 'Look how young you were, Max!' he said with wonder.

It did not feel like it was me. Just as there was an unbridgeable gap between my daughter today and the baby she had once been, so it was with me and the uniformed cop in the photograph. The passing of all that time was too big a gap to cross.

But I remembered Emma Moon. I remembered how she smelled of cigarettes and flowers.

'I was straight out of Hendon,' I said. 'I was only shaving once a week. And she talked to me, I remember. She asked me – very calmly, very politely – to let her go. When I arrived at that big house and found only her and the two dead men, and the safe already gone, she knew she was going to be locked up for a long time. And she talked to me, John. She told me about her life.'

'She was a striking young thing,' John said. 'Apparently she got the crew into the house. Got them past security. She had struck up some kind of relationship with the security guard. Been working on it for months – so they say. And when romance was blossoming, someone stabbed him. The gardener was meant to be collateral damage, an unexpected visitor as the crew were on the way out with the safe. He got hit a bit too hard and his skull caved in. I don't think it was part of the masterplan. But the Gattis could not afford any witnesses. They were a serious crew who were always going to top anyone who got in their way or saw their faces.'

'Terry was the brains behind the business,' I said. 'And Mick was the blunt instrument.'

'Terry retired at thirty from the proceeds of whatever was in that safe. His less clever kid brother Mick has played flash Harry in Spain for nearly twenty years. But Terry was smart enough to get out after his big score and keep his head down. Terry never wanted to be famous. All he wanted was the lush life of a self-made criminal millionaire and the quiet joys of happy anonymity.'

'While his girlfriend did the time,' I said. 'Because Emma Moon cut no deals. She gave up no names. Not when I arrested her, and not when she was in custody, and not at her trial, and not over the last sixteen years. Never. Emma never did what they almost always all do – offered co-operation in return for a lighter sentence. She spent the best years of her life behind bars because she wouldn't talk. That's loyalty. That's love.'

'Is it?' John said. 'Or is it stupidity? Maybe it is a bit of both, Max. Love and stupidity. That deadly combination. But everybody did very well out of that job. Apart from Emma Moon. '

'She got thirty years for armed robbery. Thirty years, John! That shocked me then. It shocks me now.'

'Joint enterprise,' John said. 'Emma Moon was a secondary offender – she might not have killed those two men or ever received a penny from what was inside that safe. Yet the court treated her as if she was as guilty as the men who did.'

There was a smaller newspaper clipping inside the glass case. It must have been printed some years after the front page of Emma Moon in my handcuffs, because it was white more than yellow. An opinion piece from one of the posh papers. *An Egregious Travesty of British Justice*, it said, next to a byline picture of a floppy-haired man.

Daniel Nevermore, it said.

'Lord Nevermore,' John said. 'He's been campaigning for years to get Emma Moon out. A bit sweet on her. Maybe totally besotted. He's Lord Longford to Emma's Myra Hindley.

'Except, unlike Hindley, Emma Moon never hurt anyone.'

'Arguable,' John said. 'I never bought Lord Nevermore's line that Emma Moon was some kind of innocent bystander. Two men died and some professional villains got very rich. Not your friend Butch — he was too far down the food chain. And not Ian Doherty, who opened the treasure chest. But the Gatti brothers, Terry and Mick — they won the lottery that night. And the law was made to look stupid. Crime was made to look like it paid — big time. And it did. Because whatever was in that safe was never recovered.'

'I can still hear her voice, John. You can't see it in that photograph, but Emma Moon never stopped talking to me until they put her in the back of the car and drove her away.'

'Then you were the only one she ever talked to,' John said.

We went out to his office, which served as the reception area to the Black Museum.

John got out a couple of mugs — one said THE BEST GRANDDAD IN THE WORLD and the other commemorated the Queen's Platinum Jubilee. He put the kettle on and took out a severely depleted pack of chocolate digestives. His tough old face frowned as he concentrated on preparing our tea and biscuits.

'Emma Moon told me she had a son,' I said. I struggled to recover his name. *'David,'* I remembered. 'His name was David. He must have been around the age that Scout is now. She must have been very young when she had him. That's why she wanted me to let her go. Because

25

of David. And she told me that the boy would not live if she went away. The kid had problems. I didn't listen. I wasn't interested. I didn't know what it meant — to have a child who totally relies on you. I was too young to understand.'

'What happened to her boy?'

'I don't know,' I said, and I knew I should have thought of Emma Moon's son before today. 'But the rest of the gang got away with it, didn't they? While she's doing time for all of them.'

'Not anymore,' John said. 'Because Emma Moon gets out tomorrow.'

5

The next morning I watched Emma Moon's release from prison on the Bar Italia TV where they usually showed the Italian football, and suddenly there she was – a woman I had not seen for sixteen years.

The gold in her hair had its first streaks of silver now and she had lost that effortless twenty-something sheen I had seen on the night I arrested her. But in many ways she seemed shockingly unchanged from the woman who I had handcuffed at the big house in Belgravia all those years ago. She had a cigarette on the go, and as she took a long drag she scrunched up her eyes, squinting as if the cigarette smoke was dazzling sunshine.

Our Murder Investigation Team had taken a break to watch her get out. There were four of us in the Bar Italia: my boss, DCI Pat Whitestone, compact, careful highlights, rimless glasses and a slow smile – more like a slightly racy librarian than a senior murder detective – and our two new recruits, the boy and the girl – man and woman doesn't really say it – Detective Constable Bear Groves and Detective Constable Sita Basu. They were two Direct Entry Detectives – meaning they had joined the force straight from university rather than doing the traditional two-year minimum in uniform, the theory being that higher education was a far better preparation for modern policing than wrestling drunks in the gutter while wearing a scratchy uniform that was originally designed in the nineteenth century.

They were from the same Direct Entry intake, and although they were new recruits to our Murder Investigation Team, they were nearing the end of their two-year probation period.

They could hardly have been more different.

DC Bear Groves was a big, privately educated rugby player from Oxfordshire. DC Sita Basu was the petite, pretty daughter of a working-class family who had a small business in Wolverhampton. In his bulk and his black-rimmed spectacles, Bear was a dead ringer for Clark Kent. Sita Basu – spelled S-i-t-a B-a-s-u, she told Whitestone and me when she met us in MIR-1, as if she knew we were doddery old wrinklies who might struggle to remember her name – was small, intense, South-East Asian heritage, also in glasses, with a head girl quality about her.

'Who's called Bear in this world?' I heard Sita demanding on their first tea break.

'I am,' Bear said, blushing furiously.

They were from different worlds. But in their bewilderment, in their *what-have-I-let-myself-in-for?* demeanour, they could have been twins. It was their first day in Murder Investigation, and so far the only thing that had happened was being shown where to get the best coffee in Soho.

And now we were watching TV.

I knocked back my triple espresso as up on the Bar Italia's screen the big steel doors of HMP Bronzefield closed behind her and Emma Moon walked briskly to where the press were waiting.

She still had the same lean, understated power of the dancer she had once been; she still had that loose-limbed leggy gait that she had when they took her away. I had not known she had once been a dancer until her trial. But you could see it now. Even after all the years of imprisonment, Emma Moon still had the easy grace of a woman who had moved her body for a living, right up until the time she met Terry Gatti. Her fair hair was pulled back into a loose ponytail. She looked like a beautiful woman who was getting older and who was done with caring too much about the way she looked. She was a striking-looking woman, and you had to look closely for her scars, for the wear and tear of prison. Most prisoners carry what they call a small props bag on their release – a bag that contains the personal property they had with them when they first checked in.

But Emma Moon did not carry one of those sad little bags. Instead she had an entourage, including a large, shaven-headed man to carry her props bag for her, and who hovered by Emma Moon's side like a guard dog.

'That's the screw who fell for Emma,' Whitestone

said. 'Luka-something. Luka the boyfriend. Luka the former warden who got sweet on Emma despite everything. You know – Luka being a prison officer, and married with children, and Emma Moon doing a long stretch, and all of that.'

DC Basu looked shocked. 'An ex-warden is her boyfriend?'

'A maybe-boyfriend. I don't know how much use she will have for him now she's out.'

When prisoners get out after a long stretch, their clothes invariably look like they are from a time capsule – the dead fashion choices of long ago. But Emma Moon wore some kind of white boiler suit, like a character from *A Clockwork Orange*, or as if she had some manual work to do, and it was impossible to tell if it was some kind of style statement or purely functional.

There were two women with her. A feral-looking girl with lank brown hair, wide-eyed and nervous, still childlike at maybe thirty, and a tall, thin beauty who looked as if she was having a bad day, or bad few years, who looked vaguely familiar from that time when it was all the rage for models to look as though they were unwell.

'Oh, I do love a bit of heroin chic,' Bear laughed, and Whitestone shot him a look, shutting him up.

'Emma's entourage,' she said. 'The *Vogue* model is Summer something. And the Artful Dodger is Roxy. I can't remember what they were inside for. But that's where they met Emma Moon.'

There was also a floppy-haired, red-faced man in his sixties, holding some notes, ready to say a few words.

'Who's the haircut?' Whitestone said. 'Is that Emma's pet peer?'

'Yes, that's Daniel Nevermore,' I said. 'Lord Nevermore.'

I recognised him from the byline picture in the clipping at the Black Museum, but with ten years on the clock.

The maybe-boyfriend, the three women, the peer — they all stayed half a step behind Emma Moon as she strode towards where the world was waiting for her. As the media pack shouted their questions, Emma Moon seemed to exhale with an infinite weariness, her pale-blue eyes moving across them with the special patience that only comes from hard time.

She turned to her entourage to confer, and I looked at our two new recruits and saw they were wondering what all the fuss was about, and if Whitestone and I were ever going to get around to investigating the odd murder.

Lord Nevermore stepped up to the forest of microphones.

'The case of Emma Moon represents the most egregious travesty of justice in recent memory,' he began, with the slow, heavy cadence of the practised public speaker.

Whitestone wrinkled her nose. 'Egregious?'

I shrugged. *Search me.* But I guessed it wasn't a compliment.

Bear and Sita exchanged a look.

'Egregious,' said Bear, and gave a small self-conscious cough. 'Conspicuously bad, flagrantly shocking.'

Whitestone and I watched the big Bar Italia TV in rapt silence. Our university-educated probationers exchanged another look that they were still too new and young and nervous to express.

Why the feeding frenzy about some old con who just got out?

'The criminal world hasn't had a lot to look up to in recent years,' Pat Whitestone said, never taking her eyes from the screen, answering their unspoken question. 'But a lot of people admire Emma Moon. Most villains would sell their old mum for a few years off their sentence. And Emma Moon's a hero to some because she stayed schtum. That old-school *omerta*. She's the last of the line. The honourable crook. The one who didn't talk. The one who didn't chuck the others under the bus for an easier life.' Pat Whitestone was a small, compact woman, and she smiled faintly as she nodded at the screen. 'Emma kept the code, and behaved with honour, and gave up the best years of her life.' She looked at our young detectives, as if they might learn something today. 'Because that's the way it's meant to be among the criminal fraternity, but very rarely is.'

Lord Nevermore was stepping back, a sign of the experienced public speaker. Be brief, be sincere, be seated. There were tears shining in his eyes.

Emma Moon stepped forward. The media pack surged

closer and the two women in her entourage, the skinny girl and fallen supermodel, instinctively put themselves between Emma Moon and the rest of the world.

She's more than admired, I thought. She's worshipped.

There was scuffling chaos and while we were waiting for order to be restored, the BBC cut away from the shambolic press conference to give the day some context.

But context for the crimes of Emma Moon was thin on the ground because they could not broadcast the faces or mention the names of Terry Gatti and his crew of armed robbers because they were all innocent men in the eyes of the law.

Instead we were shown the façade of the big house in Belgravia, and the faces of the two men who died on the night – the professional bodyguard, and the unlucky gardener.

And we saw archive footage of the safe the size of a coffin when it was discovered open and empty at a farm in the Cotswolds.

And then – inevitably – there was the old photograph of Emma Moon being arrested, and the serious face of the terrified young police officer who had put the cuffs on her.

'You were so young, Max.' Pat smiled.

Our two Direct Entry Detectives made no comment, for they did not seem to understand that the uniformed officer in that old photograph was me. The young are incapable of imaging just how fleeting youth is, I reflected philosophically, sipping my triple espresso.

Then they cut back to the prison and, finally, there she was.

'Good morning,' Emma Moon said, her face suddenly breaking into a smile. There was warmth and amusement and wisdom in that smile, and everyone fell silent, and as the camera came in for a close-up, I knew a few things all at once.

Emma Moon was a woman who had lost everything. Her family. Her future. The best years of her life.

And Emma Moon was mad as hell. Her smile could not hide the anger.

And there was something else, and at first I struggled to believe it.

She spoke of plans. Her longing for prison reform (she glanced at the floppy-haired peer behind her). Her unbroken belief in love (a smile at the shaven-headed former screw beside her). Her podcast, the publication of her memoir, her deal with Netflix.

Busy, busy, busy. I wondered how she was going to fit it all in.

Because I had seen terminal illness before.

And to me it looked like Emma Moon was dying.

6

'Time,' Fred said.

I slumped on the nearest bench, heart pumping, sweat soaking, swabbing my face with the back of the big eighteen-ounce Lonsdale boxing gloves I wore, nothing in my tank, nothing in my head, suddenly aware of the music that had been playing throughout our 48-minute circuit. Some kind of electronic dance music, a girl vocalist singing about heaven walking through the door. Another song I did not know. But I liked it.

It was early evening. The working day was done. Fred's punishing circuit would make deep, restorative sleep a strong probability. And I found I craved that physical exhaustion these days. It was the only thing that guaranteed I could switch off my mind when the lights went out.

My eyes drifted up to the big widescreen TV that always played on mute in Fred's gym. There was a wafer-thin, blank-eyed model in a pristine white boiler suit staring belligerently at the camera, and for a long moment I wondered why she looked familiar. I could not work out what she was selling, or advertising, or promoting. But I

35

could tell the blank-eyed model in her white boiler suit was meant to be channelling Emma Moon.

Because suddenly Emma Moon was everywhere. As she had suddenly been everywhere sixteen years ago. The tabloids had loved her back then. They called her the Mata Hari of the Hole in the Wall Gang, depicted her – at first – as the wicked woman whose fatal charms got the bad men inside the big house to fill their boots and do their worst.

But later, at her trial, when it was abundantly clear that she was not talking, and that she would never talk, and Emma was going to be crucified alone, it was as if a switch had been hit.

Overnight, Emma Moon had become something else – a curiously romantic figure who stood by her man, even if he did not deserve it. The way she looked helped – the way you look always helps to sell the story. The leggy, flaxen-haired Bonnie who took the hit for her Clyde.

And then Emma Moon had been just as quickly for-gotten, as forgotten as the two men who died the night they stole the safe, and the circus moved on as she disap-peared into her incarceration.

But now Emma Moon was back, and now she was everywhere.

Again.

And now it was social media rather than the newspa-pers that had their say. Unbidden on my timeline, there were reflections on the style of Emma Moon. The white boiler suit she wore to get out had hit a sweet spot. True crime bloggers, podcasters and VJs – digital ghouls of every hue – were sharing their thoughts about her, even with those of us who had absolutely no interest in what they thought about anything. A couple of books were said to be in the works. Emma Moon was rumoured to have done her own podcast, recorded in her cell, so they said, and I thought I might give it a listen if I ever got around to working out how exactly you listened to podcasts.

But I could not deny it. Something in me wanted to hear her side of things.

'Stretch,' said Fred. With his shoulder-length silver hair and deep Mediterranean tan, he looked like an incredibly fit pirate.

While he went off to see about Fred business on the other side of the gym that bore his name, I pulled off the big Lonsdale gloves and stretched my calves, my quads, my hamstrings, the pain in my back throbbing through it all, as though it had moved in for good. When I looked up at the TV screen the girl in the white boiler suit was still there, staring her challenge, and when her lips and hips began to move, I thought – *Ah. It's a song.*

I rolled out a mat and got down on my knees, the pain in my back telling me this really wasn't a great idea.

'Crazy,' a voice said above me.

It was a young woman, smiling, gently perspiring as if she was at the start of her workout. There was a rolled-up yoga mat under her arm.

I had never seen her before although new faces came and went all the time at Fred's. It was a difficult thing to stick with forever, because it was so hard, and because finding an excuse not to come back and do it again was always the easiest thing in the world.

I must have looked blank because she nodded at the big silent screen, and the singer in her white boiler suit. 'Crazy that people are so obsessed with her. After all these years. Emma Moon. Like some – I don't know – Princess Diana of true crime. They just can't get enough!'

I rolled over and stretched out into my plank.

The young woman got down by my side, in a plank of her own.

'I'm Mads,' she said. 'Mads Kool.'

I nodded. 'So your real name's Madeleine?'

Mads Kool was shocked. 'How'd you know?'

'Just guessing.'

Fred's was a serious gym. The friendliest place in town, but not one of those gyms that encourages small talk and mindless banter and social interaction when you are meant to be pushing your body to its absolute limit.

By chatting during our mutual planks, this young woman – Mads Kool, was it? – was breaking some unspoken, unwritten Fred protocol.

But then she was new.

'So what was it like?' she said.

I thought she was talking about doing one of Fred's circuits. We had just completed one of those circuits where you do not stop, where you are constantly working. Three minutes on the heavy bag, upper-cut bag and speed bag all interspersed with one minute of more work – burpies, press-ups, assorted strength exercises and jumping on and off a step for a long sixty seconds – when your body was telling you that – no, when your body *insisted* – that it should be recovering. The 48-miniute circuits were the heart of the true Fred experience.

'If it wasn't hard,' I said, reaching for one of Fred's favourite catchphrases, 'then everybody would do it.'

'No,' she said. 'Putting the handcuffs on Emma Moon. What was that like? What did you feel that night? What—'

'Who are you again?'

'I told you. I'm Mads Kool.'

'You're a journalist.'

Her face filled with scorn.

'*Influencer*. Nobody's a journalist anymore.'

Fred returned.

'Gloves back on,' he told me.

'What did it feel like?' Mads Kool repeated as I got to my feet, pulling the big Lonsdale gloves back on. There was a flicker of contempt in her eyes. 'Did you feel like a big man? Did it make you feel like some sort of pound store Clint Eastwood slapping those handcuffs on an innocent wife and mother?'

I was moving away from her, towards the line of bags. She followed me.

'This is Mads Kool,' I told Fred. 'She's an influencer.'

'Mads Kool, is it?' he said. 'She'll look funny when she's fifty.'

'Do you feel guilty that she did all those years

inside – that she gave her life – for the crimes of others?'
she said. I turned to look at her. 'And do you ever think
about her son?' she asked me.

'Oy,' Fred said, jerking a thumb towards the exit.

'Pathetic,' she told me, the smile curling with real
scorn. 'I think you are a pathetic human being. And you
won't even give me a fucking quote.'

'Now, Mads Kool,' Fred said.

And as she made her way out, he turned to me. 'Up or
down?'

'Up,' I said.

It was always best to start up, it was always good policy
to do the hardest work first. Get what you knew you had
to do out of the way as quickly as possible.

Fred got down on the yoga mat where I had done my
plank, lay on his back and lifted his heels into the air,
and called out to one of the young trainers to start the
clock.

A digital bell pinged.

I went to the heavy bag and began banging it up top,
where a man's head would be. Left-right-left-right, getting into my rhythm. After sixty seconds we would swap
and I would get down on the mat and elevate my legs for
a minute. And then we would swap again, and I would
punch the bag down below, where a man's ribs would be,
and then we would swap again.

'You're so lucky to be training,' Fred said.

Gasped, really.

He was nearly as knackered as me.

It worked for me with Fred, and it had worked for so many years, because he always did exactly what I did. He was not one of those personal trainers who barked orders at you like some kind of drill sergeant, who just stood there counting and looking superior.

Fred always did the same work as me.

And now I banged the bag like a man chopping wood, nothing in my mind but the rhythm, and the effort, and the knowledge that I had done this ten thousand times before and so I knew I could do it now, no matter how tired I was, and how loud the voice in my head was telling me to stop. I only stopped when the bell pinged again, and as I made my way to the mat I saw myself on television.

Because suddenly I was everywhere again too.

The young police officer leading away a woman who was just a few years older than him, but who seemed like she was from an older generation, the metal of the handcuffs glinting.

And the funny thing about that photograph is that it was the young policeman who looked scared of what was to come, and not the woman who was under arrest.

Emma Moon was everywhere now, or so it seemed, and I was there with her in that one photograph, bound together like mountaineers.

Half a lifetime ago.

Before Scout. Before my wife. Ex-wife, I mean.

41

Before I had any idea of what I was really doing as a cop, or a man, or a human being.

And now she was back.

A boxing glove smacked me around the back of the head.

'Protect yourself at all times,' Fred reminded me.

7

'Tonight – on *Newsnight*. A story about the criminal justice system. About a woman controlled by men. And about punishment and the possibility of rehabilitation. *Newsnight* talks to Emma Moon and the man who has campaigned, for years, for her release.'

The theme music swirled. I could see Emma Moon in the background, still in her white boiler suit, and Daniel Nevermore beside her. And the empty chair where the interviewer would sit.

'Good evening. The crime – the job, as they call it in the game – is up there with the Great Train Robbery, Brink's-Mat, and the Hatton Garden heist. Yet only one person was ever convicted of the Buckingham Palace heist.'

That had never really caught on, the Buckingham Palace heist, I thought, staring at Stan snoring beside me on the sofa. A few of the papers had run with the Buckingham Palace heist – because you could see the queen's back garden from the top floor of the big house in Belgravia – but it had never stuck. The Hole in the Wall heist is what we had called it in our game.

Not as catchy, admittedly.

The *Newsnight* presenter was back, sitting down with her guests now.

'Older viewers will remember the face of the twenty-eight-year-old woman who they took away that night.'

That photograph again. I still didn't recognise myself.

'And now – for the first time ever – she tells her side of the story. Emma Moon – and campaigner Lord Daniel Nevermore – welcome to *Newsnight*.'

Emma Moon was staring off into what looked like the distance. Somehow I knew that she was looking at her photograph. Our photograph. She had a faraway smile on her face, and it grew wider as she shook her head.

The interviewer was leaning forward earnestly.

'Emma Moon – your conviction for armed robbery has been called one of the greatest travesties of justice in the criminal justice system. Is that how you feel?'

'Well,' Emma Moon said gently, still staring into the middle distance. 'I was twenty-eight when they put me away and I was forty-four when I came out. And I think you need to be a woman to understand what that means – the scale of the loss. I look at that old fading photograph now and think – so pretty, I was, and why could I never see it at the time? Why did I doubt myself, and hate my looks, and want to change my hair, my face, my body? So pretty she was – that girl they handcuffed, the girl who stood in the dock, the girl they sent away from her life – a life that could have been a good life, full of kindness and love.' She turned her attention to the presenter. 'That's what I think.'

Nevermore cleared his throat. His face looked even ruddier than usual under the studio lights. He began to stutter.

'The – the – the case of Emma Moon represents society's longing for punishment – *not* justice, or anything *resembling* justice. This woman – this innocent woman – served sixteen years for a crime she did not commit.'

'Didn't your family own the house where Ms Moon was arrested?' the interviewer said.

The old campaigner gave a haughty twitch. 'My *father* – not my family.'

She gave him an ironic BBC smile. 'My apologies.'

'And he still does, among other properties. But of course I felt Emma's arrest more keenly as it happened, as it were, under my father's roof.'

That BBC smile grew wider. 'One of your father's roofs.'

'Indeed.'

The interviewer nodded, relieved by Nevermore's intervention but anxious for Emma to snap out of her wistful reverie and play the game.

'You say *innocent woman*, Lord Nevermore. But Ms Moon was prosecuted under the joint enterprise doctrine, meaning she was considered just as guilty in the eyes of the law as those who actively perpetrated the crime. And her sentence reflected this.'

Nevermore's face flushed with sudden fury. The old toff had been expecting a soft touch, not this line of questioning. 'That's as may be—'

The interviewer cut across him.

'Emma Moon – do you feel bitterness today?'

She was silent in the bright BBC2 lighting, so the interviewer ploughed on, looking for a question that might elicit a suitable response.

'For the length of your sentence? Towards a criminal justice system that wanted someone – anyone – to pay for a crime that was committed by others? And towards prison itself? You have spent the last sixteen years of your life in jail – what do you feel is the greatest misconception about prison?'

Emma Moon nodded.

'This is what the public always fail to understand about prison – they are not locking you *up*. It is far worse than that. They are locking you *away*. They are locking you away from everything and everyone you love. They are – ironically enough – locking you away from the only things that matter, the things that may have saved you, the things that could have forced you to be good. Like my son. Like David. My son – my beautiful, anxious boy – I could have saved him if I had been on the outside. My child would have lived if his mother had been there. And I never was. A mother's love and good professional help – I would have found the best! – and I could have saved him. They say there is no death sentence in this country, but that is a lie. Because my son – my fragile boy – was sentenced to death when they put me away.'

All this without a hint of self-pity, or a single tear. I was shamed by her goodness, by her decency. The memory of the handcuffs I put on her dug into my flesh.

'Who do you blame?' the interviewer said, and she and Nevermore both stared at Emma Moon as she thought about her answer.

'I blame – a lot of people, to tell you the truth.'

Silence in the studio.

'I was not locked away for the two men who died, and the fortune that was spirited away. I was locked away because of the man who *lived*. The man I loved.'

The interviewer touched her earpiece in frantic response to desperate words from the gallery.

But Emma Moon got it.

'The man I cannot name for legal reasons,' she said, almost smiling. 'The man I refused to betray, the man who sleeps with another woman tonight – younger, firmer, prettier than I ever was – even in my twenties! – tonight, and every night. Great crimes live in history. People remember. They do. All that money – impossible money – dragging a trail of blood and misery and ruined lives in its wake. People know the crime. But they don't know me.'

And now Emma Moon was ignoring her interviewer, and staring straight down the camera.

'But you are starting to know me now,' she said. 'And perhaps you will get to know me even better. They will

47

tell you — even now, as you did — that I served sixteen years because I was as guilty as the rest of them. That I did sixteen years for conspiracy to rob. That I did sixteen years because two men died. And I am sorry for those deaths. I truly am. But that is not the reason they put me away.'

The interviewer was touching her earpiece. Lord Nevermore was staring open-mouthed at the woman whose release he had campaigned for, his face flushed scarlet.

'My name is Emma Moon,' she said. 'And I did sixteen years for love.'

8

Buddy the Rottweiler sat in the passenger seat of my old BMW X5, as placidly stoic as a heavyweight boxer on his day of rest.

Stan was compulsively licking his paws on the back seat, his great big Manga eyes bulging with anxiety. Our dog was never fond of car rides. But Buddy gazed around calmly as we pulled into the camping and caravan site early the next morning, the glint of recognition in his eyes.

Oh, yeah, he was clearly thinking. *I know this place.*

And I looked at the caravan site too and I thought – *Whoever got rich from that job, it sure as hell wasn't Butch Lewis.*

There was every kind of mobile home on a field the size of an airstrip. Motorhomes, caravans, tents, tepees and RVs. You could stay here for a night, or a weekend, or you could stay for a lifetime. At the centre of the field were the backpackers in tents. On the outer rim there were older residents who were here for years. There were flower beds scattered about, a game attempt to give the place a homely feel, but the space was too large, and a gritty wind whipped off the London orbital.

I found the address I was looking for. It was a caravan on bricks, a mobile home that was never going to be anything remotely resembling mobile. There were faces at the window. Three young children, all girls. By the time I got out of the car, they were out of the caravan and coming for their dog. A woman appeared in the doorway, puffing on a vape. Painfully thin, her pale hair turning white. Somewhere in her fifties but looking older, much older.

It takes its toll, being married to a man with a five-dice tattoo on his face.

The woman came out of the caravan and we nodded and both watched the children fussing over Buddy, who reared his massive head back and grinned with bashful delight. Stan hovered by my side, eager to be gone.

'I'm Val Lewis. You're the one who found my Raymond?'

'Yes, ma'am.'

'And you're a policeman?'

'Yes, but I was just walking my dog on the Heath when I found him.'

The girls and Buddy took off. One of them had produced a well-chewed toy duck that Buddy apparently favoured.

'I thought they might put him down. Old Buddy there.'

I nodded. They had seriously thought about it. The Dog Support Unit had Buddy down as a dangerous dog after he took a chunk of trouser from one of the attending officers. Nobody would go near him after that. So I took him home just as an Authorised Firearms Officer was reaching for his Heckler & Koch.

'And you looked after him,' Val Lewis said.

'He's been no trouble.'

We watched the children disappear around the side of the caravan, Buddy gambolling beside them like a runaway truck. I watched the woman bend to pet Stan, wincing with pain at some protest from her thin limbs. Stan responded to her hand immediately, recognising a dog lover, always alive to the possibility of treats being offered.

'I'm sorry for your loss, Mrs Lewis.'

She continued petting Stan.

'Val,' she said.

'I am sorry for your loss, Val.'

There was an awkward silence. But an awkward silence never lasts long between dog owners.

'She's an old one,' Val said, nodding at Stan.

There was often considerable confusion about Stan's gender. He was so pretty, his ears so flamboyantly lush, that people meeting him for the first time found it hard to believe he was male.

'He's getting up there,' I said.

'Boy then, is he?'

'Stan.'

'Good name.'

We both considered Stan. His tongue lolled out the right side of his mouth as he panted with inexplicable anticipation. The bottom of my spine throbbed in sympathy, a reminder that the years were passing for me too.

51

'Stan's had a few teeth out,' Val said. 'That's how you tell their age. That's why the tongue sticks out.'

'He got on well with your Buddy.'

'Buddy's a gentle boy. They say you should never encourage aggression in a Rottweiler, because it is there anyway if they ever need to call on it. So don't try teaching them to be tough. Because they already know.'

She had the accent of the Cockney diaspora, a Londoner whose family had moved out of the city a generation or two ago. And I knew that, despite our bonding over dogs, I made her uneasy.

Not me. My job.

'I just wanted to make sure Buddy got home safely,' I said, looking at Stan, for I was keen to be away too.

Val remembered her manners.

'Please,' she said. 'I've just put the kettle on.'

So we went inside the caravan and I sat at the tiny kitchenette table while she prepared tea.

'They love him,' she said. 'My grandchildren, I mean. That mangy old mutt, I mean. They think the light shines.'

The caravan was full of the detritus of childhood. Homework, backpacks, discarded clothing everywhere.

'Your grandchildren live with you?' I asked.

She joined me at the table. 'Our daughter has . . . issues,' she said, as if *issues* was a word that she had learned to say. 'Substance abuse. She does her best with them, bless her. But sometimes her best is not good enough.' She sipped her scalding tea. 'You have children?'

'A girl. Twelve. Well, nearly a teenager now.' I picked

up my tea, It was too hot to hold, let alone drink. 'Scout,' I said.

'Like the book.'

'Yes, like the book. From *To Kill a Mockingbird.*'

She nodded in the direction of her grandchildren. 'The biggest one is doing that book at school,' she said. And then for the first time she looked directly at me. 'You've done us a great kindness,' she said. 'Finding Raymond. And then looking after Buddy. Thank you.'

I nodded, picked up my tea, took a first sip. I looked around the caravan, trying to think of something to say.

Val Lewis had a laugh at that.

'Were you expecting something grander? I know what people think. My husband was on *that job*. One of the Hole in the Wall Gang! People know – the police know – even if he never went down for it. *He must have a fortune stashed away somewhere!* But he wasn't what you think. He was just the driver. He was one of those men who are on the minimum wage for a lifetime. Raymond didn't know what he was getting into that night.' She sipped her boiling tea. 'And he certainly didn't kill those men.'

I thought of the five dots tattooed under Butch Lewis' right eye. Hardly the lifestyle choice of the innocent bystander, even if it also wasn't the move of a criminal mastermind who wanted to stay undetected. She read the scepticism on my face.

'That stupid tattoo? I told him he would regret it one day, and he did. At the first sports day of our oldest grandchild. Athletic, she is. Good at games. *Watch me win, Grandad!* But nobody was watching the sack race. Nobody was watching the egg-and-spoon race. Because all the parents were looking at the old bloke with a prison tattoo on his mush!' She sighed, and it had the weight of the years in it. 'My Raymond was not always the sharpest tool in the box. But he had a good heart.' We could hear the sound of childish laughter at the door of the caravan. 'And he lived for our girls.'

'Mrs Lewis?'

'Val.'

'I am not here to interview you, Val. Or to make judgements. I am not a policeman today. I am just a man returning a dog to their owner.'

'They all did all right out of that night,' she said. 'At least Mick and Terry Gatti did. I don't know about the rest of them. Butch got a flat fee, and I don't think they even paid him *that*. He was just a grease monkey from Lewisham who could handle a motor. He was a mechanic. That was his job. Cars – that's all he knew, and he didn't know much, it's true. But they all did all right, didn't they? The rest of them.'

'Apart from the woman,' I said. 'Apart from Emma Moon. She did sixteen years.'

Butch Lewis's widow smiled wryly.

'Well, the woman always gets the blame! My daughter gets the blame for not raising her children. But where's their bloody dad? Why isn't it his responsibility too?'

I finished my tea. I stood up.

And suddenly I saw the tears in her eyes, and felt the extent of her loss.

She was wringing her hands, and I saw they were red and raw from this life, this poverty, and bringing up her granddaughters.

And now she would have to do it alone.

'Please,' she said. 'Do they have to cut him up? I would prefer them not to.'

I nodded, my heart going out to her. 'There has to be an autopsy because your husband was found in a public place.'

'But they know already, don't they? It was his heart.'

'If you die in public, or if you die at home, then there has to be an autopsy.'

'I can't stand the thought of Raymond being all cut up.'

'I'm sorry, Val. I really am.'

'I don't know what we are going to do without him.'

I hesitated. Her husband dead, her screw-up daughter on smack, those three kids with a lot of growing up to do.

And I saw now what I had missed when I walked into the caravan. There were photographs everywhere. The proud grandparents and their granddaughters. The special kind of grandparent.

The grandparent who has to raise two generations.

'My grandmother brought me up,' I said. 'When my parents were gone.'

It was the best I could do, and it was the most I could offer.

But she took it as I had hoped. Then did not speak as she escorted Stan and me to the car.

As I took out my keys, I felt her light, feathery touch on my arm.

'What did he look like?' she said. 'Raymond. That morning you found him?'

I thought of that blank, stricken face half buried in the grass, all life flown from him, looking like they always look, like some poor imitation of life.

'He looked at peace,' I lied.

9

Scout and I still had our good days. Even when your kid is pushing thirteen, you still get those good days like the days you had when they were growing up.

Great days, I mean.

There was a growing list of things we had stopped doing together. We had – somewhere along the line – stopped walking Stan together. I had stopped reading her a bedtime story some years ago. We never watched anything on TV together, and it felt like long ago and far away when we had spent all our free time sitting on the sofa endlessly watching *Frozen*. But there was one old tradition that still remained. Every Saturday morning we still had breakfast together at a window table in Smiths of Smithfield.

I watched her ordering. She had the polite shyness of the child who had grown with a menu in her hands.

'Please may I have . . .'

When we were waiting for our breakfast, I scrolled through my phone, looking at cinema times.

'*The Little Mermaid* is on at the Everyman,' I said.

She shot me a look, as if insulted at this outrageous

slur on her twelve-year-old maturity. And then she soft-ened. Her face broke into that gap-toothed smile that always tugged at my heart.

'I guess it could be *funny*, couldn't it? Do you know the book?'

I shook my head. Stan was snoring between my feet, his tongue hanging out the way it does in an older dog who has lost a few front teeth to the vet. I thought of Val Lewis.

'Let's just say that while Disney may do *The Little Mermaid*, Hans Christian Andersen didn't do Disney,' Scout said.

I nodded, pretending I knew what she was talking about.

'She's not even called Ariel in the book,' Scout said. 'She's just the eponymous Little Mermaid.'

I stared with the slack-jawed shock of the parent who has just heard their child say *eponymous* for the first time.

'She turns into *sea foam* at the end of the book,' Scout continued. 'I can't see her turning into soap suds at the end of the latest Disney take, can you?'

'No, but – as you say – it might be funny.'

'It might be funny.'

And so we finished our breakfast and I ordered a couple of tickets for *The Little Mermaid* – because it could be *funny* – and the dog stirred as we rose, Scout taking charge of Stan.

It was a big bright spring morning in Smithfield, everyone gone for the weekend apart from the locals, the

800-year-old meat market all closed up and silent until the small hours of Monday morning.

We walked under the market's ancient arch, and past the spot where Bill Sykes dragged Oliver Twist, past the line of old red telephone booths and the plaque on the spot where they executed William Wallace, and it felt as if the city belonged to us.

There was a feeling coming over me that I vaguely remembered. Ah, yes. I was *happy*. Because I had thought that going to the cinema together was one of those experiences that were behind Scout and me now. And yet here we were – off to see the new Disney version of *The Little Mermaid*, even if we were only going for a few cheap laughs.

There was a strip of restaurants and bars and pubs and shops on the far side of the market that were all closed but, as always, music was pouring from the flat above one of them.

The sign below the window had been worn away by more than half a lifetime of weather and work.

MURPHY & SON
Domestic and Commercial Plumbing and Heating
'Trustworthy' and 'Reliable'

We went around the back of the shops and up a flight of stairs. Mrs Murphy opened the door, her large family milling around in the background.

'He's such a good boy!' Mrs Murphy cried, scratching behind Stan's ears, and I felt a surge of gratitude. Who else would look after our elderly Cavalier for us at such short notice? Biscuit, the Murphys' bandy-legged old mongrel, padded down the hallway and stared blindly at us, lifting his nose with disbelief at Stan's scent.

More Murphys tumbled down the hall to greet us.

There is this theory that ageing is not gradual. You don't look a day older every day for five years – you suddenly look five years older all at once. That was the way I felt about Mrs Murphy's tribe. Her granddaughter, Shavon, was a year younger than Scout but suddenly a head taller. Then there was Shavon's kid brother Damon, also far bigger than I remembered, and Baby Mikey, who had not been a baby for years, and must have been knocking on nine. Mrs Murphy's husband, Big Mikey, was always Clint Eastwood thin but looking actually gaunt now, his neat silver hair turned to white. And Little Mikey, always a large man, was dangerously overweight these days, and his wife Siobhan, who I remembered as a girl, now looked like a grown-up lady.

And I guess Scout and me and Stan looked older too.

The Murphy flat was always teeming with life – music and children and dogs. But now I could feel something else, and it was time passing.

We left Stan doing the circular butt-sniffing dance with old Biscuit and got out of there.

Then we caught a black cab to the Everyman cinema in Hampstead, as we had for countless afternoons when

Scout was growing up. It was nearly full with a mixed crowd of little girls with their parents and dating couples who just wanted to canoodle in the dark for a couple of hours.

And then there was us, me and Scout, cynical smirks all primed, ready to guffaw and mock in perfect harmony.

And we did – at first. We laughed so hard that we nearly dropped our cheesy fries from Spielburger next door when Ariel gave up her voice, her power to breathe underwater and her tail – all part-exchanged for a pair of human legs. But then we stilled as the story unfolded, and I heard Scout sniff in the darkness when Prince Eric – bewitched – marries the wrong girl.

I managed to hold it together quite well until Ariel's father, Triton, sacrifices himself for his daughter and is turned into what looks like sea foam by a pair of moray eels.

I dabbed at my eyes. A father did that for his daughter. Just think.

We emerged smiling into the daylight.

'That was quite good,' I said. 'Surprisingly good.'

'You were choking up!' Scout laughed.

'No, no – I just had some Spielburger cheesy fry in my eye.'

'Yeah, right.'

We walked through the Saturday crowds in silence, both embarrassed and delighted that we had been so moved by *The Little Mermaid*.

'But there's one of those songs, isn't there?' Scout said

as we looked for a cab, trying to regain some of the hard-earned seen-it-all-before maturity of a twelve-year-old girl.

'One of *what* songs?'

'You know – one of *those songs* where the hero explains how nobody understands her – and she feels very sad about it all – and now, you know, she has to *follow her destiny*. One of those songs.'

'That song, yeah. I know what you mean. That's actually always my favourite bit, that song. When they have to be themselves and, yeah, follow their dream and all of that.'

'*Why can't they see?*' Scout half-sung. '*I've got to be me!*'

'*Because*,' I croaked, '*I've just got to be free.*'

'*Please let it be – why can't they see? – it's all about me.*'

'It's all about me!' I was impressed. 'That's a great title, Scout. For one of those songs.'

She shook her head. She disliked too much praise. Perhaps all children dislike too much praise. I only knew about Scout.

She was silent, her smile fading, and I was anxious to recapture the mood.

'We should write a song called "It's All About Me",' I said. 'And sell it to Disney for a pile of money!'

We laughed together as we had not laughed for a long time.

And as we headed for home, I thought – We will be all right after all. This family is fixable.

Even thirteen is going to be OK. Even the teenage

years. We will get through them together and, even if almost everything changes, we will still be able to find things to laugh about together.

My boss called just as we were arriving home.

'The late Raymond "Butch" Lewis,' DCI Pat White-stone said. 'Whatever killed him, it wasn't his heart.'

10

His prison tattoo was fading now.

The last time I had seen those five inky teardrops etched just below the right eye of Butch Lewis, they had looked so vivid that they could have been fresh from the body artist's needle. Now the five-dot quincunx looked washed-out, and about to perform the great vanishing act of death.

Butch looked like every corpse I had ever seen. He looked like a bad photocopy of the man he had been. The spirit had flown, or dissolved, or done whatever it is that spirits do. But he was not here anymore.

And I shivered.

Because they keep the temperature just a touch above freezing in the Iain West Forensic Suite of the Westminster Public Mortuary.

Pat Whitestone stood with Elsa Olsen, forensic pathologist, on the other side of the steel table, the three of us all in blue scrubs and hairnets.

I caught Whitestone's eye. I could not fathom why we were here. It was Saturday evening and there was no real mystery in the passing of Butch Lewis. Was there?

'Thanks for opening up the shop after hours, Elsa,' she said.

'This one is worth the overtime,' Elsa said.

'Just listen,' Whitestone told me.

Elsa smiled like the perfect host. She was one of those black-haired, blue-eyed Scandinavians that defy the central casting stereotype, and she spoke the clipped perfect English of the lifetime expatriate.

'This death looks straightforward,' she began. 'No sign of foul play. No defensive wounds. And cause of death was cardiac arrest.'

'A heart attack,' I said.

Elsa shook her head.

'No, not a heart attack. The cause of death was cardiac arrest,' she said.

I shook my head. I didn't know the difference.

'A heart attack is a catastrophic problem with circulation. A blocked artery stops blood from reaching the ticker.'

'Is that a medical term, Elsa?' I said. 'Ticker?'

We all chuckled. We liked to have a few laughs in that freezing place of the dead. Then Elsa grew serious. 'But a cardiac arrest is an *electrical* problem,' she said. 'There's a malfunction in the heart and it can't pump blood to the brains, the lungs and other organs.'

She gently touched the wrist where Butch Lewis had worn his no-brand smartphone with the white strap. His heart-rate monitor. I wondered if it was back in the caravan with his widow. His skin was the colour of old milk where the strap had been.

'Mr Lewis wore that heart-rate monitor for twenty years after a scare as a younger man. Arrhythmia. An issue with the rhythm of the heart. Pressures of his day job, no doubt. But his arteries had nearly a zero calcium build-up, and were not the arteries of someone who was going to die of a heart attack. Mr Lewis had never had a heart attack – which increases the risk of cardiac arrest. And despite his history of a racing heart, in my estimation he could have lived to a hundred years old and he was never going to have a heart attack.'

'So something fatally disrupted the rhythm of his heart,' Whitestone said.

Elsa nodded. 'Strange, isn't it? Inexplicable even – especially in that idyllic setting where he died. Where you found him, Max. I can see it! The sun coming up on Hampstead Heath on a beautiful spring morning. The ponds shining in the sunshine. London smelling better than it would for the rest of the day.'

We all stared in silence at the body of Butch Lewis.

'You are both aware of the four questions of death we always have to ask in here,' Elsa said. '*Cause? Mechanism? Manner?* And *Time?* And at first glance, the answers all appear clear enough. The cause was a massive cardiac arrest. There is no evidence of foul play, so the mechanism and manner are a fatal medical emergency. Mr Lewis had an algor mortis – temperature of death – of 96 degrees Fahrenheit. Normal body temperature is 98.6. So he had not been dead for more than an hour before you found him, Max. The five triggers of cardiac arrest are a heart attack, a severe haemorrhage, electrocution, a drug overdose – and hypoxia.'

Whitestone and I waited.

'Hypoxia is a sudden drop in oxygen levels,' Elsa said. 'Look at his lips and fingernails.'

We leaned in closer to the body on the steel table.

'What do you notice?' Elsa said.

'Blue,' I said. 'His lips and fingernails are blue.'

'You can see it more on the lips than the nails,' Whitestone said. 'But, yes, I see it now. They're blue.'

'The blue lips and nails you can see are the main distinguishing feature of hypoxia,' Elsa said. 'There's suddenly not enough oxygen available to the blood and tissues. The lips and nails turn blue.'

'So – what? He suddenly could not breathe?' Whitestone said. 'And it killed him?'

Elsa nodded again. 'And if Mr Lewis here had been an accountant or a delivery driver then I would sign the paperwork and think – that's a bit odd. Why did he suddenly stop breathing so quickly that it killed him? But he wasn't an accountant, was he? And he wasn't a delivery driver. Mr Lewis was a career criminal who participated in one of the most famous robberies of the century. A career criminal who, as I understand it, was never convicted for what he did. For what they all did that night.'

'What are you suggesting, Elsa?'

'It's just a hypothesis, Max.'

67

'Something – or someone – stopped him breathing?' I said. 'Is that even possible? I mean, as a medical fact – can it actually happen?'

'That would be a conditional *yes*,' Elsa said. 'If a person is subjected to sufficient pressure – and I mean a terror unlike anything they have ever known in their life – then adrenaline is pumped into their system as the heart attempts to get more blood to the muscles. And that can cause a cardiac-related event that can prove fatal. In 1938, Orson Welles put H. G. Wells' *War of the Worlds* on his radio show and thousands of people thought it was all real – they thought the earth was actually being invaded by aliens. And thousands took to the streets, looking at the skies, waiting for the invader. And a contemporary report in the *Washington Post* said that one man died.' She paused. '*He died of pure terror.*'

We all stared at the body of Butch Lewis.

I shook my head in disbelief.

'What are you saying happened to Butch Lewis?' Pat Whitestone asked.

'Someone scared to him death,' Elsa Olsen said.

11

DCI Whitestone and I stood on the steps of Westminster Public Mortuary, and I was aware that something had changed in the air while we had been inside. You could smell it, hear it, taste it. The evening was scented with something burning. In the distance were shouts that rose above the eternal hum of the city. And then the sirens. Trouble, I thought. Trouble out there on this Saturday night. Riot time in the city.

'But why would you scare someone to death?' I said. 'Why not just stab them? Or shoot them? It seems so much more – I don't know – final.'

We began walking towards New Scotland Yard, and towards the sound of tonight's trouble, whatever it was.

'Talk me through that night,' Whitestone said. 'The night you put the handcuffs on Emma Moon.'

Pat Whitestone was my friend, and she had been my friend for years. But she was also my boss. I removed my hands from my pockets, took a deeper breath.

'I was just a week out of Hendon,' I said. 'Wet behind the ears, and everything else. Still self-conscious about wearing my uniform. Walking the beat in Knightsbridge – in the days when a pair of coppers still walked the beat. There were meant to be two of us, but my mate went home sick halfway through the shift. So I was alone when I got the call – robbery in progress, all units attend. And it turned out I was closest. And I saw the bodies before I saw her. The gardener, just inside the front door. He was young, not much older than me, a New Zealander. A good-looking kid with his head caved in. George Eapia. His name was George Eapia. The bodyguard was down the hall. Sitting down. Against the wall. Eyes open. Heavyweight, shaven head. He looked like a bodyguard. He was ex-Special Forces, so they said, but you never know if that's true. Andrew Wojcik. He had been stabbed more than once.'

'You remember their names.'

I shook my head. 'I have been reading about that night since I went to the Black Museum and learned that Butch Lewis was the driver. The thing I really remember – the thing I have never forgotten – is that I had never been so scared in my life. I looked at those dead men and I thought I was going to be killed next. But they were all gone. The Hole in the Wall Gang. The Gatti brothers and company. Butch Lewis had chauffeured them off into the night. Apart from her. Emma Moon. She was in some kind of study. A library, an office. Sitting at the desk. There was a big ragged hole in the wall where the safe had been ripped out. It was as if she was waiting for me, or as if it was too late to run. But it wasn't that at all.

70

She was waiting for her boyfriend to come and claim her. And he never did.'

'Terry Gatti,' Pat said. 'He lives very quietly now, and very well. Beautiful young wife – Helen something – the Emma Moon upgrade. Men always go for a younger version of what they've got at home already. I wonder if he was ever planning to come and get her?'

I had a foggy memory of a car slowing down outside that big house just as I went inside the front door. It did not stop. And I wondered if that was just a curious passer-by watching a policeman walk into a crime scene or if that had been Emma Moon's ride. The driver, whoever he was, saw my uniform and did not stick around.

'She didn't run because she thought that he loved her as much as she loved him,' I said. 'When I found her, it was like she was just starting to understand that she had been abandoned. And she talked to me, Pat. We could hear sirens, almost immediately, coming for them, coming for her, and she said – *Just let me walk away, please*. That struck me – she said *please*. She had nice manners. *Because I have a son*, she said. *And he is twelve years old. And his name is David. And he will not survive without me. So please let me go. Not for me – for my boy.*'

'That was a tad optimistic, wasn't it? Two dead bodies, blood on the walls, a safe gone containing God knows what – and she asked you for a free pass? You must have kind eyes, Max. And what did the young constable say to her?'

'Nothing. I did what I was trained to do. Subdue and

71

control. It wasn't hard. I didn't have to use any force, and I was very happy about that. We were quite gentle with each other. I was all fingers and thumbs with the cuffs. I had never done it for real before. I had only done it in training, up in Hendon, giggling with my mates. And she said to me – *Please let me go home to my son.* And I was concentrating on locking her cuffs because I wasn't very good at it. And she said – *One day you will understand. One day you will have a child of your own, and you will remember today.*'

'And you do. How old was Emma Moon when she had her son?'

'Young. I worked it out. She must have been sixteen.'

'Too young. Babies having babies.'

'And then the heavy mob turned up and she didn't say anything else to me. I didn't even know there was a photographer outside until I saw the papers the next day.'

It should have been a fifteen-minute walk to New Scotland Yard but our mob were out in force, blocking off the streets around Westminster. The trouble was much closer now. Sirens, breaking glass, shouts and screams only a street or two away. A young copper with a sweaty red face blocked our way just before Parliament Square. He looked as though he had been chasing someone, or perhaps running away. I was reaching for my warrant card when he recognised DCI Pat Whitestone.

'You don't want to go this way, ma'am. It's all kicking off.'

So we walked down to the river and took the long,

picturesque route back. It was a beautiful evening down by the Thames.

'If I was Emma Moon, then I would wish Butch Lewis dead,' Whitestone said. 'And I would wish the lot of them dead for not coming back to get me. You must do a lot of thinking in sixteen years.'

'But she was still inside when Butch died,' I said. 'And she's – unwell.'

I did not like to say the word. In my family we always had a fear of the word, a reluctance to name the disease, as if speaking it out loud would conjure it up. Whitestone was staring at me.

'She has cancer,' I said.

'What kind?'

'The end-of-the-road kind. Her lungs. I put in a call to the governor at Bronzefield after we watched her get out. And wishing someone dead – it's not the same as making it happen, is it?'

'I wonder what was in that safe,' Whitestone said. 'It was enough for Terry Gatti to retire to his big mansion. It was enough to keep his brother Mick in the good life in Spain. That night – when you were standing there with that big hole where the safe had been – she never even mentioned the score?'

I shook my head.

'I don't know if she even knew. She didn't talk to me about the job. She didn't talk to me about what was in the safe. She didn't talk to me about the two dead bodies. She only talked to me about her son.'

'And what happened to the boy?'

'I don't know.' But it was starting to matter to me.

We were at New Scotland Yard now.

They were bringing in the protestors. All ages. Children fired up by the cause as if it was a sugar rush, wrinklies who had been carrying placards for a lifetime, everything in-between. We let them pass and took the lift up to MIR-1. Sita Basu and Bear Groves, our two shiny new Direct Entry Detectives, were watching from the window, chuckling together, enjoying the show. Their faces got serious when we showed up.

'The duty sergeant in the holding cells says you might want to come down for a chat about tonight's intake,' DC Groves told me.

'That's not really what we do up here, Bear,' I said, but even as I said it, I felt my stomach fall away.

Fresh from some happy campus, DC Bear Groves was still young and soft-hearted enough to be embarrassed, God love him.

'One of the protestors is your daughter,' he told me.

12

It was knocking on for midnight by the time I signed her out. We drove home in silence. This was, I realised, how Scout and I maintained our uneasy peace. There was a mutually assured destruction if we started talking and so we stayed quiet, our verbal nukes stored in their silos during the cold war of her pre-teen year.

My daughter had been sitting outside the holding cells, scrolling through her phone. And I felt a flood of emotions that almost overwhelmed me. Relief – relief like I had never known – that she was unharmed. Bewilderment – that goofy-guy how-can-this-be-happening? parental bewilderment – that she was not at home doing her homework. And anger – anger that she put us both through this mess, anger that she was sitting outside a holding cell in New Scotland Yard when it was past her bedtime.

And yet I said nothing as the city slipped past and I kept my eyes on the road ahead. We drove along the Victoria Embankment and then turned north for home. We were passing under the great white dome of St Paul's Cathedral gleaming in the moonlight when Scout cleared her throat with a self-conscious cough, as if about to address the nation.

'I'm not sure I approve,' she said, looking away from me, staring down empty Fleet Street.

I glanced at her, dumbfounded. I had no idea what she was going on about.

'What don't you approve of, Scout?'

'This . . . nepotism.'

I opened my mouth and nothing came out.

'What nepotism?' I managed after a while.

Now she looked at me, lifting her chin, her brown eyes shining.

'I don't get put in a cell because my father is a police-man. And I get to wait for my father to pick me up and take me home when everyone else is getting charged. It's nepotism,' she concluded haughtily. 'And it's *wrong*.'

I didn't know where to start.

'Scout, this is not nepotism. If I am the CEO of Micro-soft and I get you a million-buck job on the board with share options – *that's* nepotism. Do you think they didn't lock you up with the rest of them because of some special favour to me? Scout – *you're a kid*. You're *twelve years old*. They are not going to lock up any child without first trying to contact a responsible adult. Because if they can't find a responsible adult then they have to contact social services and go through all that crap.'

'So they were being kind, were they?'

'Kindness has not got a lot to do with it. They just don't want all the extra paperwork. Why would they?'

What is she, Max? Twelve? a cheerful duty sergeant had asked me. *I've got twins a year older. It gets worse!*

'You don't even know what we were protesting about,' she said. 'You never even asked. Unbelievable! Do you even *care* why we were on the streets tonight?'

'Not really, Scout. It feels like everyone's always got a very good reason to stick a brick through someone else's window or deface a war memorial or scream and shout that they are mad as hell and not going to take it anymore.'

But my heart softened at the sight of her. I could still see the baby girl in her, and I could still see the child. And I could still see the smart, knowing, funny kid who only a few hours ago had interesting things to say about the soundtrack to *The Little Mermaid*.

'Look – I just want you to be all right, Scout. When I know that you are all right, I will worry about the world. But I can't worry about the world when I have you to worry about.'

The tears came at last. She fought them under control but her large brown eyes filled with them.

'But how can I be all right when there are people sleeping on the street? How can I be all right when kids just like me – *just like me* – are *not* all right?'

The neighbourhood was sleeping when we got home, the ancient meat market all locked up and dark and silent until the working week began on Sunday night. We had reached our apartment block when an emaciated figure emerged from the shadows.

'Sir Max?'

It was Suzanne, in tears of her own. Scout hovered behind me as I approached her. Suzanne was clutching her tatty stuffed rabbit to her chest. I touched her arm.

'What's wrong?'

'There was a policeman tonight.' She stared wildly out at Smithfield. 'A young policeman who said he was arresting me for vagrancy. He showed me his card and made me get in his car.' She shot a look at Scout. 'To interview me about the charges he might be bringing, he said.'

'A squad car? A police car with markings?'

She shook her head.

'Just a regular car.'

'Was he in uniform?'

She shook her head. 'Ordinary clothes. Like you.'

'Then how do you know he was a policeman, Suzanne?'

She looked bewildered. 'He said so, Sir Max.'

'Did he show you his warrant card?'

'His card. Yes. He showed me his ID.'

Was it real? I wanted to ask, but stopped myself. How the hell would Suzanne know? How does anyone ever know? I took out my warrant card and showed it to Suzanne.

'Did it look like that?'

She licked her cracked lips, trying to control her breathing, looked nervously at Scout then back at me.

'I don't know,' she said. 'I think so. Yes.'

We stared at each other in silence.

'Are you OK?'

'I got out of the car. He didn't stop me. He just laughed.' She glanced towards the meat market. 'Sir Max, I am afraid he will come back.'

'If he comes back, then you call me.' I gave her my card. Our mob were probably the last people in the world who still carried business cards. 'Are you sure you're all right, Suzanne?'

She nodded, suddenly embarrassed. I palmed a £20 note into her hand as we parted. She needed more. A roof over her head. People who were on her side. All the things that we all need. But I didn't have the time or the heart to give her more than twenty quid.

Scout and I went up to our apartment in silence. *You see?* I wanted to say to my daughter. *You see how hard it is out there?*

But she already knew, of course. That's what she was protesting about. How hard it was out there.

Mrs Murphy was all smiles and good humour, and as always, both Scout and I felt the need to echo her sunny mood.

But Mrs Murphy knew us.

'Is this a good night for one of your group hugs?' Mrs Murphy laughed, and Scout and I both did our best to chuckle along. 'I think it might be, you know!'

Mrs Murphy had first come to work for us when my wife left me and she had been deeply touched by four-year-old Scout's belief in the healing power of the group hug – and they were very minimalist group hugs because back then there was only Scout, me and a reluctant Stan, a skittish puppy.

But we did our best to have a group hug at moments of crisis – the hell of every sports day, because my daughter was not remotely sporty, and on parent-teacher evenings when Scout realised that most children had two adults in their lives and nearly all of them had a mother, and at those other moments of crisis and melancholy that come to every growing child, whatever the size or shape of their family.

But we *were* a family. We became a family, Scout and I – and Stan too.

You don't need very many for a good group hug, Mrs Murphy taught us. And you don't need many people to become a family.

'Look at this good boy,' Mrs Murphy said, and the three of us watched Stan snoring in his favourite corner of his favourite sofa. He always enjoyed his social calls to the Murphys', but liked to return home at bed-time. It was only when Mrs Murphy had taken her leave that the uneasy silence between Scout and I fell once more.

Scout went to her room. She couldn't get there fast enough.

Despite our tradition of group hugs, we were never the most tactile of families. But when she was younger, I always kissed her on top of her head before she went to bed. A kiss on top of the head was unthinkable now. Even without a goodnight, I assumed I would not see her again until the morning.

Stan watched expectantly and then, realising there was no more food on the way tonight, settled himself on his favourite sofa. I sat alone at the kitchen island, firing up the laptop.

Everyone had said that it would never work out between Scout's mother and me.

And everyone had been right.

Scout's mum and I – Anne, the beautiful Anne – were one of those unlikely couples that sometimes end up staying together for a lifetime, despite all the odds. We managed five years. It turned out that we were one of those painfully predictable couples that were always going to come apart.

Everything we had liked about each other was what had ripped us apart.

Anne was a model – although not really a model, because she was not earning enough to live on, and although she looked like the most beautiful girl in the world, she was working in a coffee shop in Chelsea when we met, a bored barista immune to the double-takes of the stunned clientele.

And I was a policeman – although again, not really, because I was still doing my training at Hendon when I worked up the nerve to talk to her in a King's Road café where I couldn't afford the bill.

The pretend model and the pretend policeman, trying to make it work.

And although in the end it did not work, I would never accept that our marriage was a failure. Because it produced Scout.

Contact between Scout and her mum had always been sporadic as Anne embarked on her long and winding journey of a second marriage, a second family, a second divorce, and the fragile relationships that followed. Even when it was good – in the early days, which were the only days Scout saw her mother on anything like a regular basis – Scout had to be fitted in around the edges of a jagged, complicated life.

People who did not know us – or did not know human nature – were always stunned when they realised that Scout never saw her mother now.

I envied them their sheltered lives. Because I knew it happened all the time.

And I knew the banality of the problem, the cliché of the absent parent who means well at first but becomes ever more absent with the passing years. Talk to the children of divorced parents – they are legion. And they will tell you that the absent parent often dissolves into the mist of their new life. It is usually the father who slips away from the child. But not always.

They say you divorce your partner but you don't divorce your children.

But that's not true. Plenty of people out there divorce their children. Ask their children.

But we were a family, Scout and I. And I always thought that we were going to make it. I believed that Scout was going to get to adulthood largely unscathed by the stupidity of her parents. Somehow I always thought that we would pull through. But lately not so much.

Not after she threw a party for the local homeless in our flat.

Not after seeing her sitting outside a police holding cell.

Scout's bedroom door creaked open and she came slowly out.

We stared at each other, my beautiful daughter and I. My heart leapt and I smiled, eager to make up, desperate to know that we were going to be all right again. And I knew – I knew in my heart – that all our problems were because Scout was a kind, compassionate girl driven mad by the cruelty and injustice of the world. I should be proud of that fact.

I watched her cross the vast open space of our loft. I thought perhaps she had come back for a group hug. A light kiss on the head. A kind word.

And I was wrong.

When they are four years old, they accept everything, But when they are pushing thirteen, they accept nothing.

'I spoke to Mum,' Scout said.

13

As the coffin appeared, the music began.

'What a Wonderful World' by Louis Armstrong.

A touching choice for a funeral, I thought, and it was certainly a lovely spring morning beyond the doors of the ancient church, the kind of dazzling new day to make you glad to be alive. But had it really been a wonderful world for Butch Lewis?

He did hard time and had the stupid tattoo to prove it. He and his wife had raised their troubled child and then had to raise their troubled child's children too. Butch was living in a caravan when he died. Like a lot of career villains, his life made me think – wouldn't it have just been easier to get a regular job?

But as his wife and his three young grandchildren followed his coffin into the small rural church, I thought that perhaps they were the reason Butch Lewis thought that yes, on reflection, this *was* a wonderful world. Because their hearts clearly broke at his passing.

The congregation stood, and the pain in my lower back came so quickly that I gasped out loud. The man next to me – small, dark, erratic eyes – assessed me with a knowing smile. He shook his head as if he had seen it all before.

'Are you going to live with that pain?' he whispered. 'Or are you going to do something about it?'

I stared at him as Louis Armstrong growled poignantly on and the coffin slowly advanced down the aisle.

'What?'

His grin grew broader. He was dressed in some kind of lightweight grey tracksuit. He was not dressed for a funeral. But then most of the mourners in here looked like they were going anywhere but a funeral.

'You're not getting old,' he said, slightly louder now. 'You just need to stretch.'

A woman in front of us turned around in fury.

'Will you shut your cakehole, mate?' she asked.

She was a tiny Cockney, but not a lovable salt-of-the-earth East Ender that you might find being all bright and breezy on a TV soap. She was the real thing, from a deeply discontented wing of the Cockney diaspora. Her family probably moved out of London a generation or two or three ago and she was possibly unhappy with the way the world was going. She was still turned in her pew, waiting to see if my knowing, wild-eyed neighbour had anything else to add. He studied the Order of Service with a grin. But he slipped me his business card. There was not much on it. A tiny emoji of a woman on her knees with her hands together in prayer. And the name of his business.

Mindful Yoga with Keith Jones

I stared at him. So this was Keith 'The Nutjob' Jones. This was a man transformed from a violent young criminal with multiple addictions into a yoga master and wellness guru. I nodded in recognition and gave him my own card. He slipped it into his jacket without looking at it, as if he would throw it away the first chance he got, winking and touching the side of his nose.

His voice was a whisper.

'I already know who you are, mate,' said Keith 'The Nutjob' Jones.

The church was full and I scanned the crowds to see the rest of them. The old Hole in the Wall Gang.

I wanted to see what they looked like now, if they came. Those men who had never paid for the crime.

And Emma Moon clearly wanted the same thing. Because she was there, among the mourners, flanked by her entourage.

The shaven-headed ex-warden maybe-boyfriend on one side, the floppy-haired peer Lord Nevermore on the other, like the before-and-after pictures of a hair-loss campaign.

And the two women at Nevermore's side. The feral-faced youngster squinting myopically at the light hitting a pane of stained glass, and the older one who looked like a model who had gone off the rails. They all kept their eyes on Emma Moon as she scanned the congregation.

This was the first time I had seen her in the flesh since the night I led her from the big house in handcuffs and a senior police officer had looked at me like I was the hired

86

help and said, 'We'll take it from here, sonny.' She had impressed me on that night and she impressed me still. There was an ethereal beauty about her even now, especially now. She was tall and thin and impossibly pale, and she looked very beautiful and very ill, and the two states were impossible to separate.

She was looking for them, the old gang. But they were not there.

And it was all a long time ago, and the church was full of men and women who knew Butch Lewis from more recent times.

Louis Armstrong ended with a growled affirmation and the doors of the church were slowly closed.

And then at the last moment they swung open again and they were suddenly there. Terry Gatti, with his matinee idol good looks even in his forties, following the almost universally ignored dress code – black suit, white shirt, black tie. Terry and I were the only ones wearing a black tie. His brother, Mick Gatti was a bigger, coarser, more casual man with a deep Spanish suntan and a shirt so loud it made him look like he had wandered in from an Ibiza beach.

They took their place in the back row.

The Hole in the Wall Gang's all here, I thought.

Well, almost. The only absentee was the safecracker. No Peterman. No Ian Doherty.

'Dearly beloved,' said the young lady vicar, and we all faced front.

My eyes drifted to Butch Lewis's widow and their tiny

grandchildren in the front row. Little girls too young to be dressed in black, and too young to be in a church mourning their grandfather. Their sobs filled the silence, and I saw again how deeply Butch Lewis had been loved.

There was a photograph of Butch on the cover of the Order of Service. Butch smiling in some lost English summer. A much younger man. The five-dot tattoo by his eye already absurdly out of place, and something to regret. But he looked happy.

I leafed through the little booklet. Entry music. Welcome and Introduction. Hymn, Eulogy, Reflection, Prayers, Poem. It all washed over me. The hymns and the prayers and the readings. *Sun and moon, bow down before him. Give us this day our daily bread and forgive us our trespasses. I was a stranger, and you took me in. Amen.*

I zoned out until right near the end.

Because Terry Gatti was the Poem. Which was not really a poem at all. Chief Tecumseh, it said in the Order of Service. Shawnee chief and warrior.

'So live your life that the fear of death can never enter your heart,' he read, his face like a good-looking actor doing some provincial rep, but glancing only occasionally at the A4 sheet he held. Because these were words he knew by heart, words that meant something to him, words he had thought about and believed. 'Trouble no one about their religion. Respect others in their view and demand that they respect yours. Love your life – perfect your life. Seek to make your life long and its purpose in the service of your people. Show respect to all people and grovel to no one.'

There was a murmuring of voices, restless simple souls unused to the discipline of sitting perfectly still for an hour.

Terry Gatti raised his handsome head sharply, and I could understand why he had once been feared.

He looked back at the A4 piece of paper, pausing for a moment to find his place, then looked up at us.

'When you arise in the morning give thanks for the food and for the joy of living. If you see no reason for giving thanks, the fault lies only in yourself. Abuse no one and no thing, for abuse turns the wise ones to fools and robs the spirit of its wisdom.'

He paused. Someone quietly cleared their throat. Terry Gatti let it go.

'When it comes your time to die, be not like those whose hearts are filled with the fear of death, so that when their time comes they weep and pray for a little more time to live their lives over again in a different way.'

He was folding the piece of paper. He knew the last line. He did not need reminding.

'Sing your death song – and die like a hero going home,' he said.

Then it was over.

I was suddenly worn out by it all, and I could not face the thought of watching Butch Lewis's coffin being lowered into the ground while his widow and grandchildren sobbed. I just wanted to go home. I wanted to take off these miserable black clothes and order Deliveroo and huddle in my nest. I wanted wine, I wanted life, I wanted to be with my daughter and my dog. I wanted to go to Fred's and exhaust my mind and body so that I would sleep through the night.

But I found I could not resist. Their story – the story of Emma Moon – held me, and I wanted to see what happened next.

I took them in more closely as we filed out of the church and the Gatti brothers walked with the crowd to the graveside. Terry and Mick looked like rich men, and they were still relatively young. That is what shocked me.

Emma Moon had grown paler and more fragile in prison, but the Gatti brothers had thrived on their proceeds. The lowliest members of the crew may have squandered the biggest payday of their lives.

But not the brothers. They looked like they had invested wisely.

The Gattis seemed like rich relations, moving through the crowds, shaking hands and smiling and nodding, and then sad-faced and offering their condolences to Mrs Val Lewis. Mick Gatti crouched to pat the tear-stained face of the oldest granddaughter. She recoiled with an instinctive disgust, and I wondered if it had been this prosperous middle-aged man with the Mediterranean tan who had taken two lives in that big house sixteen years ago.

And I wondered again what was in that safe.

Emma Moon and the Gattis ignored each other. It was as if they had never met, as if there were not merely years between them, and secrets kept, and high prices paid. They looked like total strangers.

Out of the confines of the church, the fields of Kent stretched away under blue sky and fluffy clouds.

The mourners were filing past, dropping a single rose onto the coffin in its freshly dug grave.

Emma Moon was towards the back of the line. When it was her turn, she dropped the rose, lowered her head as if in prayer.

And then she laughed. A laugh that was clearly audible above the sounds of mourning. She touched her mouth, as if the amusement had been instinctive, rather than designed to offend, and turned away, still gently amused, with an apologetic shake of her head.

Then Mick Gatti was screaming something and trying to get to her while Emma's boyfriend, the ex-warden with the shaved skull, crashed into him with full force and one of Emma's female companions, the whey-faced kid, hung on Mick's big back, ripping his Hawaiian shirt so badly that you could see the Millwall FC tattoo – a lion rampant – he had on his right shoulder blade.

Terry Gatti shook his head and did nothing.

But the man who had been sitting next to me in church, the one who told me I had to decide if I was going to live with my back pain, Keith Jones, moved forward with impressive speed and grabbed Mick Gatti in some kind of restraining hold, hugging him, pinning his arms to his side, then lifted him off the ground, swinging him away.

Keith The Nutjob Jones.

After fifteen years sober. After cleaning up his act and getting born again with yoga asanas, green tea and kale smoothies.

As Keith Jones wrestled Mick Gatti to the ground, one thing was clear.

Even after all that yoga, and all those kale smoothies, and all those gentle Namastes, even after all of that – The Nutjob could still handle himself.

14

My plan had been to attend Butch Lewis' funeral and slip away. But in the crush to leave the church I had found myself face to face with Butch's widow, Val Lewis, as I tried to make my getaway.

'You'll join us after,' she had said, meaning the wake, and I did not have the heart to refuse.

Show my face and escape, that was my latest plan, as I crowded into the bar of a dying pub with all those displaced Londoners. But there was food all over the bar and my stomach rumbled with desire and the sausage rolls called to me, bidding me to stay for a few minutes longer.

'It's you, isn't it?' said a voice behind me, in one of those old London accents that you don't hear so often these days, an accent untouched by the outside world. I turned with my paper plate in my hands and the Gatti brothers were staring at me.

Mick – beefy, belligerent, his tanned face bruised high on one cheekbone, his print shirt ripped on one sleeve. Hair highlighted with a defiant blond. And Terry – older by a couple of years but looking younger because he was several kilos lighter than his kid brother and had not done all that time in the Mediterranean sun. A younger woman hovered behind them, glossy and bored, in a minidress that had not been originally designed for mourning, scrolling through her phone with elaborate nails. The second Mrs Terry Gatti, although Emma Moon had been what they used to call his common-law wife.

It was Terry who had spoken. 'You're the one who found Butch,' he said now.

'Yes, and he's a bit more than that,' Mick said, leering at me, as if we shared a secret. 'He's the one who nicked *her*.' He turned to the woman, his voice thick with mockery. 'He's famous, this geezer, Helen. He's the arresting officer!'

'What?' the woman said, not looking up from the screen.

There was no sign of Emma Moon at the wake. Whatever she had come here for today, it was done by now. I could see Keith Jones talking earnestly to Butch Lewis's widow. He had the glazed look of the religious convert, all touchy-feely empathy. But he looked like a reformed character.

Unlike the Gattis. They may have been straight for years, but they still had the smell of criminality about them. Both of them.

Mick Gatti was the more obvious thug, used to throwing his weight around in the bars and pubs and restaurants of tourist Spain. But Terry had the same air about him, for all his polish, despite his immaculate suit and quiet demeanour – that feeling that it could turn nasty in a moment.

That's what career villains have. And the police have it too.

'So the gang's all here,' I said, taking a bite of my sausage roll. 'Apart from your Peterman.'

They laughed at that. 'Peterman. Listen to him,' said Mick.

'What's he up to these days?' I asked. 'Ian Doherty? Your safecracker?'

'Don't know who you're talking about, mate,' Mick Gatti said, the first air of threat in his voice.

'Ian's an underground poet,' Terry Gatti said, amused.

I took a bite of sausage roll. 'What – you mean an alternative poet?'

'No – he works for Transport for London. On the underground. And he writes poems on a little sign outside of tube stations to give the commuters something to think about.' He shook his handsome head. 'But here's what we want to know – are you going to nick her again?'

'Who?'

The brothers exchanged irritated glances.

'That bitch Emma Moon,' Mick said. 'Are you going to arrest her?'

'For what?'

Terry Gatti seemed genuinely surprised. 'For those children crying over there because they are not going to see their granddad anymore. For Val – the wife who should have had years more with her husband. *For what?* For topping Butch Lewis.'

He had a flair for the dramatic, did Terry Gatti.

I placed my paper plate on the bar, brushed crumbs from my hands. I stared at Mick Gatti's hands. They were clenched into tight fists, ready to be thrown.

'Cardiac arrest, it says on the death certificate,' I said.

Mick snorted with derision. 'You dumb copper,' he said. '*She did it.* Or she got someone else to do it for her.'

'Careful,' I said to Mick, and for a long moment we just stared at each other until he slowly unclenched his fists. 'She was still in HMP Bronzefield when your friend died.'

'Ah,' Terry Gatti said. 'But her little cult – the Manson Family – all those freaks – were out and about. Her little entourage. That screw. Her former cellmates. The friends of Emma Moon.'

I had to smile.

'Wait a minute,' I said. 'You actually want *me* to protect *you?*'

Terry Gatti shook his head.

'We are not asking for your protection – we just want the death of Butch Lewis properly investigated. We want it to be treated with the seriousness it deserves. We just want you to do your fucking job, DS Wolfe. Don't look surprised. Oh, of course I know your name. And your rank.'

'We know everything about you,' his brother said. 'Everything.'

I stared at his coarse face. I was still staring at it when Terry spoke again, more reasonable now.

'Emma is a psychopath,' he said. 'That's what you have to understand. I know you think you have some kind of insight into her. You are dead wrong. You don't know her at all. And she will not rest until all her old friends are in the ground with Butch. She blames us for things that had nothing to do with us.'

I stared at him with disbelief.

'And she blames me,' he said, 'for what happened to David, for what happened to our son.' Then he smiled. 'And she blames you, too.'

I remembered the night I put the cuffs on her. I remembered that her boy was the reason she wanted me to let her walk away. I could believe that she blamed me too for what had gone wrong in her life.

'What happened to your son?'

Terry Gatti shook his head, no longer able to look at me.

'David killed himself,' Mick Gatti said. He touched his brother's arm. 'Ten years ago. Out of his head after years on the wacky-baccy. It's different these days, the wacky-baccy. Industrial strength. Too strong.'

'I'm sorry.'

'I don't want your pity,' Terry Gatti said, eyes blazing. 'But some very bad things will happen if you do not put Emma back where she belongs. It has already begun.'

It always makes me laugh the way everyone hates the police until someone is climbing through their bedroom window. Then suddenly we are everyone's best friend, everybody's daddy.

'What was in that safe?' I said, and they stared at me with their belligerent no-comment eyes.

I saw the tiny old Cockney lady who had told Keith Jones to shut his cakehole leading Val Lewis and her grandchildren out of the pub. I could feel the base of my spine pulsing with pain.

It was time to go home.

'Don't you get it?' I said to the Gatti brothers. 'Emma Moon is not going to come looking for you. Because Emma Moon is *dying*.'

'I think you're the one who doesn't get it,' Terry Gatti said. 'Emma has a list of people who have to pay for what was done to her. And what you have to ask yourself is — am I on that list?'

15

Ian Doherty was not a poet after all. The former Peterman for the Hole in the Wall Gang was more of a self-help guru. A positive thinker.

When I discovered Ian outside Belsize Park tube station the next morning – a small, neat man in a dark blue Transport for London uniform, settling into his comfortable middle years – he was writing on a whiteboard as the late commuters rushed to their train, and the words he wrote were more motivational quote than poem.

> *One step must start each journey.*
> *One word must start each prayer.*
> *One hope will raise our spirits.*
> *One touch can show you care.*

Nobody looked at him – or his words – twice. You would never have guessed that this man was a renowned safe-cracker in a previous lifetime. Until perhaps you noticed his fingers. His fingers were long and tapered and curiously elegant, like a piano player's fingers, but that was the only clue. He was a man somewhere in his early forties and his criminal past had been left behind in the outskirts of youth. I recalled the man who had sold flowers at Waterloo station when I was a kid – it was Buster Edwards, the former Great Train Robber, gone straight in his later years. Probably every single tube station in London has some reformed villain outside trying to earn an honest crust.

Ian saw me reading as he put the top back on his Sharpie.

'There's a bit more,' he said, 'but I don't have room.'

'What's the rest of it?' I said, genuinely interested.

'*One voice can speak with wisdom,*' he said. '*One heart can know what's true. One life can make a difference – you see, it's up to you.*'

'Yes, that's a bit long. I think what you've got is fine,' I said. 'Who said it?'

'Unknown,' he said, grinning, showing me his smoker's teeth. I looked at his hands again and saw those long thin fingers were tinged with nicotine. I wondered if he had smoked back in the day when he was cracking combinations. Squinting in the cigarette smoke as he worked, just as Emma Moon squinted in cigarette smoke as if it was too-bright sunshine.

'I love it, don't you?' he said. 'The author has been forgotten but their words will never die. That's . . . that's something special.' He stared thoughtfully at his whiteboard. 'Words for the spiritual wanderer, to help them on their way as they head for the southbound Northern line.'

'Unknown,' I said. 'I used to read my daughter a lot of stories by unknown. When she was little.'

He laughed. 'Unknown wrote some great stuff.'

I smiled along with him.

He was grateful that someone had stopped to talk about his whiteboard. I guessed that people rarely did.

'You weren't at the funeral,' I said conversationally, and he shook his head, bewildered. 'Butch Lewis,' I said. 'Yesterday. Everyone was there, Ian. The Gatti brothers. Keith Jones – you know, The Nutjob, although I don't think he goes by The Nutjob anymore. Even Emma Moon. Yes, she's out, isn't she? But not you, Ian.'

He looked around wildly. It was a beautiful sun-dappled morning in Belsize Park. And he could suddenly feel the past crowding in.

'That's got nothing to do with me anymore,' he said. 'None of it. Not anymore. Not for a long time. Who are you?'

He knew I was police. I raised my hands, pleading for calm.

'I'm not here to make trouble for you. I just wanted to ask you a couple of questions. And it's nicer in Belsize Park than an interview room. How did you get into that game anyway? Safecracking?'

He shook his head, right on the edge of – 'no comment'.

I smiled at him. 'Come on, we both know what you did for a living.' I held my hands wide, as if for a body search. 'I'm not wearing a wire. This is just a friendly chat.'

101

'My dad was a locksmith,' he said slowly. 'Maybe the best locksmith south of the river. And locksmiths – the good ones – they get brought safes. All kind of safes. Because people lose the key and they forget the combination. Or they drop dead before they tell anyone else the combination. And it started there. Watching my dad opening safes for the relations of the dead who hoped they were about to win the lottery. And my dad was fascinated by the safecrackers in the Second World War. Talked about them as he worked. Eddie Chapman and Gentle John Ramensky. These Petermen who became big war heroes because they could crack safes in Nazi occupied Europe. So it started there. Learning from my dad. Seeing the magic in doing this thing that ordinary men could not do. And I was good at it.' His face hardened. 'And I will tell you when it ended – the day I learned that two men had died on that job sixteen years ago. And I know you know who I am – and I know who you are. You're the copper in the photograph with Emma Moon – the same copper but with a few more miles on the clock.'

'And what was in that safe, Ian? The safe you opened at that farm in the Cotswolds for the Gattis?'

'Is that what you came to ask me? I never knew. That was above my pay grade. But as you're asking so nicely – and as you're not wearing a wire – I'll reveal that, like the others, I was on a flat fee. I don't give a damn what the Gattis found in the safe. And when I learned about that dead security guard and that dead gardener, that young kid, I had had enough to last me a lifetime. Because it all seemed a long way from my old man in Catford telling me stories about brave safecrackers fighting the Nazis.'

He looked into the station. He was not actually paid to write motivational quotes on a whiteboard outside Belsize Park. He had other duties to attend to, and they were calling.

'Has anyone threatened you, Ian?'

'What you talking about? Why would anyone threaten me? Listen, I've got to go.'

'Do you know how your old friend Butch Lewis died?'

'Heart attack, wasn't it? That's what the *Guardian* said in the obituary.'

'Cardiac arrest. Not quite the same thing. And there's a theory – and it's only a theory, Ian – that someone scared Butch to death.'

He laughed.

He thought it was funny.

My phone began to vibrate.

I looked at it and saw the caller ID that every parent dreads.

SCHOOL CALLING, it said.

I gave Ian Doherty my card.

He stared at it, still smiling.

'Shall I give you a call if someone tries to scare me to death?' he said.

I nodded.

'And if you remember what was in that safe,' I said.

*

103

'So you didn't know that Scout was absent from school today?'

The headmistress on the other side of the desk was a good woman. A nice woman. An Australian in London, dedicated to educating the children in her charge, trying to do her best. But as I gazed out at the teeming playground, all those hundreds of kids with growing pains and hormones raging, I detected a weariness in her voice.

She had seen it all before, not least the single parent who, in the end, found it all a bit overwhelming.

'All this – all this *trouble* – it's all new,' I said, wanting her to understand, wanting her to see that we were different in our little family. 'Scout's a good kid. A compassionate child. She cares about the world. It can distract her.'

I had been called in to see the headmistress because Scout had failed to put in an appearance at registration that morning, just as – it turned out – she had failed to make an appearance all of last week.

This was breaking news to me.

Twelve years old and my daughter was not where she was meant to be. Twelve years old and instead of going to class, she was off to destinations unknown, and the first I heard about it was when the call came to come in to the school from some bone-tired receptionist, ready to call in social services. The headmistress looked at me, friendly enough, but with the edge of accusation.

How could you let this happen?

'I understand that Scout is not in contact with her mother,' she said.

MURDER FOR BUSY PEOPLE

All those kids out there: you look at them from a distance, and you feel like you are the only family in the
world that has fallen apart. But it is not true, of course. It
just looks that way from a distance. It's only from a distance that everybody else's life runs so much smoother
than your own.

'Does Scout *ever* see her mother?'

'They have been in contact again recently. While she
was growing up, contact was . . . sporadic.'

Sporadic! That was a good word for it.

The headmistress brightened, keen to hold on to some
good news. 'That's great, isn't it?' she smiled, suddenly
sounding more Australian. She smiled. 'That they are in
contact again? That's . . .'

'Normal?'

'I was going to say – *natural*. That Scout would want
to form a healthy relationship with her mother.'

I nodded. 'Of course. But we were a happy family.'

'You mean – before the divorce?'

'I mean – all the time.'

'Excuse me?'

I needed this truth acknowledged. That Scout and I
were not some problem family. We were not the kind of
family – despite all the evidence! – where the child did
not turn up for school and the feckless lone parent had to
be hauled in to see the headmistress. Except that is exactly
what we were now. That's exactly who we were. But it
wasn't always this way! That's the point I was trying to
make. Somehow it was very important to me.

'Scout and I. When she was growing up – we were a happy family. Scout and me – and Stan.'

'Stan is her brother?'

'No – Stan is a dog.'

The headmistress shook her head. 'A dog?'

'Our dog. And we were happy. We were! All of this trouble – not turning up for school, disappearing – it's all new. We were happy.'

The pain started up in my back.

The pain seemed to be on the move, growing in confidence, advancing from the base of my spine up to just below the right shoulder blade, settling in for a lifetime.

'Perhaps – forgive me, Mr Wolfe – perhaps *you* were happy,' the headmistress said. 'And perhaps Scout acted brave and cheerful because she knew that was what *you* wanted – that was what *you* needed. That Scout wanted to reassure you that things were OK when they were far from OK. Is that a possibility?'

It was more than a possibility, I saw now. Pretending – putting on a brave face – was exactly what Scout would do. It would be the *caring* thing to do. To make believe we were happy.

'You can be proud of your daughter,' the headmistress said, and I thought perhaps she did know us a bit after all, or at least she knew Scout, and I fought back the sudden blur of hot tears. 'I see how liked she is among her cohort. There is a maturity about her that other children of her age lack. As you say, she's a compassionate child. She believes in kindness. She cares about the world.'

106

'Oh, yes.'

'But sometimes she drives you nuts.'

'Because she can't heal the world.'

'But she's *young*, Mr Wolfe. She has to try.'

It was Detective Wolfe, but I let it go.

'It's all true,' I said. 'But she's twelve years old and bunking off school on a regular basis – so let's not make her out to be Nelson Mandela.' I stood up to go. 'I'll make sure Scout starts coming to school again,' I said, wondering if such a simple task was already beyond my power.

We shook hands.

'It's quite unusual,' the headmistress said. 'To see a man bringing up their child alone.'

'We are not quite as rare as we used to be,' I said. 'There's a few of us now. It's not just me and David Bowie anymore.'

'And – if I may ask – what happened?'

'What happened?'

'With you and your ex-wife.'

The headmistress was not prying. She was just doing her best to understand how a sweet, smart, caring kid like Scout went off the rails because of her fucked-up folks.

But there was no great mystery.

Adults cock up their lives and their children pay the price.

'It was the same old story. Scout's mother – Anne, my ex-wife's name is Anne – was very young when we married. I was young, too. Then a few years went by and

107

Scout was born and then Anne met someone else who she liked quite a bit more than me.'

The headmistress was starting to look uncomfortable. Too much information? But there was no gentle way to tell the story.

'This guy – this new man – he was the love of Anne's life – so of course you try to understand. And we broke up. And it was painful for everybody. Especially Scout, I know. She was so young. Four years old. How can a four-year-old even begin to process the mess that men and women make of their lives? Then Anne started a new family. More children, all of that. A new life. I know she tried her best to find a place for Scout in her new life. She really did. But it's not so easy, fitting your old life into your new life. Then Anne moved out to a big house in the suburbs to live happily ever after.'

'I see.'

I paused at the door.

I had almost forgotten the punchline.

'And that didn't work out either,' I said.

Then I went to look for my daughter.

16

I fought down that feeling of simmering terror, the parental panic attack that is well known to any father and mother. You get it when they are little, and out of your sight for just a sickening moment or two in the park or a shop. But this just in – *it never goes away*. I knew that feeling when Scout was two. Now I had it when she was twelve. I knew I would feel it again when she was twenty-two. It's the feeling – the knowledge – that you can't protect them from everything that wants to hurt them.

It is the worst feeling in the world.

When I parked the car in Smithfield, Suzanne came out of the shadows, looking like the ghost of a girl, clutching her stuffed rabbit to her thin chest. Mr Flopsy.

And I just wasn't in the mood.

Being a parent makes you selfish. As soon as your child is born, they matter more than the rest of the world put together. That is always true, but you only notice it when they are in danger. Until then, you can kid yourself that you care about humanity as this great entity. And perhaps you do. But not as much as you care about your child.

Suzanne trailed after me as I headed for the great arch of the meat market, all closed up at this hour of the late afternoon.

Scout would not have gone far. That was my guess – that she had stayed within the neighbourhood where she had grown up, the city streets that she knew so well. She was a smart kid, a cool kid.

But still. So young. Nowhere near as worldly-wise as she believed herself to be. I fought down the mounting panic.

Suzanne was grinning by my side, trying to keep up.

'Sir Max?'

'Not now, Suzanne, please.'

'He came again.'

'Who?'

'The policeman.'

I stopped, sighed, stared at her.

She was suddenly tearful, gripping Mr Flopsy so tightly his ragged ears shook.

'He wanted me to do things to him.'

'You got into his car?'

'He made me. He said I was under arrest. He showed me the card, that card you have.'

'His warrant card.' I felt like we had already had this conversation. 'Where did this happen?'

She gestured towards the river. 'Fleet Street. There's a lot of empty buildings down there now. A lot of people sleep there. People like me.'

'Listen, Suzanne, I am going to sort this out for you. I

am going to find this creep. But I can't right now. I suspect this guy is impersonating a policeman. Trying to take advantage of you. And I'm going to make some enquiries, OK? And I'm going to stop this happening. I promise.'

She brightened, happy for any show of kindness, showing her teeth. I was always shocked when I saw Suzanne's teeth.

'But right now – I'm busy,' I told her.

'Are you looking for Scout?'

'Yes.'

'I know where she goes every day.'

Between Bart's hospital and the meat market, the Rotunda Garden sits in a secret corner of Smithfield. As the city roars and frets all around, this little stone garden is an island of tranquillity. It is built around a drinking fountain and a Victorian statue in bronze representing Peace – ironic, as this spot is where they executed heretics, dissidents and assorted rebels for five hundred years or so.

My rebel daughter was sitting on a bench, scrolling through her phone.

I took a seat next to her.

She registered me with those bright brown eyes.

And as the relief ebbed away, I felt that feeling I increasingly felt with my daughter. That weary, bone-tired, where-do-I-begin feeling.

'You've got to go to school, Scout.'

111

'This was where they executed Mel Gibson. Did you know that?'

'They did not execute Mel Gibson here, Scout. William Wallace. Braveheart. That's who they executed. I think Mel Gibson is still in reasonable health.'

She sighed, with all the world-weariness that only a twelve-year-old can muster.

'School is just so . . . stupid. A waste of time. The girls trying to be all cool for the boys. The boys trying to look tougher than they really are. All those tired teachers who wonder why they chose to devote their lives to all these ungrateful brats.' She looked at me directly. 'It just doesn't seem to have much to do with education.'

'You *liked* school,' I said, with an edge of desperation.

She looked pained. 'I liked school when I was *a little girl.*' She looked at me with what may have been pity. 'I'm not a little girl anymore.'

'When you don't show up, they are going to call me and I am going to have to go in. You get that, right?'

'Sorry,' she said, actually sounding truly sorry. 'I mean – sorry.'

I resisted the urge to reach out and hug her. Sitting there on a bench in the Smithfield Rotunda Garden in the middle of the day – she just looked so lonely.

In the silence, we were aware of Suzanne shuffling her feet nearby. She smiled at us and I felt a surge of gratitude. I fought back the urge to ask her if she needed anything. Because Suzanne needed everything.

'I'm going to look into that thing for you,' I said.

It felt like the least I could do. As Scout and I got up to go, I palmed Suzanne another £20 note. But I wasn't going to invite her to eat lunch with us at Smiths of Smithfield, and I wasn't going to invite her into our home, and I wasn't going to do anything to put a roof over her head. I should have felt at least some shame about these things. But I was just happy to find my daughter, and that overwhelmed every other emotion.

'Thank you, Sir Max,' Suzanne said, the £20 note in one hand, her stuffed rabbit in the other.

There were messages waiting for me when we got home. A follow-up phone call from the same knackered receptionist saying the school were legally obliged to contact social services if Scout continued to bunk off and spend her days sitting in the Rotunda Garden with dreams of executing Mel Gibson. When I hung up, Scout promised that she would start showing her face. But I knew that a big change was coming, and nothing could stop it.

'Mum said this thing,' Scout said, staring at Stan snoring on the sofa.

I waited.

'Mum said – she didn't leave *us*. She left *you*.'

And for the sake of my beautiful, school-skipping rebel girl, with all my heart I wanted that to be true.

When night came, Scout retreated to her room, and I stood for hours by the window because my back hurt more when I sat, and I watched Suzanne from the high

113

window of our apartment above Charterhouse Street, a thin, young figure moving unacknowledged and unseen like a spirit through the white-suited porters of Smithfield, and I felt a pang of disappointment in myself that I had yet to do what I promised.

And as I watched from our window, Suzanne disappeared under the great arch and into the shadows of the meat market, as if all my feeble, half-hearted promises would never be enough to save her.

17

There was one other man in the early morning yoga class.

He was a fat-free elderly gentleman, his silver-white hair tied back in some kind of topknot, and he wore a sleeveless vest and baggy trousers that made me think of magic carpets and Aladdin. Barefoot. We were all barefoot in the yoga class. And at first I thought he looked at me with irritation – I suspected he preferred being the only man in the class – but took pity on me when he saw that I had no mat of my own. A novice. I had no idea you were meant to bring a mat of your own. But my classmates – apart from the old chap with the topknot, they were women of all ages and shapes, but all with the same air of enlightened affluence about them – all had their own mat. I was invisible to them. But the old man showed me where to find a spare mat and I was unfurling it on the floor when our teacher, Keith Jones, came into the hall, wreathed in smiles and with his hands clasped together in some kind of prayer.

'Namaste.' He beamed. 'Let's just find a moment to connect with our breath.'

I was anxious that my stiff, aching body would immediately be found wanting, but the class was not like that at all.

Keith Jones eased into a pose – asanas, he called them – and we copied him to the best of our ability, and some of the women were as bendy as pretzels, and others were almost as stiff and unyielding as me, and the old bloke with the topknot was one of the more advanced students, his supple old body reaching for the sky into the sun salute that was where we began. And later I was on my knees, my forehead pressed against the mat that smelled of rubber and someone else's sweat, my arms reaching forward, when I felt the pain that had been in my back start to melt away. From where my face was pressed against the floor, I could see the bare feet of Keith Jones out of the corner of my eye.

'Breathe,' he murmured.

And when the class was over and they were rolling up their mats, he sought me out and gave me a triumphant smile.

'How do you feel?' he asked, already knowing the answer.

'Better,' I said.

'Only better?'

'More than better. Some of those moves – those asanas – just made the pain go away. It's just *gone*. You should be able to get yoga on the NHS.'

The class was emptying. We stood in silence, watching them go.

Keith Jones was still smiling. 'And why else are you here, Detective? Apart from your back.'

'I just wanted to ask you a few questions about what happened that night.'

He kept smiling. But it was more of an effort. He was looking at my T-shirt.

'Do you mind?' he said.

'Go ahead.'

His palms lightly tapped me down. Arms, chest, crotch. Thorough.

'Can't be too careful. There's no statute of limitations in the UK.'

'I'm not wearing a wire. If I wanted to ask you difficult questions, it wouldn't be in a yoga class. But I think you can help me. I think perhaps we can help each other. I saw you break up that fight at the funeral.'

He grimaced with distaste.

'Violence solves nothing. It never did.'

'You've changed your tune, Nutjob. If I may call you Nutjob?'

I caught of flash of anger in his eyes. 'Please don't. Not even in jest.'

All the green tea and kale smoothies and downward-facing dogs in the world could not take the South London out of him entirely.

He shook his head with distaste.

'If you think I am still the man that I was twenty years ago – you're wrong. That man – the one they called

Nutjob? – he doesn't exist anymore. I was out-of-control crazy back then. We all were.'

'Ah, but that's too easy. The whole I'm-a-changed-man routine.'

'There's that old zen puzzle. If you change the handle of a knife – and then you change the blade – is it still the same knife? I am that knife, Detective. Sometimes I think we all are – or we will be. We change so much in the course of a lifetime that we become someone else. The transformation is so total that the man or woman you think you know truly no longer exists.'

'But there's still bad blood. Between your old colleagues. Butch didn't die of a dodgy ticker. Whatever it says on the death certificate. Whatever his widow chooses to believe.'

'Then what killed him?'

Something scared him to death, I thought but did not say. Because it was crazy – wasn't it?

'Beats me,' I said.

'I hope that Butch is at rest,' he said. 'I hope Emma finds peace. I hope she heals.'

'I understand she has cancer. Advanced. It's not so easy to heal from that.'

'Then I hope she heals in any way she can in the time that remains. I hope we all do. But it was all a long time ago.' He looked me in the eye for what felt like the first time. 'What we did.'

'I always wondered – what was in that safe? The Gatti brothers look as if they have been living the high life for the last twenty years.'

He laughed.

'Good for them. Good for Terry and Mick! What was in the safe? I have no idea.'

'I don't believe you, Nutjob.'

A flash of temper, and I wondered how far you could push him before he reverted to his old ways. When other criminals call you Nutjob, it is meant to be a compliment.

'Believe what you like,' he said, curt with me for the first time. 'I never knew what the score was. I was nineteen years old. I was a wild teenager, and that's what I was there for. *To bring the wild.* To bring the terror. Like at the Brink's-Mat heist. Before they started asking the guards questions, they doused their trousers with petrol. That's what armed robbery takes – a bit of wild, a bit of terror. That's what I was there for. Terry and Mick Gatti know what was in the safe. But me and Butch and the safecracker were on a flat fee. I got my wedge and then I put it up my nose, and in my arm, and down my throat.'

He showed me his lower arm, the pale skin still bearing the pinpricks of heroin addiction.

'I blew my share on coke and smack and booze and whores and horses. And then it was all gone. The money runs out. And one morning my mother was trying to wake me up as I lay in a bed full of my own filth, and she was crying, and I knew I had to clean up or die. And so I cleaned up.'

'Very noble. And good for you. But two men died that night.'

'Nothing to do with me.'

'And you all got away with it.'

'Did we? I don't feel like I got away with anything. I feel like the money I made that night tried to kill me, and came very close to succeeding. That night has distorted my life. Shaped my life. And nobody wanted those men to die. I didn't kill them. I didn't want anyone to die.'

'But they died anyway, Nutjob.'

Finally he had had enough of me.

'Why are you *here*, man? I'm glad your back is feeling better. But that's not it, is it? Not really.'

It was difficult to explain. Even to myself.

'I was there too. That night. And I saw those two dead men. And I put the cuffs on Emma Moon. And in some ways it has driven my life, too. It's shaped my life too.'

His eyes had the hard glitter of the religious convert. 'I know you were *there*,' he said. 'But why are you *here*?'

'Because I don't think that night's really over, Nutjob,' I said. 'I think it's just begun.'

18

I came out of Fred's gym close to my bedtime, the meat market already in full swing on the far side of Charterhouse Street, and I saw him waiting for me in the doorway of a shuttered shop, the tip of his cigarette glowing red in the shadows.

Nils was painfully thin, almost skeletal, his beaky nose, all-black clothes and milky complexion making him look like a hard-living old crow. Nils was one of those vintage rock and rollers who had retained the spiky, feathered haircut from another century. He had earned a crust on the fringes of the music business around Camden for decades, with a side-hustle of criminal informant. And he was good at it.

'Someone is impersonating a police officer,' I said.

Nils sucked hungrily on his smoke. 'No small talk,' he coughed. 'I love it. No – *How are you then, Nils? How are the wife and kids?*'

'I didn't even know you had a wife and kids.'

'I don't. But still. The principle of it, Max. Impersonating a police officer – how?'

'This guy flashes what he claims is a Met warrant card

at vulnerable women. Threatens them with arrest. Generally chucks his weight about. Sexual coercion. I know of one woman he's abusing. He's not in uniform and he is acting alone.'

'Vulnerable women? What? Like when they're walking home alone? Drunk? Stoned?'

'This is a homeless woman.'

Nils raised his thick black eyebrows.

'So – what? – he gets them in the back of the squad car to inspect his truncheon?'

'It's not funny, Nils.'

'And I am not laughing. But – what happens? He makes them perform sexual acts? What does he do to them? What did he make this homeless woman do?'

I thought of Suzanne. 'She doesn't tell me everything,' I said.

'You sure it's someone *impersonating* a cop, Max? Are you certain – absolutely certain – it's not one of your own?'

I had considered the possibility, of course. But I badly wanted to believe that my mob – the Met in particular, and the police in general – were what we had always been. I wanted to believe that we were the protectors of the weak and vulnerable. Rather than their tormentors.

Nils read my thoughts. 'No offence, mate.'

'None taken. My gut feeling is that this guy is a fake.'

'I'll look into this matter,' he said. He gazed around. 'Any other business?'

'This is the business, Nils. It's important to me. Ask around. Find him for me.'

He hesitated. 'But if we are looking into cops abusing women, I have to say – we might be spoilt for choice.'

'How's that?'

He looked pained. 'Come on, Max! You and Dixon of Dock Green are the last of the line! The Met is full of them. They're the new generation, Max! Bullies, sexual predators – and worse. Look at the headlines. Guys attracted to that sense of power that comes with the gig.'

'This job has always attracted its share of bullies. You know that, Nils.'

'Ah, but this new lot – they're different. They grew up watching porn every day of their lives and it has done them no good at all. They're not just bullies – they're bullies who have dined on poison every day of their lives. May I be brutally honest?'

'Go ahead.'

'This is why nobody is that keen on your lot any more, Max. Why – frankly – the reputation of the police has never been lower. When I was growing up in Kentish Town, the old dears used to say that our police are the best in the world. You don't hear that so much these days, do you?'

'Not so much.' I hefted my kitbag, more than ready to go home and sleep.

'Let's just find the bastard, Nils. I want him off the streets.'

'And we will do, Max.' His voice called after me as I turned for home. 'But do you really think there's just the one?'

19

I woke up early to a dozen missed calls and one voice message.

This is the Intensive Care Unit at Whittington Hospital . . .

Scout, I thought, my heart falling away, and ready to do deals with God.

But then I could hear her murmuring on the phone in her room, and the sound of Stan's snoring behind her closed bedroom door.

I called I C U at the Whittington.

'Are you the next of kin? Of a Mr Keith Jones?' the woman said.

'What?' My mind struggled to catch up.

And then I understood. Someone had found my business card in the jacket pocket of Keith Jones, the yoga master formerly known as The Nutjob.

'There's been an accident,' they told me.

I stood outside the Intensive Care Unit and stared at Keith Jones as he clung to life.

A profusion of tubes, wires and cables seemed to snake

into every part of his body. A feeding tube ran up his nose. There were IV lines in his arm. There was a thick blue pump hanging from his mouth that was keeping him breathing. A thin catheter wound into his bladder draining urine. There was a light blue smock draped on top of him but because of the tubes keeping him alive he was not actually wearing it and his shoulders were bare. His nose had been broken and his eyes were blackened by the damage. His skull was shaved and bandaged. He looked as if he had been dropped on his head from a great height.

Machines crowded around him like anxious relatives, monitoring his heart rate, blood pressure and other bodily functions.

But there were no anxious relatives. There was only me.

A doctor came and stood by my side. I glanced at him. Tall, glasses, youngish but ageing fast. He looked exhausted.

'Who did this to him?' I said.

The doctor glanced at his iPad.

'Mr Jones did it to himself. We haven't done the full bloods yet. But my guess – he did it with a mixture of ketamine, crack and alcohol.'

'But that doesn't make any sense. This man didn't touch any of that stuff. He has been clean for years.'

The tired young doctor smiled. 'It's a war that has to be refought every day. That's the struggle, I'm afraid. *God, grant me the serenity to accept the things I cannot change, the courage to change the things I can, and the wisdom to know the difference.* And you can lose at any time.'

The Serenity Prayer.

I looked at him more closely. He wasn't as young as I had first thought. He smiled wryly, and I wondered if he was in AA or NA, and I knew enough not to ask.

'Keith Jones has been on the wagon for years,' I said.

'Looks like he fell off the wagon,' the doctor said.

'Or somebody pushed him,' said Terry Gatti.

Terry and Mick Gatti. Recognisably brothers, but so different. There was a prissy vanity about Terry's good looks – he looked like the kind of man who had a skin regime. In contrast, Mick was defiantly heavy and rough, toasted somewhere way beyond golden brown by years in the Spanish sun. Like Terry, Mick was burnished by the good life but he would always carry the rough edges of his old neighbourhood with him.

'She did this to him,' Mick said, and below his tan his features were twisted with a bitter mix of grief, rage and fear. 'Emma fucking Moon. She did it to Butch, whatever you lot say. And she did this to Keith. It's all on her.' He turned to bare his teeth at me. 'Don't you get it yet? *She's got a list.*'

The doctor quickly made his excuses and left us.

'What kind of list?' I said.

'A kill list. A shopping list of people she wants to bury. And you lot do nothing. And you lot make me sick.'

Terry was all calm as he contemplated Keith Jones in his hospital bed.

'Mick? Please remember your manners.' Then he

turned to me, almost apologetic. 'But my brother's right. This didn't come out of nowhere. First Butch. Now Keith. And he has been clean for years.'

I shook my head. I didn't buy it.

'Do you really think that Emma Moon – or anyone else – could make your pal smoke, snort and drink himself into a coma?'

They stared at me. That's exactly what they thought.

'Don't you get it?' I said. '*She's dying*. From what I can see, Emma Moon is in no position to hurt anyone. And you – all you old faces – are all scared witless of her. So what did you do to her? What did you do to her that makes you so terrified of her now?'

Terry Gatti smiled politely. His brother was always a blunt instrument.

But Terry probably always had this easy charm about him, I thought. It didn't just come with money they stole.

'With respect – you don't know her,' he said. 'Because if you knew her, then you would be scared, too. That famous photograph of the pair of you is deceptive. You don't have a relationship with her, even if you think you do. You don't have any special insights. You think Emma's some poor little waif who can do no wrong? That butter wouldn't melt? Who got caught in the crossfire? Detective, you know nothing.' Terry Gatti exhaled softly, more in sadness than anger.

I looked at what was left of Keith Jones. I wondered if somewhere inside that broken mind, he could hear any of this.

'But how do you make someone smoke crack?' I said. 'How do you get them to go out and score some horse tranquiliser? How do you make them drink a bottle of gin?' It was the stink of gin that was on him still, that ripe smell of juniper, and it filled the room and mingled with that hospital smell of bleach and bad food. 'How do you throw someone off the wagon when they have been on it for sixteen years?'

'Forgive me,' Terry Gatti said. 'Isn't answering that your job?'

The Gatti brothers exchanged a look.

'Well, go on,' Mick said. '*Tell him.*'

'I think he knows already,' Terry said. 'I think he can feel it in his blood.'

'No,' Mick insisted. 'He's just a stupid policeman. He really doesn't get it. So you explain it to him, Tel.'

Handsome Terry Gatti stepped closer and he smiled at me. It was a lovely smile, wide and white, one of those smiles that make you feel important, that make you feel noticed.

'If Emma Moon has a kill list, Detective Wolfe,' Terry Gatti said, 'then you're on it.'

20

There was an interview with Emma Moon on YouTube. Some true crime channel. I recognised the interviewer – Mads Kool, the woman from the gym, the influencer that Fred had chucked out. And it was not like *Newsnight*. It was not like some grown-up TV show where things had to be put into a wider context, and difficult questions were obliged to be asked.

Mads Kool just let Emma Moon talk.

And what Emma Moon talked about was the night she was taken into custody.

And she talked about me.

'I remember the night they took me away. The arresting officer was just a kid. Around ten years younger than me. I had never seen a uniform so blue. There never was a Metropolitan Police uniform so . . . pristine. It was just out of the box. And so was the policeman. He was so young. But that is no excuse, is it? And I begged him. *This will kill my son.* There was no doubt. If he took me now, if the prosecution got under way, then it would not stop. Justice would never come into it. But there was nothing in his eyes. Nothing in his heart. Nothing in his head. He could have freed me. I had done no wrong. He knew – I believe – that I had done no wrong.'

I rolled my eyes at that one. *I had done no wrong.* And yet there were two dead men on the floor, Emma, and a stolen fortune on its way to a secret location in the Cotswolds. But I had no doubt that Emma Moon believed in her total innocence. The criminal class has a genius for delusion. Her voice was calm, but there was something in those pale-blue eyes that was not calm at all, that seemed to rage at the injustice that had been done to her. By the men she protected. And by the young and dumb copper who had put the handcuffs on her.

'There was evil – true evil – done that night,' she said. 'But not by me. And not by my son. Though we were the ones who would be punished for the sins of others.'

'How do you feel . . .' Mads Kool shyly ventured, but Emma Moon did not need her questions.

'That young policeman,' she said, as if thinking aloud, as if unloading the thoughts of sixteen years in prison. 'There was only him and me in the huge house. But the front door was open. There was no other living soul any-where near. You could not even hear the sirens. There was a brief moment in time when he could have let me go. Just walk away, out that open door and back to my son. And the moment passed. He was just doing his job. Just obeying orders – history's great cop-out. And I was just trying to do mine – you know, the biggest job we ever do, the biggest job we ever have – *to protect the lives of those we bring into the world.* I failed at my job and I will carry that open wound to my grave.'

'Tell me about David. What kind of boy—'

'David was twelve years old when I was arrested. Already a troubled boy, an anxious boy. Unable – totally unable – to live up to his father's warped idea of macho masculinity. His father's idea of what a boy should be, a man should be.

'Twelve years old. Which sounds like a child. It *should* be a child. But he was already doing drugs. Smoking – strong stuff. He was already embarked on a path that would lead to psychosis by the time he should have been doing his first important exams. Smoking – just that – as far as I knew. But smoking was enough. Smoking – the potency of what they smoke now – was enough to poison his mind.' Emma Moon fought to control her breathing. Dry-eyed, as if all the tears had been shed long ago. 'I had been away – as they say – for six years when my son was found hanging from a door handle. They let me out for his funeral but I never had a chance to hold him. And it should have all been different. With kindness. With humanity. With compassion.'

Mads Kool cleared her throat. 'Do you—'

But Emma Moon may as well have been alone, all alone with the crowded, broken-hearted past. She drew another ragged breath, a long-term smoker's breath.

'But they chained me up and they took a mother from her son and he took the drugs that were such fun, and made him feel so grown up, right up until the moment when they were not fun at all, and he heard the voices, and he felt the terror, and was living in more pain than he could endure. My husband's cleaning lady found David hanging from his neck until dead.'

She smiled. A terrible smile full of nothing but hopeless regret.

'They say there is no capital punishment in this country but it is just not true. Because they sentenced my son to death when they put me away. And they sentenced me to a kind of death too. For no parent is ever fully alive again after they bury their child.'

Mads Kool was silent now.

'And I see it all so clear,' Emma Moon said. 'I see a uniform so brand new, and so blue, that it almost blinded me. And I remember my boy, my son, my David. And I forget nothing.'

21

I shut my laptop, looked at my watch and went to the window.

Scout should be home by now.

The meat market burned in the night and I stared at the familiar sight without really seeing any of it. The lines of vans and lorries, the shouts of the men, their white coats.

Emma Moon's podcast had unnerved me. That voice – so slow, so measured, as if she had all the time in the world.

And I remembered that night too, although the details were sketchy, a series of fractured images that were already half a lifetime away. The truth was that Emma Moon had faded in my memory. I remembered the shock of seeing those two dead men, and the ripped-out hole in the wall where the safe had been. Yet I had never thought of her, and I had never thought of her son. And over the years I had grown accustomed to, and bored sick with, the great plea of the arrested – *It wasn't me, guv.*

Yes, I was just doing my job. What else was I supposed to do?

And Scout should be home by now.

Scout was out with her mother. Dinner in Chinatown, I had been told. A chance to talk, to reconnect over Peking Duck. But it was knocking on for midnight. This was not what we'd agreed.

Home by 10 p.m. was what Scout and I had negotiated, and then only because Scout assured me that her mother would bring her to our door. And now it was long past 10 p.m. Now it was the fretting hour.

I was, I knew, a nervous father at the best of times. I always feared for my daughter until she came home, until I heard her key in the lock. I can't rest – I am not at peace until I know she is safe and sound. Perhaps all parents feel this way. But it is worse when you have done it all alone, when you are the single parent, the last line of defence between your child and the rest of the world.

I thought it would get better as she got older.

But tonight I feared for my daughter, and I could not shake the feeling that something terrible was going to happen.

Stan opened his eyes and sleepily watched me putting on my Rag & Bone flying jacket.

'Be right back,' I told him.

I went down into the night.

I began walking down Charterhouse Street towards Farringdon tube, expecting to see Scout and her mum coming towards me, all of us recognising the shape of each other at the same time. But the streets were empty, and there were no late-night travellers arriving at Farringdon tube.

I carried on to the Rotunda Garden.

It was crowded tonight with people who had nowhere else to go. A drunk who had missed the last train. Faces of the homeless that I recognised, and some faces I would never see again.

I walked out of the little square and back towards the meat market. The streets, I saw now, were not empty, because these streets were never empty.

Someone was watching me.

I saw him – too casual – leaning against the closed door of a café. I moved towards him and he turned.

'Wait!' I shouted as the figure broke into a run. I went after him. And I only stopped when I saw the skip.

The skip sat at the end of a side street that was being renovated. It was one of those narrow back roads that are little more than a glorified alley. Work was being done, the constant tearing down and rebuilding of a city. Scaffolding was all over the hollow block that had once been some kind of storage facility for the meat market, and was now about to be turned into luxury flats.

The skip was piled high, far too high, with rubble.

And there was something else.

One pale hand fluttered over the side of the skip.

I began walking towards it.

Something scuttled away and my heart pumped – a fox, very young, scrawny as a wild cat and not much bigger.

135

It cringed away from me and then settled, head bowed, protective of some prize it held in its mouth, watching me as I approached the skip.

The hand was milk-white in the glow of the street lights.

And then I was standing beside it, and I saw Suzanne's face, and I pulled away, stumbling backwards on the rubble-strewn street.

I turned my face away and stared at the fox and I thought I saw, limp in its mouth, a stuffed toy, a forlorn-looking rabbit, for all the world as if it had been thrown away, unwanted and discarded, like a part of childhood long since outgrown.

22

'*How to tell if you're a Golden Retriever*,' Scout read, staring at the phone in her hand.

She was still in her pyjamas. Morning had broken some time ago and she should be dressed for school by now. She should have brushed her teeth, and she should have had breakfast. None of this had happened.

I was at the window, staring down at the street, pole-axed with the exhaustion of a sleepless night, and in the distance I could see the lights that we had set up in the side street where I had found Suzanne.

As always, from a distance the crime scene looked like a movie set. It looked like something clean and glamorous when what was happening was the polar opposite. I could see the Scenes of Crime Officers in their white suits and blue face masks and gloves and shoe covers going about their business in their meticulous, slow motion pace. Our yellow-and-black *Do Not Enter* crime scene tape fluttered in a faint breeze.

'*How to tell if you're a Golden Retriever*,' Scout repeated, her voice small and mechanical and flat in the growing daylight.

I turned to look at her. She was cross-legged on the sofa, one hand holding her phone and the other absent-mindedly stroking Stan. I tried to smile.

'I already know that I'm not a Golden Retriever, Scout.'

'Not *you*,' she said. How impatient children can be with their slow-witted parents. She indicated the bundle of red fur curled up at her bare feet. 'Stan.'

'Go on then.'

'*How to tell if you're a Golden Retriever,*' she began. '*You sleep with a ball in your mouth?*'

'No. Stan never sleeps with a ball in his mouth. Wouldn't dream of it.'

'*You like rolling in muddy water?*'

I shook my head.

'Stan's idea of hell.'

'*You are the happy-go-lucky type who just wants to have a good time?*'

Now I smiled at her.

'That sounds like him.'

'*You beg shamelessly for food,*' she said, and I heard something crack in her voice, and I went to her as she began to cry, these small, desperate sobs that were all the more terrible for being totally silent. I put my arm around her and I held her as she let it out.

'Listen to me, listen to me, Scout,' I said, but there was nothing I could say to make any of it better. 'It's not fair. I know it's not fair.'

'But it should be,' she said. 'It should be fair!'

It had been nearly one in the morning when Scout had

finally arrived home, citing problems with the tube and buses that may even have been true. No sign of her mother, who she claimed had dropped her off at the end of our street and then kept the black cab.

I was waiting for her in our apartment.

She had not noticed the side street where the full cast of a murder investigation had already begun setting up. But I had told her about Suzanne immediately, and that she was gone, because it felt necessary and right that I tell her immediately, but it was only now, all these hours later and in the light, that it was starting to feel real.

The key turned in the lock and Mrs Murphy came into our loft.

'A terrible thing,' she said, more to herself than me, nodding, her focus totally on Scout. 'I've got her now,' she said. 'I'll take care of my girl. You go and do whatever it is you need to do.'

And so I went down to the street.

The process was already some way down the line. The divisional surgeon, there to pronounce death, had come and gone a few hours ago.

The SOCOs had made their preliminary pass, recording and photographing and bagging, and Suzanne's body had been whisked away in a blacked-out mortuary van. A tent had been erected above the street. The blue lights of our squad cars pulsed in the morning light.

I ducked under the tape and went to where DCI Pat Whitestone stood staring at the skip. She wore blue latex gloves and covers on her shoes.

'Bad body,' Pat said, meaning that there were no witnesses, meaning that this would not be simple. A good body would be one where we instantly knew what had happened and who had done it. She looked up and down the narrow side street, blue eyes glittering behind her glasses, finally jabbing a blue-gloved finger up at the scaffolding that covered the building. 'And no CCTV,' she said. 'At least not down here. There should be plenty on the main streets – some of it might even be working. But we have no weapon, no gloves, no photo ID on the victim. I understand you identified her?'

'Her name was Suzanne. She lived on the streets. A recovering addict, I always assumed, but I never knew if that was true or how the recovery was going. She spoke to me because she was getting harassed.'

'A young woman living on the streets,' Whitestone said. 'Well, yes. I imagine she was living in a world of harassment.'

'Some guy who claimed to be a cop.' I remembered Suzanne on the sofa of our apartment, the TV remote in her hand, watching the videos of dancing girls in bikinis on yachts. Could there be anything more remote from her own life? 'She was a sweet kid, Pat. She always had this toy with her, this stuffed rabbit. Some young fox had it in its mouth, I think. That's how I knew it was her.'

Whitestone looked interested.

'Hey, Carmen,' she called to a passing SOCO with a camera in one hand and an iPad in the other. 'Your people find any sort of toy on the deceased or in the vicinity?

Because Max here thinks he saw a fox with it. You bag anything like that?'

The SOCO pulled off her blue face mask. 'A toy?'

'A child's stuffed toy,' I said. 'A rabbit.'

The SOCO consulted an iPad. She shook her head. 'Nope. Not yet, at least. I'll let you know if it turns up.'

'Fox got it,' I said, staring at the skip piled high with the rubble of building work, seeing her so clearly in my head. 'Her name was Suzanne,' I said, and I felt a flood of shame that I did not know her family name. 'Shall I start knocking on some doors?'

Whitestone nodded. 'CCTV would be handy. And take the new kids with you,' she said. 'If they're up to it. You'll find them in there.' She indicated an old glass-fronted pub across the street, the faded brass and tobacco-stained twilight already teeming with life. 'Catching their breath.'

At this time of the morning the pubs and cafés were serving the great old meat market of Smithfield after the end of the long night. The work was over for the porters of Smithfield and now they were refuelling, wilting in the dawn, many of them with pints of lager in their fists.

As soon as I walked into the pub, I could tell what they did by the bloodstains on their white coats. The wholesalers, the men and the few women who buy and sell the meat, wore coats as pristine white as a laundry commercial. The men who worked with pork, which is carved while hanging up, had Jackson Pollock-style splatters of blood on their coats. And the men who worked with lamb – always butchered on thick wooden blocks, always carved by slicing towards you – were drenched in blood. Some of them still wore their cut gloves – the thick leather hand-wraps butchers wear to avoid losing their fingers.

Our two Direct Entry Detectives sat alone at a table in the corner. DC Sita Basu and DC Bear Groves. Two glasses of tap water in front of them. They had been up all night. They had seen the body. And they did not look like junior detectives from Scotland Yard's Homicide and Major Crime Command. They did not look like university-educated probationers nearing the end of their two-year apprenticeship.

They looked like a couple of scared kids.

Sita was pale with shock but composed, her head-girl demeanour shaken but trying to keep a grip. The lad – Bear – looked like he was coming apart. He was staring at two porters soaked with the blood of slaughtered lambs. He was starting to annoy the men. But he couldn't look away.

I pulled up a chair and joined them.

'We were just coming to find you,' Sita told me.

Bear stared at me without recognition. His big broad rugby-player face was slick with sweat. He took off his glasses and wiped his face with his palm. Clark Kent in pieces.

'Take your time,' I said. 'Finish your drinks.' I stared at them both, wanting them to calm down and then do what they were trained for, what we were here for. My voice was brisk and as businesslike as I could make it. 'We're going to be checking CCTV this morning. We're going to be interviewing the locals for anyone who saw a man having an altercation with a woman. And – I promise you – we are going to find the bastard who did this.'

DC Sita Basu was sipping her water and paying attention, just about holding it together.

But DC Bear Groves was still looking at me as if we had never met.

And I knew the feeling.

Because I had felt exactly the same way on a night long ago.

I had been that shocked boy.

It is the way you feel when you see your first murder victim.

And for the first time in your safe, protected life you understand that human evil is real, and close, and it never goes away.

PART TWO

The playlist at
Fred's gym

23

Ian Doherty's voice message had been left in the middle of the night, when I was lost in fitful sleep, but it was right there waiting for me at first light.

'Please . . . please . . . I meant no harm . . .'

Sobbing, blubbing regret. Incoherent, for the most part. But I got the gist. Ian Doherty, the old safecracker, was in fear of his life.

The rush hour had not quite begun when I arrived at Belsize Park.

There was no sign of Doherty outside the station. But the whiteboard where he wrote his motivational messages was there, as always. Three little words scrawled in his spidery black Sharpie.

Enjoy every sandwich.

I stood there staring at it as the commuters rushed by. It did not look like an inspirational quote.

It looked like last words, wry final thoughts. It looked like a suicide note.

*

He was on the platform of the southbound Northern line, walking up and down, addressing the same words to oblivious commuters who stared at their phones, totally ignoring him.

'There is a normal service on all other lines,' he said, dry-eyed and cheery. 'There is a normal service on all other lines . . . there is a normal service on all other lines . . .'

I grabbed his arm.

He stared at me in alarm, as if he had never seen me before.

'You called me,' I reminded him. 'What happened? Did someone threaten you? Who got to you?'

He pulled his arm away.

'Threatened me? Why would someone threaten me?' He was defensive, mad-eyed. 'I told you – I haven't done anything *wrong*.'

I followed him down the platform. It was filling up now. He treated the commuters as though they were familiar old friends. They treated him as if he was invisible.

'There is a normal service on all other lines!' he chanted. 'There is a normal service on all other lines! There is a normal service on all other lines!'

I grabbed his arm again. His long, pianist fingers fluttered with fear in front of his face.

'Hey, pal – you don't call me blubbing in the middle of the night and then get to walk away,' I told him.

'I'm sorry. That was a mistake. I shouldn't have done

it. But everything is clear now. Everything is decided. Please – please let me go. There is a normal service on all other lines.'

He removed his arm from my grasp. But I called after him as he marched on down the platform.

'What does the thought-for-the-day mean, Ian?' I said. '*Enjoy every sandwich* – what's all that about? Is that one by unknown, too?'

But he was no longer listening to me.

His voice faded as he moved to the end of the platform and then turned to come back, a slight, anonymous man in his neat blue TfL uniform, smiling at the crowds who were not aware of his existence. I could see his mouth still moving.

'There is a normal service on all other lines. There is a normal service on all other lines. There is a normal service on all other lines.'

A train was coming into the station.

The snaking headlights appeared in the black tunnel, getting closer, and suddenly it roared into the light as Ian Doherty stepped off the platform and fell onto the rails, his hands held out in front of his face as if to protect himself.

There was a sickening moment when I saw him on the tracks – no more than a moment – and then he was gone and the train just kept coming. Then there were the screams – the screams of the emergency brakes on the train, and the screams of the commuters who had seen Ian Doherty step off the platform.

Then all was chaos, and panic, and questions.

'What happened? Did someone push him? Oh, God! What just happened?'

But I knew.

Someone had scared him to death.

A few hours later, I was driving the old BMW X5 up to the gate of the big house on The Bishop's Avenue. Like every other property on that strange street of decaying mansions, Lord Nevermore's London house was barely visible from the street.

But even at this distance, it was clear that the property was one of the smaller and better-preserved residences on The Bishop's Avenue.

I got out of the car and pressed the buzzer by the gate but there was no sign it was working until the two women emerged from the house.

It was Emma Moon's two-woman entourage – the one who looked like a former model who had taken too many of the wrong drugs, all gawky limbs and frazzled beauty, and the younger one, the lank-haired, childlike girl, like an urchin from Dickens.

As they got closer I saw that the woman who looked as if she had been blown from the catwalk by chemical substances had her lips and cheeks heavily rouged, giving her the appearance of a discarded doll. The younger one grinned up at her, then stared at me.

'It's him,' the urchin said through the iron bars of the gate. 'Him from the photo.'

'But older,' said the fallen supermodel. 'And he's no spring chicken anymore, is he?' She tried hard to disguise it with elaborately stretched cod-Essex vowels, but there was a lifetime of privilege in her voice. Her face contorted with amusement. 'We *know* you. We know who you are. You're *famous*.'

The urchin was from the poor side of a smaller northern city, and more hostile.

'*He's* not famous,' she snorted. 'He only *arrested* someone who's famous. That doesn't make *him* famous.'

'Morning, ladies,' I greeted them, jovial Old Bill that I am.

They both flinched at my greeting, but the catwalk casualty was still trying to be amused at my presence.

'Oh, Constable,' she drawled. 'You really should have called.'

'The way it works,' I said, taking out my warrant card and holding it up in a gap in the black iron gate, 'is that I am a police officer – so I don't have to call anyone. I just show up.'

'Got paper, have you?' The urchin looked as if she was ready to cave my head in. She was enquiring if I had a search warrant.

'I don't need a warrant because I am not here to search or arrest. It's just a friendly chat.'

How they sneered at that.

A man appeared in the doorway of the grand house, which was not quite so grand on closer inspection but crumbling slowly with an air of genteel decay.

I recognised the gleaming shaven head of Emma's maybe-boyfriend, the ex-screw. He quickly ducked back inside.

'Can I get your names?' I said, as friendly as a flight attendant prior to take-off.

The tall, thin one was still looking at my warrant card.

'I'm Summer and she's Roxy,' she said. 'And we are wondering – how do we know this is genuine?'

I thought of poor dead Suzanne – *I don't know if it was real, Sir Max* – as the electric gates suddenly began to creak open from a command issued deep inside the house.

Summer and Roxy stepped aside.

Even in the clean, affluent air of north-west London, they both had that prison aura around them. People whose luck had been mostly bad, people who had made some bad choices, people with nothing to lose. I was getting back into the car when Summer seized my arm and pulled me close. I could feel the warmth of her breath on my face.

'She cut my cord in prison,' she whispered. 'Emma did. The cord that joined me to my baby. Emma cut it. In my cell. In Bronzefield. *Emma cut it with her teeth.*'

'Emma looked after you, didn't she, Summer?' Roxy said with a sudden warmth, her face lighting up. 'Emma looked after all of us.'

Their devotion was living proof that Emma Moon had been a model prisoner during her sixteen-year incarceration. When I spoke to him, the governor had given her a rave review. Despite those two dead men in the big house in Belgravia, and the unrecovered riches that were whisked away, Emma's time inside was a textbook of good behaviour, a model of successful rehabilitation. And although she was still in her twenties when she was sent down, she had clearly become a mother figure to her fellow inmates in HMP Bronzefield.

With all that time on her hands — years and years of time — she had taken her Certificate in Counselling and Mentoring (duration 200 hours, Level 4 Prisoner's Education Trust). She had taught her fellow prisoners to read. She taught them to stop cutting their own flesh. If Summer, the fallen supermodel, was telling the truth, then she had shown them how to deliver their babies. The governor could not praise her highly enough. The wardens were so fond of her — he joked, straining a bit, it is true — that one of them was now engaged to be married to her.

But even a model prisoner is released on licence.

Even a counsellor and mentor and mother figure is bound by strict rules, regulations and restrictions on their release. And one of the multiple conditions of Emma Moon's release was that she had to reside permanently at an address approved by her supervising officer and obtain the prior permission of that supervising officer for a stay of one or more nights at a different address.

So I knew exactly where I would find her. At Lord Nevermore's city residence on The Bishops Avenue.

The tall stooped old toff was waiting for me at the

house, smiley and bashful and apologetic with his long fringe hanging over his spectacles, like a Richard Curtis hero grown into gouty old age. The bald, burly ex-warden hovered behind him like some thug butler.

I told Nevermore my name and rank as I showed him my warrant card.

'But of course I know who you are,' he smiled, apparently at ease with my unannounced presence, although his face flushed an alarming red. He soundlessly clapped his hands. 'It's *you*! And I am delighted to meet the famous PC Wolfe in person. I've seen your photograph a thousand times, of course. Ten thousand.'

'I'm not a police constable anymore,' I said, churlish in the face of such enthusiasm for the old days.

The women had trailed me into the house.

'You know Emma's done nothing *wrong*, don't you?' demanded Roxy.

'Apart from fall in love with the wrong man,' sighed Summer.

'I know she did her time,' I said.

And even that's not the whole truth, I thought.

Because she also did time for the rest of them.

Terry and Mick Gatti. Keith 'The Nutjob' Jones. Butch Lewis. Ian Doherty. It was not only her time that she had served. It was their time, too. Nevermore turned to the motley crew that had gathered around to gawp.

'I see you've met Summer.' He nodded to the fallen supermodel with the mad light in her ravishing eyes. 'And Roxy, of course.' The aggressive urchin glared at

154

me. 'And Luka Brady I imagine you know already,' he said, indicating the former warden, as though law and order, the prison service and the police, was some kind of private gentleman's club in St James's and we had all known each other from public school. With the glorious arrogance of the upper class, Nevermore didn't bother to introduce himself.

'Did you wish to see Emma? I am afraid she has an appointment in Harley Street.' He was still smiling but some of the warmth had gone out of his watery eyes. 'She begins her treatment today.'

He let that settle. 'And may I ask why you are here, Detective?'

'Yeah, because that's what I was fucking wondering,' muttered Roxy, and Nevermore gave her a swift withering look that instantly silenced her.

For all his self-deprecating manner, for all the polished politesse, I could see that there was no disguising who was in command here.

'I wanted to tell her something,' I said. 'Something I should have told her years ago.'

Nevermore sized me up and saw me as no threat to whatever it was he was protecting here.

'Then I must take you to Emma immediately,' he said.

A hospital on Harley Street. A private room.

And on the bed Emma Moon rested with her long dancer's limbs stretched out, languidly drawing on a cigarette, the red pack of full-strength, high-octane Marlboro on the dressing table next to her, and beside her the bleak paraphernalia of chemotherapy – a small pump, an intravenous drip, all the kit for the long, nausea-inducing hours of continuous infusion chemo – untouched and unwanted on this day, and – I was guessing here – on all the other days of her life.

Nevermore was outraged. 'But Emma – this is so wrong! The treatment – it has been paid for and scheduled and – the hours I have spent with your oncologist, the bloody *hours*, Emma! – I really must object in the strongest possible terms!'

She exhaled a cloud of smoke with a kind of sighing relish.

'Well, after some reflection I have decided that I will opt for *quality* rather than *quantity* in my time that remains,' she said. 'All this' – she indicated the chemo hardware – 'is likely to give me *less* quality time, not more quality time. It will give me *less* time to do what I have to do.' She chuckled quietly to herself, and I wondered if anyone had ever chuckled with such amusement in that expensive chemotherapy room before today. 'And a lot less hair, of course.'

'But Emma—'

She shut him down.

'Look – just get lost for a bit, would you, Boy?' she said. 'Thanks, awfully.'

And then she finally turned her pale-blue eyes on me,

sucked hungrily on her cigarette and smiled, the smoke curling out of her thin lips.

And I smelled that old scent from long ago, that smell of cigarettes and flowers that she carried with her on the night I first met her.

'Long time no see,' said Emma Moon.

24

Emma Moon lay on the bed in that deluxe chemotherapy room in Harley Street, a brace of pillows at her back and neck, sucking a full-fat Marlboro as she spoke of her mother.

'I remember this thing my mum said when she was at the end with her lung cancer,' said Emma Moon. 'She would say – *This is not me*. As if there was a point when terminal illness robs you of yourself. And she would look so – I don't know – stricken. So – sad. *This is not me*.' Emma Moon nodded at the untouched chemotherapy kit all around. 'And I don't want to say the same thing. *This is not me*. But that's what my mum said, and she said it all the time. And then she died.'

The door to the private room flew open and a cheery overweight nurse bustled into the room, her face falling and flushing an appalled red when she saw Emma Moon smoking.

'There is no smoking,' she managed eventually, and I knew she was looking at something she had never seen before.

Emma Moon smiled. 'Get him to arrest me,' she said.

'This fine young man by my bedside. It wouldn't be the first time.'

'I'll get the doctor! That's who I'll get!'

'Oh, get who you like.'

'Madam — you are dying.'

'Then it doesn't make a whole lot of difference, does it? And we are all dying, dear. It's just that some of us are doing it a bit faster than others.' Emma winked at me as she relished another puff. 'Nobody here gets out alive.'

The nurse left, shaking her head in distress, and we sat in silence, Emma smoking, staring off into the distance, lost in her thoughts, and me staring at her face.

She was changed by the years, but not in the way I had anticipated. This close up, she was still unexpectedly stunning. When I had met her in that big house sixteen years ago, and when I had put the handcuffs on her, Emma Moon had been a pretty, skinny, long-limbed dancing girl who had met the wrong man. And you could understand what that wrong man had seen in her. But now she was one of those women who had grown into her looks. Now she was something else.

There was a steely confidence about her. The generic good looks of youth had been chiselled into something more meaningful over the years. She was no longer that pretty young girl I had arrested. But there was a worn, hard-earned beauty about her that would not fade with time.

Emma Moon may have been dying. But there was nothing remotely weak about her.

'How long have you got?' I said.

'I think visiting hours are until four o'clock.'

'You know what I mean.'

'Long enough, I hope. Long enough to – what's the phrase? – *put my affairs in order*. This desperate clinging to life that is always expected of us – I never understood it. Not after watching my mum die. But of course there is always unfinished business. And I suppose we all get pushed for time in the end.'

'And you're getting married.'

She snorted. 'To Luka Brady? My disgraced screw? So they say on social media! Well, let's see, shall we? I'm not really looking for love, to tell you the truth. I'm hoping to avoid it.' She considered me with amusement. 'You've gotten older,' she said. 'You looked like a scared little kid that night! I almost felt sorry for you. Almost.'

'We've all gotten older.'

She nodded. 'But I was the perfect age for prison. There is never a good age to be locked up for sixteen years. But there is an optimum age – the age when you are most likely to survive more or less intact. The age when you are young enough to be strong and resilient but old enough to not fall into the trap of despair. And I knew that it was my life now, HMP Bronzefield, as the years came and went. That helps – when your brain adjusts to the new reality. I knew I wasn't leaving anytime soon.'

Because you cut no deals, I thought. Because you would not talk.

'You learn a new language inside, a different way of being alive,' she said. 'Blue code, red code. Blue code being when someone is turning blue – mostly an attempted suicide; there's lots of that – and red code when there is blood; mostly self-harm. You would not believe the number of inmates who seek relief by cutting open their own flesh.'

This was the rhythm of her speech. She had the accent of the self-educated working class. There were lots of parentheses – she broke off to digress, or to expand her point – but what struck me most of all was that her monologue was totally free of self-pity.

'Prison found me in my prime,' Emma Moon said. 'I was kind to the people I encountered until they gave me good reason to not be kind. I was young enough, strong enough, loved enough to be kind. And young enough, strong enough, loved enough to survive. And I *was* loved in there. In prison. It's the only word for it.'

'I met your friends,' I said. 'Those two women. Summer and Roxy.'

'Roxy and Summer. They're not really my friends – they're more like my family. The closest thing to family that I have left.'

'Summer told me you had helped her in childbirth.'

Emma Moon smiled. 'Only in her head,' she said. 'Summer has these . . . fancies; these delusions that seem completely real to her. And she gets confused about where the dreams end and where real life begins.' She stubbed out her cigarette in an empty glass. 'But Summer can't have children.'

And then finally she looked at me. Really looked at me.

'And why are you here?' she said.

'Because I'm sorry about what happened to your son,' I said. 'I'm sorry about David. I learned what happened. And I can't imagine what it must be like to have a child who takes their own life.'

We sat in silence.

'I did tell you,' she said quietly, her mouth tight. 'I did predict what would happen to David if I was locked away.'

I nodded.

'And he snapped. He just broke. Children do that these days, you know. They are more fragile than we were. The pressures are stronger, and so are the drugs. But David would not have died if I was out. He would have lived. He would have had a happy life. If someone had helped him to carry the load – just for a bit, just for a bit, just for a bit.' She reached for her packet of Marlboro. 'And so – are you *sorry*? Do you feel *guilty*? Do you wish you had let me walk away?'

I remembered the dead gardener. I remembered the dead bodyguard. One with his skull cracked like a soft-boiled egg hit with a hammer. The other stabbed more times than I could count.

'With two men dead? And that safe – and whatever was in it – gone for good? I couldn't let you just walk away, could I? Then we would have both ended up in jail.'

'The men who died had nothing to do with me. And from first to last, I behaved with honour. Tried to.'

'Please. You got them inside the house. Your colleagues. Your boyfriend Terry. And it's true – you never threw the others under a bus for a lighter sentence. A bit of that old South London *omerta*. But so what? They deserved to go down. They should have been locked away. And you – you were arrested at the scene of an armed robbery and double murder. It's a bit of a stretch to see you as completely blameless, Emma. But I am – and I will always be – truly sorry about your son. About David. No parent should have to bury their child. And I wanted to see you. And I wanted to tell you that I am so sorry about what happened to David.'

She took her time lighting another cigarette. There were raised voices outside the room. Nevermore and a nurse or two, it sounded like, his patrician authority competing with their Harley Street bossiness.

'Someone said – in times of peace, children bury their parents,' Emma Moon said. 'And in times of war, parents bury their children. Herodotus. He was one of my favourites. I did a lot of reading inside. I was never much of a reader outside but I became a reader inside. And it was a time of war – those mad years running with Terry and his brother and the rest of them.'

'But why did you take the punishment for all of them, Emma? Why didn't you start talking and keep talking until they let you go home to your son? That's what I still don't understand.'

163

'I was a fool in love.'

'And that's all? You did sixteen years because Terry Gatti was a good-looking boy?'

'I *loved* him.'

'And why didn't he help with David? Why wasn't he there for his son?'

'Terry had his own life to live.'

'And now they are all dying. All your old friends.'

She laughed softly, shaking her head.

'You get out,' I pressed on, 'and bad things start happening to them. Butch Lewis dead from some kind of heart attack. Keith Jones killing himself with whatever poison he can score. And this morning Ian Doherty threw himself under a tube train. What's going on, Emma?'

She shrugged and looked around the chemo room.

'Do you think I'm settling old scores? This sick old woman before you?'

There were more noises beyond the door now. I could also hear the voices of the women raised in angry expletives – the northern accent of Roxy, and the cut-glass tones of Summer, her Essex vowels discarded at a moment of social conflict.

And I didn't want to see any of them anywhere near my home, I thought.

The two old jailbirds and the disgraced warden, all those graduates of HMP Bronzefield. I didn't want to look out of the window of my apartment one night and see them standing in the street. I didn't want them anywhere near me. None of them.

'I was the one who found Butch Lewis.'

'Dodgy ticker. Poor old Ray. I always liked him. A simple soul. Doted on those kids. Those little girls. His granddaughters.'

Someone scared him to death.

'And Keith Jones. He died a few nights ago. Did you know that?'

Her face twisted with contempt. 'Keith was an addict. A raving mad man. Drink, drugs – The Nutjob was up for anything that was going.'

'When he was a kid maybe. Not anymore. Not for a long time.'

He didn't fall off the wagon – somebody threw him of the wagon.

'And why did Ian Doherty kill himself today? First time I met him, he seemed like a quiet, philosophical soul, quite content with his self-help quotes and his job on the underground.'

'Oh, *come on*! Do you really think any of this mess had anything to do with me?'

'I don't know. But you bear a grudge. I can feel it.'

'Ask me. Go on. We both know you want to.'

We stared at each other.

'Did you – or any of your associates – have any contact with Butch Lewis or Keith Jones or Ian Doherty prior to their deaths?'

'I was still inside when Ray Lewis had his – what shall we call it? – funny turn. Keith is – was – a junkie. And the other one – Ian Doherty – I never met the man in my life. Not that night, and never since. I have been inside for the last sixteen years.'

'I know you were. But your friends – your *family* – were not inside, were they? I understand that Summer and Roxy were released years ago.'

'Is this crap why you are really here? Do you actually give a damn about David? Or are you just interrogating me?'

'I'm asking you. Something scared Butch Lewis. And Keith Jones. And Ian Doherty. Something – someone – put the fear of God into them. Something – someone – scared them to death.'

She laughed out loud. She laughed in my face.

'Is that the theory, Max? That I *scared* Butch to death? And that I somehow forced Keith to stick a gram of God knows what white powder up his snout? That I shoved Ian under the eight fifteen fast train from Hendon Central? You give me too much credit! I'm not that smart. And I am not a killer. It takes a lot to take another human life. I don't have it in me. I just don't. But I do know this – *death is far from the worst that can happen to you.* Being alive and tormented for every living moment – waking and sleeping – ah, that's a lot harder! This is what you have to understand – *I thought about what happened for sixteen years.* But I never wanted to kill them, Max. Not even my ex-husband. Certainly not poor old Butch with his dodgy ticker. Or Keith with his pathetic born-again new age tofu-munching, yoga-mat bullshit. All I ever wanted is this – *I wanted to see them suffer as I have suffered.* That's not much to ask, is it? After sixteen years inside. After losing the best years of my life. *After losing my son.* After protecting people who abused me. I never wanted them harmed, not any of them. But – yes – I wanted them to suffer.' She leaned back with a smile, contemplating her unlit Marlboro. 'Because do you really think that dying is the worst thing that can happen to you? Trust me – it's really not. Living . . . sometimes nothing hurts like having to go on living.'

The door opened, slowly this time, almost deferentially, and they all hovered in the doorway. Nevermore and the ex-warden. Summer and Roxy. Beyond them there was a young doctor and a couple of nurses in the corridor, trying to peer into the room. The door was gently closed in their faces as Emma Moon's entourage stepped inside.

Nevermore and the others carefully approached the bed. I could feel them behind me. And more than this, I could smell the same thing on all of them. They all had it, even Nevermore after all those visiting hours over the years.

That prison stink. There is a silent desperation in it, and it sticks to everything.

'You're tired,' Nevermore said, and this time she did not slap him down. 'You've had enough for one day.'

I stood up to go.

'Lovely to see you again after so long,' Emma Moon said to me. 'Thank you for coming. And I believe that you became a parent yourself during the intervening years?'

'A daughter.'

And I waited. '*Scout*,' she said, and she let that settle between us, smiling to herself. It was very quiet in the room. 'Like the book. Like the little girl in *To Kill a Mockingbird*.'

'Yes,' I said. 'Just like the little girl in the book.'

'A beautiful name,' said Emma Moon. 'Anything else on your mind?'

I nodded.

'Yes,' I said. 'Stay away from my family.'

25

'Shall we wait a bit longer?' DC Sita Basu said. 'Give it five minutes? See if a few more of them come?'

It was the morning after my Harley Street reunion with Emma Moon. Our team were in the media room in the basement of New Scotland Yard. The press conference should have begun by now but there were still row after row of empty seats. In the centre of a low stage, just to the side of a table with four chairs, there was Suzanne's face – her passport photo, massively enlarged, looking younger, healthier, more full of hope than I had ever known.

DCI Pat Whitestone stared out at a handful of bored journalists checking their phones and chatting among themselves. We stood to the side of the stage, waiting for the room to fill.

'They're not coming,' Whitestone said, staring at Suzanne's photograph. 'They only come in significant numbers when the victim is attractive. A beautiful woman – preferably a young wife and mother. Or an innocent little child with a sweet smile. But it has to be a *beautiful* little kid. *Then* they come. But Suzanne? A foreign drug addict sleeping on the street? Who cares if she gets her neck snapped? Who cares if she gets her body dumped in a skip?'

DC Basu exchanged a glance with DC Bear Groves. The head girl and Clark Kent, uncertain what to do next. They both looked at me.

'Give it five minutes, Sita,' I said, and at the sound of my voice, Whitestone turned on me, as if I had done something wrong.

'*This* is our murder, Max. You understand that, right? Not Butch Lewis, who had a dodgy ticker. Not Keith Jones, who topped himself with whatever poison he put into his body. And not Ian Doherty, the old safecracker who could take this wicked world no more. *This* is our murder. *And I want you to care.*'

I took a breath.

'I do care, Pat. I knew her. I knew Suzanne. And I promise you – I do care.'

'Oh, good! Because I heard you were down at The Bishops Avenue yesterday. Yes, I know all about that. And I heard that after that you were gallivanting down Harley Street.'

'It was hardly—'

'And I know because Nevermore called the boss of *our* big boss. The man at the top of the Met. Apparently him and Nevermore were at school together.'

'A complaint's been made?'

'Not a complaint. These big shots like Nevermore don't make complaints. They don't have to. They *talk* to each other. So a word to the wise. Just stay away from Emma Moon, will you? Butch Lewis, Keith Jones, Ian Doherty – that's not our investigation, they are not our murders – in fact, they are not anybody's murders. She's under your skin, this Emma Moon, and you really don't want her under your skin.'

'Ma'am?'

It was the FLO – a Family Liaison Officer. She was another bewildered middle-class kid, another university graduate, not unlike our two Direct Entry Detectives, looking like she was wondering what she had got herself into. There was an older woman and a younger woman with her. Suzanne's mother and sister. I could see her in both of them. Their eyes were fixed on the blown-up photograph of Suzanne.

'I'm afraid their English is not good enough to participate in the press conference,' the FLO said.

Whitestone stared at the two women. 'Talk to them, Max,' she told me.

And so I tried.

'I'm so sorry for your loss,' I said. But they clung to each other and they did not give any indication that they had heard me.

'I knew Suzanne,' I said. 'I spoke to her many times.'

No reaction.

'I promise you now that I am going to find the man who did this,' I said.

And finally they looked at me.

*

171

They were winding it up in Smithfield.

Witness statements had been taken. The white-suited SOCOs were no longer on the scene. The countless hours of CCTV were back at MIR-1 at the Yard, being pored over by Pat Whitestone, DC Sita Basu and a dozen uniforms.

We had one promising lead so far – sixty seconds of foggy images of Suzanne walking past a strip of Smith-field shops in what looked like a heated argument with an unknown man. This one minute of CCTV had already been handed to the digital assistance team for circulation Met-wide to see if it produced any hits on the Forensic Image Management system.

Back in Smithfield, DC Bear Groves and I watched them taking down the DO NOT CROSS police tape at either end of the side street where Suzanne had been found. The skip was gone now. There was still a Rapid Response Vehicle parked at either end of the street – a glorified alley, really – but this was misleading. Because we were done here. We had reached that point where the investigation had moved on from the scene of the crime.

I looked at my young colleague's exhausted face.

'You all right, Bear?'

'I'm fine. Just a bit of a downer back there. At the press conference. Just a few journos showing up. Nobody really caring. It's dispiriting.'

I watched the police tape fluttering in the breeze like the flag of some defeated army. 'DCI Whitestone is right,' I said. 'Some murders matter more than others. Or at least, they matter more to the public.'

He nodded, ran his fingers through his thick black hair, hair good enough for a shampoo commercial, and I wondered if he would stick with us.

'The job – is it what you expected?' I asked him. 'When you were – I don't know – punting down the river Cam?'

He smiled. A big, good-natured smile.

'I was at university in Manchester so there wasn't a lot of punting involved, I'm afraid. Sita – D C Basu – is the swot. She went to Trinity, so she may have done some punting down the Cam.' Then he thought about it. 'I can't pretend it is not a bit different to what I was expecting. Because theory will only take you so far. Because people lie to us, don't they? The public lie to the police. There was a couple that I interviewed with Sita – D C Basu. This couple – this man and woman – they gave Suzanne money. They gave her twenty pounds. They were kind to her. We had them on CCTV. They gave Suzanne this money before they went to the hotel.' He gestured towards Charterhouse Square. 'The Malmaison. And we talked to them at the hotel. They were a married couple. But the thing is – *they're not married to each other*. And they looked at me and D C Basu and they swore blind that they had never given money to any homeless girl.' He shook his handsome head. 'People don't like us very much, do they?'

'They used to like us more,' I said.

The head of the Specialist Search Team came to tell me that they had completed their work.

'Suzanne had this stuffed toy she always carried with her,' I said. 'This toy rabbit. Mister Flopsy. If we have it, then I want it for her family.'

The head of the search team bristled, as if I was questioning her work. 'My search team just completed a three-mile-radius search of the crime scene,' she said sharply. 'No Mister Flopsy. Maybe the wildlife got it. I'll let you know if it turns up.'

We watched her walk away. I slapped Bear on the back.

'Let's get a beer,' I said. 'I live right over there.'

I took DC Bear Groves back to my apartment. He gawped at all the wide open space, taking in the view of the dome of St Paul's Cathedral, shaking his head in disbelief.

'Wow,' he said. 'You don't share this place with anyone?'

I was getting a couple of Tsingtao out of the fridge.

'My daughter. My dog.'

Stan – who loved everyone – stirred on his favourite sofa, stretched out a perfect Downward Facing Dog and padded over to make Bear fall in love with him immediately and forever. But Scout was not home. Out with her mum again, she had told me.

I knew what DC Bear Groves was thinking – what people always thought when they saw my home. *How does someone on Metropolitan Police wages afford a loft in Smithfield?* I don't tell them that my parents died when I was a kid. That my grandmother brought me up and left me everything she had in the world. I didn't feel like explaining. I never did. And if that inspired anyone to think I was a bent copper on the take, then that was their problem, not mine.

I gave the boy his beer. We clinked bottles.

He got a secret smile on his face.

'Can I show you something? I was going to show you at the office but after what DCI Whitestone said about concentrating on our murder I thought – better not.'

He scrolled through his phone and held it out to me. It was a picture of a boat.

A 70-foot motor yacht. '*With unique, graceful and seductive lines, let yourself be carried away by her design,*' I read. '*The V40 quintessentially showcases the sleek exterior, performance and exceptional seakeeping of the Princess V Class Range.*' The asking price was mid-six figures.

'And look at this,' Bear said. 'Same neighbourhood. Marbella, Spain.'

A white villa with a red roof. '*Nestled within the luxurious enclave of Los Cotijas at La Cala Hill Club, this gorgeous villa offers an unparalleled blend of sophistication and panoramic views.*' Price on application.

'The boat?' Bear said. 'The villa? They're both owned by Mick Gatti.'

I looked at the boat, the house. Both for sale.

'How did you find this stuff?'

He laughed. 'I just did some digging. That's what we do, isn't it? Dig until we find buried treasure. And I thought you might be interested.'

I thought about it. 'So Mick Gatti is selling up.'

'What does it mean?'

I sipped my Tsingtao.

'It means his money is running out.'

My phone vibrated.

Whitestone calling, it said.

'We got him,' she said. 'The man who murdered Suzanne. I'm sending the images to you now.'

I stared at my phone and waited a moment as the blown-up CCTV images began to arrive. It was the old homeless soldier. The big bearded man who kept his kit so neat and tidy. The one who never said anything, who never asked for anything. The clearest images had him in the doorway of a shuttered shop with Suzanne. Walking down Charterhouse Street with Suzanne. And in what looked like Smithfield Long Lane late at night, his arms raised in what looked like protest – with Suzanne staring up at him, Mister Flopsy clutched to her chest.

'It's not him, Pat,' I said. 'I know this guy. It's not him.'

Whitestone exploded.

'Why not him? Because he doesn't fit your theory about some fake cop?'

'Come on, Pat. Does he look like he's got a warrant card? Even a fake one?'

'We've got him on CCTV! With the girl. With Suzanne.'

'Doing what exactly?'

'Arguing with her! Confronting her! Having a violent, emotional argument with Suzanne. All right?'

'Pat, it's not enough.'

'Listen to me, Max. *It's enough.*'

I could hear the voices behind her in MIR-1.

I could hear their excitement.

'We're bringing him in now,' Whitestone said, her voice cold. 'Want to watch?'

26

Early doors at Fred's.

That first shift of the day, when the high-flying, habit-stacking finance sector boys and girls were in for their high-intensity primary health care, lifting the free weights and banging the bags and pumping the blood and raising the heart rate on every bit of machinery in the gym, and on every free bit of space on the floor. Later the clientele would be far more diverse – people of all ages and shapes and sizes coming in for perfect abs and gorgeous glutes, for rehab and healing, or just to keep the rubber tyre of time off their waistline. But here at the start of the day was hardcore. The music was turned up to eleven – guitars from the last century that sounded as though they were playing live. I recognised the song – prime-time Clash running amok on, ironically enough, 'I Fought the Law'.

And in the middle of it all, in the centre of an ancient boxing ring, two men were attempting to beat the other unconscious.

Terry Gatti – tall, lean, with the kind of fitness you

have to work hard for in the middle years – wore all the appropriate kit. Headguard, pristine white T-shirt and shorts, and when his mouth twisted in a grimace of effort, his upper lip bulged with the mouthguard wedged beneath his upper teeth.

His kid brother Mick had none of these things. Mick was in his street clothes, as if he was in a street in tourist Spain at closing time – a short-sleeve shirt with palm trees open to his beer-belly girth, baggy knee-length shorts and bare feet. If you didn't have the proper foot-wear for the sacred canvas of the old ring, then you did it in your bare feet. They both wore heavy Lonsdale sparring gloves, eighteen-ounces. And they were taking it seriously, this business of battering another man to the floor.

Mick charged forward, swinging wildly, prepared to take a punch to the cakehole, or even two or three or four, if he got to land a good one of his own. Terry skipped backwards, looking the part but clearly not quite as sharp as he would like to be, slipping most of his kid brother's shots but staggering backwards with shock when he caught one on his headguard.

Fred stood in one corner, watching them with aca-demic interest, and it looked like he was admiring their effort if not their technique. He was giving the odd com-ment and word of advice, but I couldn't hear it above the racket that The Clash were making until I was standing right by his side.

'Triple jab,' Fred said. This to Terry. 'And the last jab has to be the hardest – to keep them off and show them you mean it and finish your combination with a bang.'

Terry did what he was told. Three short lefts to his brother's flushed, sweating face, the third with some real welly behind it. Mick's head snapped back with the shock – and it is shock more than pain – you invariably feel when someone punches you hard in the face.

'You're so lucky to be training,' Fred smiled at them, and then he glanced at the clock as it counted down. 'Time,' he said, and the pair of them knew enough to stop immediately.

Fred turned to me. 'We should have a day – every week – when we only play bands that played the Rainbow.'

I knew he was thinking about when he saw The Clash at the Rainbow in Finsbury Park when he was a teenager from just down the road in Kentish Town. It felt like we had had this conversation before.

'Joe and the boys,' I said. 'The Clash, of course.'

He nodded. 'And Buzzcocks. The Faces. The Who.'

Mick Gatti was bent double behind us. Terry was hanging on the ropes, not quite as fit as he thought he was. Fighting exhausts you faster than anything in the world.

'Iggy Pop,' I said. 'Bob Marley and his Wailers. Slade. T. Rex.'

'Kool and his Gang. Pink Floyd. Jimi Hendrix.'

'Hendrix? Really?'

'Oh yeah. Back in the Sixties when the Rainbow was the Astoria. That's where Jimi first burned his guitar.'

Fred nodded to the Gattis – they gasped their thanks – and he went off to supervise his kingdom. And then the brothers were staring at me.

'You didn't know we know Fred, did you?' Mick said, looking like he was contemplating having a stroke.

'Knew him when we were boxing as lads,' Terry said, starting to look more like his smooth self again. 'He was North London and we were South London. Different weights, of course. Fred was much lighter and smaller than us, so neither of us ever had to fight him.'

'Thank fuck,' said Mick.

'What do you want?' I said.

'We want to help you,' Terry said. 'You got some snitch asking questions – this murder across the street from here, the homeless girl – about someone using their warrant card to harass women.'

'He's not a snitch.'

Mick Gatti guffawed. 'Ooh, is he a *criminal informant?* Is that his job description? Is he your *CI*? La-dee-da!'

Terry shot his mouthy brother a look.

Then he turned back to me.

'Point is, Max – if you want to know what's going on, you can always come to us. You don't give the task to some bottom-feeder like that clapped-out rock and roller. What's his name?'

'Nils.'

'Yeah, Nils, right.'

181

'Don't get too snotty, Max,' Mick said. 'We know all about you.'

I stared at him. I could smell the booze on him, smell it coming out of his pores. He either had a heavy night or he had started early. And I thought about the yacht for sale, and the Spanish villa for sale, and I wondered if he saw me as some kind of payday.

'Haven't you been smacked about enough for one day?' I asked him.

But Mick Gatti was undeterred. He grinned like he had something on me.

'You got a QPM, right? A Queen's Police Medal. Officer A, right? That was you. That suicide bomber that was stopped outside the railway station. That was our hero Max. But then your career stalled. What happened? Your career stalled but – funny thing – our hero's climb up the property ladder just kept going.' He grinned stupidly. 'How does a lowly detective in the Met get to live in a big loft in Smithfield? They don't go for peanuts. You didn't get that on a plod's pitiful salary, did you?'

I didn't hit him. I reached out with my right hand and I wrapped it around his throat and I squeezed. And he let me. He was not stupid enough to start chucking his telegraphed punches at me. And he laughed at me, or tried to, as I kept squeezing until he finally stopped laughing and his eyes began to bulge.

Terry Gatti placed a gentle hand on my arm. He was still wearing the big black gloves and the leather was slick with sweat.

'Max,' he said. 'Please. This is not about you. It's about Suzanne. Honestly – we are only here to help.'

I took my hand from Mick Gatti's throat and turned to look at Terry. Kool and the Gang were on the sound system now, celebrating good times. Fred was serious about this they-have-to-have-played-the-Rainbow philosophy.

'What do you two know about Suzanne?' I said.

'We know you picked up some homeless old soldier for her murder,' Mick said, massaging his neck. 'With the Met's usual knack of cocking everything up. If you – I mean the Old Bill, the filth, the Met – were doing the job you're paid for, then that poor little cow would still be alive.'

'That old soldier,' Terry Gatti said softly. 'The one you took into custody last night? What's he had to say for himself?'

'Not a lot,' I admitted, and the Gatti brothers laughed.

Nothing, in fact. The old soldier's name was Robert McKay. Age forty-one. No fixed abode. Winner of the OSM with clasp awarded for service in the Afghanistan theatre of operations. McKay had come quietly when we lifted him from his doorway. He towered above the arresting officers but came without protest, as if this had all been arranged long ago.

We still handcuffed him as we read him his rights. Now we had him in a holding cell awaiting mental assessment because he had been discharged with PTSD after two tours in Helmand.

'He didn't kill Suzanne,' Terry Gatti said.

I said nothing. I already knew that Robert McKay did not kill Suzanne. Despite the CCTV images of them arguing. Despite his total lack of any denial.

The brothers were looking at me.

'But we know who did,' Terry Gatti said.

27

'Talk,' I said.

We were the only men in the pub who were not dressed in the white coats of Smithfield meat market. A cosy corner table. A double shot of Grey Goose for Mick Gatti and sparkling mineral water for Terry and me. The pub was packed. The rest of the city was clutching the first coffee of the day and on their way to work but these blurry-eyed white-coated men with pints in their hand for breakfast were at the end of their night shifts.

'Who gave you this old soldier?' Mick Gatti leered, lifting the shot of vodka in his meaty fist. 'This CI of yours – Nils? Or – what? Don't tell me! You got him on CCTV with the girl? But you don't have him topping the girl, do you? No, I bet you don't! Your CCTVs not that good. Because he didn't do it.'

He bolted his drink in one go and bared his expensively veneered teeth, toilet bowl white, always a mistake, staring around the pub, shaking his head.

'This country,' he said. 'On the last day of all time there will be men sitting in pubs knocking back pints and talking about the football. Bloody rain-soaked, strike-riven dump, dreaming of past glories.'

'Is that why you're selling up in Spain and coming back?' I said, and he shot me a look as I turned to his brother. 'Get a move on. Talk or I walk.'

So Terry Gatti talked.

'We know there is not one serving policeman using his warrant card to apprehend, arrest and abuse young women,' he said. He held up his hand, showing four fingers. 'There's four of them.' He let that settle between us. Mick got up for a refill and Terry laid a gentle hand on his arm. 'Slow down, cowboy, you haven't even had your Coco Pops yet.'

Mick did as he was told and sat down.

'And you are telling me these serving policemen had something to do with the murder of Suzanne?' I said.

Terry flinched, not quite a denial.

'That would be out of character for these guys. But what I am telling you is that we know – for a fact – that there are serving officers in the Metropolitan Police who are currently using their warrant cards for – what shall we call it? – sexual opportunities.' He sipped his mineral water. 'And I know that this has been one of your lines of enquiry.' His smooth, handsome face twisted with disgust. 'Even if your boss, DCI Pat Whitestone, has gone for the easy option of chucking some homeless vet to the wolves just to keep down the Met's murder statistics.'

'Who are they? These four cops?'

'Chap called John-Paul Ledoux and his three mates.

186

They call themselves the Beatles. John-Paul and the Beatles – geddit? And they have this one-room flat near the Angel in Islington where they take these women who they have arrested on false pretences.'

'And you know this – how?'

'Because we sold them the flat,' Mick Gatti said. 'We met all four of them. We always knew what they wanted it for. They were laughing about it.' He raised his empty glass in mock salute. 'Best police force in the world, eh?'

'This was a couple of years back,' Terry admitted. 'Mick and I were having a few cashflow issues and decided to unload some of our property portfolio.'

So the money had been running out for a while for the Gatti brothers.

'And it is an open secret in that part of the Angel that a bunch of cops use that apartment as their own private – excuse the expression – shag pad,' Terry continued. 'Come on, Max – who do you like more for that dead homeless girl – *Suzanne* – a bunch of cops who use their limitless powers to coerce women, or some blameless old soldier who dosses in a doorway?'

'Best investment in the world, London property.' Mick grinned. 'But then you would know all about that, wouldn't you, Max? We all know about that des res you've got around here. Not many coppers can afford a big loft in Smithfield. But good for you, Max. Good for you! Funny career you've had, though. That shining QPM medal and yet here you are – Pat Whitestone's bag carrier.'

I ignored him.

'Where do they work?' I asked Terry.

Mick Gatti pointed an index finger at me and smirked as he pulled an imaginary trigger. 'They're shooters. The Met's bang-bang boys.'

'They're all AFOs.' Terry nodded. 'John-Paul and the other Beatles are all Authorised Firearms Officers. Do you know any AFOs, Max?'

My oldest friend in the world was a senior AFO.

I wasn't going to tell the Gattis that. But Jackson would know these guys. This John-Paul Ledoux and his friends. He may even have instructed them in the use of firearms.

'And why are you sharing this information with me?' I said.

'Because we want to help you,' Terry said. He held up his hands. 'Full disclosure – we want to do you a favour so that you are more inclined to help us.'

'Keith Jones died.' Mick frowned. 'You heard about that.'

'Addiction is a terrible thing,' I said.

Terry shook his head. 'Addiction didn't kill The Nutjob. No more than a dodgy ticker killed Butch Lewis. Or Ian Doherty just suddenly decided to end it all. Whatever the official line is – whatever the autopsies may claim. You know what killed them, Max. You know who killed them. And it wasn't natural causes, was it?'

I smiled at them. 'You're scared of her! You big hard men from South London – retired – are scared witless of a dying woman.'

'You don't know her,' Mick said.

'And you don't know what happened that night,' Terry said. 'You think you do, Max. But you really don't.'

'I know two men died,' I said. 'I saw their bodies. I know someone lost their rag and things got out of hand. One of your team lost control. Was it you, Mick?'

He rattled his empty glass. He really needed a refill of Grey Goose. Functioning alcoholic, I thought for the first time. Not that Mick Gatti functioned very well.

'It was a tragedy,' Terry said. 'Someone said – every murder is a tragedy that echoes through countless lives.'

I laughed. 'What a fount of human compassion you have become in your old age, Tel. You know, I talked to the governor of HMP Bronzefield. He sent me a full list of Emma Moon's visitors – *over sixteen years*. And you never went once, Terry. None of you did. You dropped her in it and then left her there to rot while you all got on with your lush lives. You can hardly blame her if there's a few hard feelings.'

Mick Gatti leaned across the table, his face flushed with anger. 'Look, we've given you John-Paul and the Beatles on a plate and now we just want you to keep that bitch off our backs, all right?'

'You've given me tittle-tattle,' I said. 'You've given me rumour. You've given me malicious gossip. Maybe a couple of armed robbers with a guilty conscience are not the most reliable witnesses in the world.'

Terry Gatti shook his head sadly.

'It's more than gossip, Max – you know it is. It is

happening now – John-Paul and the Beatles. They are running wild with their warrant cards in one hand and their cocks in the other – and everyone is turning a blind eye. And they are *exactly* who you are looking for. So if we ask you to please watch our backs – off the book, of course, a strictly freelance operation – then that doesn't seem like too much to ask.'

'Come on, Max,' Mick said, as if we were old mates. 'You never do any work off-book? Then how did you ever get that lovely open-plan penthouse?'

I looked at them with disbelief.

'Why the hell would I help you two?'

'Because there's a list,' Terry Gatti said simply. 'And you're on it.'

I got up to leave. I was sick of the sight of them. Sick of their sense of entitlement, of their unpunished crimes, and of their pathetic need to be protected by the forces they had spent a lifetime laughing at. And, yes, I was sick of hearing what they were saying – that disturbed me more than any of it.

'So you going to follow this up?' Mick Gatti said, with that imbecilic frown that came so naturally to his coarse, suntanned features. 'These dirty AFOs – John-Paul and the Beatles?'

I shrugged, uncommitted. And they stared at me, their pity glazed their contempt.

'You don't get it, do you, Max?' Terry said. 'The police are not the good guys anymore.'

28

Alone outside the pub, I checked to see that our conversation had been successfully recorded.

'*You don't get it,*' Terry Gatti said again, his voice distant and metallic as it came out of my iPhone, and far friendlier than I remembered. '*The police are not the good guys anymore.*'

And then there was only the background sound of that Smithfield pub as I had got up to go, and then even that faded as I had stepped out into the night, and I could hear the sound of my breathing as I had pressed the stop button.

DCI Pat Whitestone was shaking her head.

She had said nothing as she had listened to my conversation with the Gatti brothers.

Now she looked around Murder Investigation Room 1, deserted apart from the two of us, and then she finally looked at me.

'What exactly are you asking me to do, Max?'

'Well—'

'Wait. Do you honestly think – even for one second – that I am going to set the dogs on serving police officers

191

in the Met on the word of . . .' She stared at my phone. 'What are they, these Gatti brothers? Retired armed robbers? Ageing gangsters? Maybe we can settle on scumbags. Yes, let's call them scumbags, shall we?'

'Pat—'

She held up a hand. I could not remember when I had seen her this angry. She removed her spectacles, her watery eyes owlish and blind without them, and began to furiously polish the lenses.

'Max,' she said, struggling to control herself. 'We already have Suzanne's murderer. He is in a holding cell downstairs. He has signed a confession. Robert McKay is going to be charged with her murder.'

'He's mentally ill. He doesn't understand what he is confessing to.'

'We have him on CCTV with his hands on Suzanne. We have skin samples scraped from under his fingernails that are currently at the lab – which I strongly suspect will be from Suzanne.'

'This is a seriously damaged man.'

'No doubt. Perhaps that's why he did it – because he is so seriously damaged. My guess is that in the end he will be sent to Strangeways rather than Belmarsh. But, just between you and me, Max – I don't really give a toss where they lock him up. And – no, let me finish, please – if you think that I would ever take the word of some low-life villains *over our own* – our own, Max – then you don't know me at all.'

'These AFOs – this John-Paul Ledoux and the

Beatles – you're not interested in any of that? I can't believe it, Pat.'

'I think we – our mob – get a hard time these days. I think we get called every name under the sun. I know we get spat on, literally and metaphorically, by people who call us before anyone else when someone is kicking down their front door. And these AFOs? They have it worst of all. The shots get the shortest straw. We all go to work in the morning not knowing if we are going to be coming home. But the boys and girls with guns – and there are plenty of female AFOs, Max – they go to work wondering if they will get charged with murder for doing their job. Because they *do* get charged with murder – and it happens all the time. They put down some wannabe gangster or drug dealer or terrorist and the first thing that happens is they get suspended. I don't know who these guys are, Max. I don't know if it is true that they have a flat near the Angel where they take women.'

'After flashing their warrant cards, after using their position of power to apprehend, arrest and coerce.'

'My job is to find who killed a young woman that the world doesn't give a damn about. And I feel pretty good right now, Max. Or as good as I can under the circumstances. Because I've done my job. And when I charge Robert McKay with murder, I will enjoy it.'

'Let me talk to him first.'

She exhaled, long and hard, and I felt she was giving up on me. 'You can have fifteen minutes with him.'

I headed for the door.

'And Max?'

Pat Whitestone was a small, unassuming woman in glasses who was probably the most experienced murder detective in New Scotland Yard. She had given her life to this job. She was under no illusions about who we were or what we were for. But she knew whose side she was on.

'Don't believe what they tell you,' she said. 'We are good people.'

And I wanted to believe her.

Robert McKay didn't remember me, even though I remembered him clearly in our flat – huge, bearded, bewildered, staring out of the window with one of Scout's sandwiches in his hand. He looked different now, wearing a grey tracksuit and black slip-on plimsolls.

'Robert, I am DS Wolfe, I work with DCI Whitestone, who conducted your interview.'

My words did not appear to register.

Robert McKay sat on the low bed in the holding cell, built close to the ground so that drunks could not fall off and crack their skulls and potential suicides could not attempt to break their own necks.

'You came to my apartment once.'

Nothing.

'My daughter – Scout – invited you and some other people round.'

His eyes stared at his hands.

'Suzanne was there that night.'

And now he looked at me. His face was weathered by years on the streets and by whatever life had come before that.

'You knew Suzanne, didn't you? She's dead now. Someone killed her. And they think it's you.'

Robert McKay looked at me without emotion.

'You understand what's happening here, don't you? They tell me that you signed a confession. They are going to charge you with Suzanne's murder.' Silence. 'Did you kill Suzanne, Robert?'

He cleared his throat. 'Suzanne was my friend,' he said softly.

'But you argued with her, didn't you?'

He shook his head slowly, not a denial but in memory of Suzanne.

'She did things that she should not do. That she did not have to do. There was a man . . .'

'One man?'

'He came round our way and then he kept coming round our way – for her. For Suzanne. And she would get into his car. And I told her not to. I told her . . . this will be bad.'

'Did you put your hands on her?'

'What? I don't know.'

I leaned closer. 'You don't know?'

'I take this medication. Sometimes I forget. Or I can't get there – the place where they give me the medication.

And then I can't remember things. Or there are things that happen that I don't know if they were real or if they only happened in my head.'

'You are going to have to try to remember, Robert, because if you don't—'

And he went for me then.

Out of nowhere he was on his feet and before me and I lifted my hands to protect myself and he just sort of slid between them with his own arms, some basic martial arts movement, and I could smell the stink of him as he turned me around and picked me up and he rushed me across the room and slammed my face against the door.

He managed to do it twice and was rearing me back for a third when the duty sergeant and a couple of uniforms got inside and pressed the Taser against his thick neck and pulled the trigger.

'That bastard,' gasped one of the young coppers, when Robert McKay was unconscious on the holding cell floor.

'He served in Afghanistan,' I said, as if that explained anything.

'He should have died there,' the duty sergeant said. 'It would have been better for everyone.'

I rode the lift to the top floor, my head ringing and a lump on my forehead, gingerly probing the scuffed lost layer of skin above my eyebrows.

Good people, I told myself. Pat Whitestone was right. We were good people, forced to clear up the mess that nobody else even wanted to think about.

'Done?' she said, smiling ruefully at my damaged face when I got back to MIR-1.

'Done,' I said, and she patted me gently on the back as she went off to charge Robert McKay with the murder.

I was suddenly violently sick into a wastepaper basket.

Good people, I thought, yes, who never get the credit we deserve, and who never get cut any slack, good people who get spat upon and shat upon and smashed against a metal door.

Bloody hell, my face hurt.

Good people, I thought, as the sound of wild, mad laughter drifted down the corridors of New Scotland Yard.

29

'There he is,' Jackson Rose said as I came up the stairs to his top-floor flat two at a time.

My oldest friend was holding his front door open with one arm and in the other was a baby girl, her plump, perfect face creased with a frown at my presence, and I knew she had to be coming up to one year old because I could remember, clear as if it was yesterday, the length of Scout's hair at that age, and the way that it grew into this silky fringe that you could brush to one side with two fingers.

'And there *she* is,' I said, stopping on the landing to smile and admire my friend's daughter. 'The famous Rosie.'

'Rosie Rose,' laughed Jackson, jiggling her up and down in his arm, and I knew he would never tire of saying her name, not if he lived to be one hundred. 'Come on in, Max.'

Jackson did not shake my hand. We had known each other for too long for that stuff. Instead I felt his palm pat my back twice as I went inside his home, a gentle touch of welcome. The flat was small but airy and light, the top floor of a Victorian terrace that had once been an attic and was now a one-bedroom apartment. There were framed prints on the wall. A Hockney exhibition at the Royal Academy. Warhol at the Tate Modern. I had never heard Jackson express one single thought on the doings of the art world, but I could see how happy he was, and how much he belonged in this flat. *This is who we are here*, the prints said. *This is who we are now.* And my oldest friend looked home at last.

'You haven't been here before, have you?' Jackson said, and I hesitated a moment before shaking my head, as if I had to think about it, when we both knew that I had been invited round for dinner multiple times and had always found an excuse to cry off.

Music was playing, as tasteful as the prints on the wall. Solo piano that sounded vaguely familiar. The small dining table was neatly set for three, plus a high chair for Rosie Rose. From the tiny kitchen came the smell of something that made me realise I was very hungry.

A woman – smiling, American-Taiwanese, slightly built – came out of the kitchen and took Rosie from her dad.

'Max, you made it at last!'

I kissed Nini, Jackson's wife, who I had not seen since I was best man at their wedding two years ago. Then we all admired Rosie as she solemnly stared at the three of us, and I guessed that she had not seen her parents doing much entertaining. The flat was a bit small for inviting people round, but Nini and Jackson had clearly pushed the boat out for me tonight, and I was touched, and guilty that I had got out of dinner so many times before. What the hell was wrong with me?

'Congratulations,' I said to Jackson and Nini. 'Rosie is lovely.'

And it was true. Both Jackson and Nini were mixed race and Rosie Rose looked like she could come from anywhere in the world. The beauty of the entire human race was in her face.

'Such a shame that Scout couldn't make it,' said Nini, who had not seen my daughter since that wedding day two years ago. 'Is she still into her boxing?'

Two years ago. How long ago it seemed.

When Scout was younger she gamely took part in my pastimes. As a little girl, I would regularly help her put on a pair of miniature boxing gloves and, getting down on my knees, encourage her to bang away at the training pads I wore on my own hands. Two years, the gap between ten and twelve, and it felt like another lifetime.

'Not so much,' I said.

Dinner was great. Taiwanese beef noodle soup.

'Nini's masterpiece,' Jackson said proudly.

A big pot full of beef, vegetables, noodles and a thick steaming broth sat in the centre of the rickety table and filled the top-floor flat with an aromatic mist. We helped ourselves, all three of us drinking Tsingtao beer. Rosie sat on her mum's lap sucking a biscuit until she began to grizzle and Nini took her off to the cot that sat at the end of their bed.

Jackson grinned at me, happy that I was at last here in his home, delighted for me to see how happy he was, how well his life had turned out, how blissed-out he was with his family. We didn't talk about it. We didn't have to. We clinked glasses and smiled at each other and that said it all.

'You all right?' he said.

'Good,' I said. 'All good. You?'

'Fine. I'm fine.'

It was Nini who drew us out. When she came back from putting the baby to bed, she got another round of Tsingtao from the fridge and wanted to hear the full story of my lifelong friendship with her husband.

I realised I had met Nini exactly three times. In a too-loud bar in Mayfair when Jackson had just started dating her. At their wedding, very briefly, because the rest of the world wanted to talk to her. And tonight. Nini was smart, beautiful, clearly in love with my friend, who totally adored her – but I didn't know her at all, and she didn't know me. I asked about her work – she was an art teacher, which explained the prints, in a notoriously rough local school – and she told me how much she was loving maternity leave. It sounded unlikely that she would ever want to go back to the day job. And then she wanted to hear about her husband and me.

'Jackson always says – *my best friend is my oldest friend,*' Nini said. 'And Jackson says – *you can make new friends but you can't make old friends.*'

Jackson and I both grinned with embarrassment.

I looked at the gap-toothed smile that I remembered from back when he was the same age that Scout is today.

'Jackson says the sweetest things,' I said.

But it was true for me too. Jackson Rose was one of those childhood friends that you never replace, one of those friends that you never find the like of again. There had been a gap – some thirteen years – when we had lived without each other and probably never even thought about each other very much. He had served his country in Afghanistan and Iraq. I had become a policeman and then a detective. I had married the most beautiful girl in the world, become a father and been left by the most beautiful girl in the world. After some early success, my career had not thrived as expected. All without the consolation of that childhood friendship. A lot of water and a lot of bridges. It was a miracle we had found each other again.

Nini already knew some of it.

'And you *found* him,' she said. 'After he left the forces. Before he became a big-shot AFO training officer. When he was sleeping on the street. Is that true?'

We all smiled as if it were a heart-warming anecdote but the truth was that it had broken my heart to see Jackson Rose, holder of the Medal of Military Valour, dossing in a doorway. But it was true that Jackson's dialogue was original, even at his lowest moment.

'What did you say to me?' I said, turning to him.

He laughed. '*Spare fifty grand, mate?*' he remembered.

'It's a good line!' Nini said, and she squeezed his arm across the table, and I was struck by it again. *Crazy about each other.*

I had taken him home with me the night I found him on the streets and he had met Scout — and I had been the proud father on that night, showing off my incredible daughter, wanting my friend to see how happy and proud I was. We gave him a roof, a chance to catch his breath, to start to put his life back together.

And he did.

'Jackson was never going to stay on the streets,' I said. 'With or without me.'

'I'm not so sure,' he said.

Rosie Rose began to cry, and I recalled those distant days when everything seemed to revolve around a baby sleeping, or waking, or needing changing, or feeding, or just being held.

Nini disappeared into the bedroom and stayed there.

'Ha,' Jackson said, shaking his head, and I expected him to recall some old adventures and good times had, and all of that. But he knew me too well.

'What's on your mind, Max?'

I looked innocent, surprised — tried to — and sipped my Tsingtao to give myself a chance to think. But Jackson nodded — *Get on with it* — as I heard Nini soothing Rosie Rose as she paced the only bedroom with the crying baby in her arms.

'Suzanne Buksa,' I said. 'She's on my mind, Jackson, to tell you the truth. That's the case we are working on.

203

Suzanne was a homeless woman, sleeping rough in Smithfield. And she got murdered.'

He shifted in his seat. 'I thought you charged someone for that. Another veteran sleeping on the streets.'

'Robert McKay. He's – I don't know – he's a badly broken man, Jackson. And he doesn't defend himself. He does himself no favours. He signs whatever they put in front of him. And they have CCTV of him shouting at Suzanne. And he's . . .' I instinctively touched the scuffed lump on my forehead, feeling it begin to throb. 'He's volatile. He did this to me. But he didn't murder Suzanne, Jackson.'

'And you know this – how?'

'Suzanne was being harassed by a guy who used a Metropolitan Police warrant card to approach her. He made her get into his car, threatened her with arrest. The truth is – I don't know what he did to her, or what she was made to do to him, because she was always too shy to tell me.'

'Wait a minute – this is a genuine Met warrant card he flashed?'

'She didn't know. How would she know? How would any young woman know? But I think it was the real thing.'

'And what does your boss say?'

'Pat Whitestone is happy with her collar. She thinks we've got our man. She is looking to see Robert McKay go down.'

Jackson looked towards the bedroom, where Rosie Rose had been coaxed back into a fretful sleep.

'The warrant card,' I said. 'That's what Suzanne always said to me – *he had a warrant card like you and so I had to do what he said.*' I took a deep breath. This was hard. 'And, Jackson – I have been told there is a group of serving Met officers who use the same technique for getting girls.' I paused. There was no easy way to say it. 'And they're in your lot. Four of them. They're serving Authorised Firearms Officers. They're shots.'

There was a sudden hardness in Jackson's eyes, but when he spoke his voice was very soft and calm. 'Names?' he said.

'Ledoux,' I said. 'John-Paul Ledoux. That's the only name I've got. He has three mates. They call themselves the Beatles.'

We sat in silence for a long moment.

'I know John-Paul,' Jackson said finally. 'I trained him.' He sighed. 'He's a good man, Max.'

'Maybe he is a good A F O, Jackson. But maybe he's not such a shining light of virtue in the rest of his life. Because what I hear is that this John-Paul Ledoux and his three pals have this one-room flat near the Angel in Islington where they take women who they have arrested on false pretences.'

'Look, I know Ledoux from work, and I don't know anything about some flat near the Angel.' And then he thought about it, and I knew in those seconds that I was on the right track. 'I don't know, Max. I guess I may have heard about some place . . .'

'Go on.'

'Some crib where some of our single guys go to have a few beers and watch the match and let off a little steam. Maybe have some recreational sex between consenting adults.' He showed me his thick gold wedding ring, still hoping we could laugh this off. 'I'm a family man, Max! I don't know anything about it. While the single guys are having a wild time, I'm changing Pampers.'

I was not laughing. 'I'm not talking about stressed officers letting off a little steam, Jackson. I'm not talking about watching the match over a few beers. I'm talking about sexual coercion. I am talking about serving Met officers using the power vested in them to apprehend, control and abuse women.'

'I know exactly what you're talking about, Max. You don't have to talk to me as if I am a fucking simpleton. I get it.'

'See, I'm not sure you do, Jackson.'

'No, it's all completely clear. This girl – this young woman – Suzanne – is – was – out on the streets every night of her life. You know how dangerous that is? How many scumbags she is absolutely guaranteed to encounter? Because I think I may know a lot more about it than you do, Max. *Because I've been there.* And shall I tell you what happened? Someone approached her. Flashed his warrant card – or more likely his driving licence. Took her in the back of an unmarked car for fifteen minutes of fun. You think he's a cop? *On what evidence?*' He took another breath, trying to calm his heart. 'You get it, right? Everybody hates us these days. I don't just mean the police – I mean the *armed* police. Slot a drug dealer who is reaching for what might be his firearm – *murder charge*. Slot some terrorist who may be about to blow himself up – *murder charge*. Everybody wants to chuck us in jail! You do appreciate that cruel fact? Morale is rock bottom. People want to leave the department. Officers are handing back their firearms. We – the law – all go to work every day of our lives not knowing if we are going to come back home at the end of the day. The difference is that shots don't know if they might be on a murder charge by the end of the day – just for doing our job.'

'Whitestone said the same thing.'

'But *you* – you, Max – you want us to go hunting cops.'

'Not innocent cops, Jackson. I'm not talking about going after clean cops. I'm talking about going after dirty cops. Corrupt cops. Exactly the kind of cop that makes the public hate our guts.'

'And where does it come from? This intel about John-Paul Ledoux and the others?'

I took a breath, exhaled slowly. 'It comes from the Gatti brothers. Terry and Mick Gatti sold these guys their flat at the Angel when they still had a property portfolio.'

Jackson shook his head, more in disbelief than anger now. 'So Mick and Terry Gatti, a couple of lowlife wide boys who never got the hard time they deserved, they point the finger at serving A F O s – *my people*, Max – and you expect me to believe them?'

Nini came out of the bedroom, holding Rosie, red-faced and watery eyed, her lower lip trembling with despair.

'Look who will be joining us for dessert!' Nini said.

'Sadly Max has to go now,' Jackson said. 'Don't you, Max?'

'Yes,' I said, getting to my feet. 'Got to get back to Scout.'

I thanked Nini for a lovely dinner, and smiled at a deeply unimpressed Rosie, and let Jackson walk me to the door, one arm slung casually around my shoulders.

Old friends saying goodnight at the end of a wonderful evening.

He stepped outside, the door ajar, his voice as soft as a prayer.

'You're my oldest friend and I love you,' he said. 'So please – don't shine your detective's torch on my boys. Max – I promise you – this is not us.'

'If they've done nothing wrong then they have nothing to worry about,' I said.

Jackson shook his head.

'It's not them I'm worried about, Max,' he said. 'It's you.'

30

I sat by the big window overlooking the market, and I waited for Scout to come home.

We had reached an accommodation. I gave her all the space she needed in her developing relationship with her mother. I left them alone. My input was not needed or wanted – by either of them. I had the strong impression that Scout's mum had no burning desire to ever see my face again, or even to talk to me. ('Daddy, if Mama wanted to chat with you, don't you think you would have her new number?') And that was all fine – as long as I knew that Scout was safe.

But she had to get home by 10 p.m. on a school night – no excuses – and her mother had to accompany her to Farringdon, the tube station at the end of our road. 'Mama will be with me all the way!' Scout always promised, although I still could not quite imagine Anne, my ex-wife, on the tube – even during the hard times when we had no money, black cabs were Anne's idea of public transport. I didn't need to know where they went, or what they talked about, or even how their relationship was going. But I needed to know that Scout was safe.

Because that was my job. Scout was twelve years old, for God's sake, and already I thought I had conceded far too much parental authority. But I saw how much this meant to Scout. I felt it in my blood and bones and I saw it in her eyes and the flurry of excitement when she was getting ready to go out – how crucial this was to her. Of course I did. The mother who she had only sporadic contact with was back in her life. Scout was free to meet up with her without my interference and I was free to fret by the window, waiting for her to come home, sick with anxiety, because, between you and me, when we bring a child into the world, life holds us hostage forever, life has us chained to a radiator, anticipating the next punishment beating.

The market was in full swing with a long line of white vans outside the main building, the men in their white suits and hats at the start of their night.

At my feet Stan gnawed on a giant bone gifted to him by some admiring porters, pausing to look up at me with watery, myopic eyes.

Shouldn't we all be in bed by now?

And when I looked back to the street Scout was there outside our block, almost home, thank God, and I released the breath I was not even aware I had been holding. I resisted the urge to go to the door and greet her. She let herself in and padded to her room.

Subdued, uncommunicative, tired, still immersed in a world I could never enter. And twelve years old.

'You OK?'

MURDER FOR BUSY PEOPLE

'Fine.'

'How's your mum?'

'She's fine.'

I resisted the temptation to say that I was fine and as far as I could tell, the dog appeared to be fine, also.

'I have to go out, Scout. A work thing.'

She nodded, not caring, just about acknowledging the information. I listened to the bathroom and bedroom sounds of her getting ready for bed. Her door briefly opened to allow Stan entry and the old Cavalier limped into her room, tail wagging with a happiness that knew no bounds, and then I heard her murmured voice as she settled the dog down for the night.

Then I grabbed my jacket and went down to the street where I knew they would be waiting for me.

Suzanne's mother and sister wanted to see where she had been found.

I understood the impulse but I was not convinced it would make them feel any better. On the phone, the Family Liaison Officer had mentioned some clichés about closure. But in my experience, for some things – the worst things – there is no closure. They remain open wounds.

But if they wanted to see where Suzanne died, then I would show them.

The two women, Suzanne's mother and her sister, were waiting for me at Farringdon tube station with the same FLO from the press conference, the one who had talked about closure.

I could see in her eyes that she too had her doubts about tonight. Suzanne's mother was still in shock, but the sister was animated, almost euphoric, determined to do this before they flew home.

The homeless were out in force tonight, I thought, as I led the way into Smithfield.

You did not see them at first, in those ancient alleyways around the tube station, but as we reached Smithfield's 500-year-old arch with the market beyond, they began to appear, settling at this late hour in the places they had picked to spend the night. The shuttered shops, cafés and abandoned pubs.

The FLO and I did not say much as we crossed the street to the market, Suzanne's mother and sister between us, clinging to each other. We answered their questions. The sister's English was better than her mother's and she did the translation.

'Suzanne had a toy,' the sister said. 'She slept with it as a child.'

I knew immediately what she was talking about. It was Mister Flopsy, the stuffed rabbit who had seen better days. I remembered again how the toy rabbit had seemed like an affectation to me when I first saw Suzanne, a way of making her look younger, a way of getting sympathy in those hard, uncaring, unsympathetic streets.

But now I realised it was her last bond to home, and childhood, and a life that had been lost forever.

'I know the toy you mean,' I said. 'That old rabbit Suzanne always had with her. I'm afraid it hasn't been found. I will certainly make sure it is sent to you if we find it.'

They nodded, grateful, and I felt a surge of real shame.

We had not found Suzanne's murderer – whatever we told ourselves. And we could not even find her stuffed rabbit.

Suzanne's mother and sister were wary of the homeless. Of course they were. Robert McKay, the man who was to stand trial for Suzanne's murder, was one of them. But there was a white van giving out clothes and food, and when they saw the homeless more closely, and in all their heartbreaking diversity – the young, the old, the ones who were there because of bad luck and wrong choices – the fear faded. Because of course Suzanne had been one of them too.

A small crowd, perhaps a dozen people, were queuing patiently at the back of the van.

'Who are these people feeding them?' Suzanne's sister said.

'I don't know,' said the FLO. 'Good Samaritans, perhaps.'

First I saw the shaven head of Luka Brady, hefting pallets of bottled water from the back of the van. Then Summer, the starved beauty, the fallen supermodel, and Roxy, looking like a wild child who was up past her bedtime. They were all silently handing out the supermarket sandwiches. Lord Nevermore was nodding and smiling, his floppy locks falling over his forehead, his patrician charm turned all the way up to ten. He wore a button-down shirt on top of neatly pressed jeans. Toff casual.

And Emma Moon was at the heart of it.

She looked younger, healthier, animated by the work of the night, her blond hair pulled back in a loose ponytail.

And she was staring at Suzanne Buksa's mother.

Then she was moving towards Suzanne's mother, her blue eyes locked on the other woman's gaze, and the crowd parted to let her pass, and at last Emma Moon and Suzanne Buksa's mother were face to face.

'I know what it's like to lose a child,' Emma Moon said, and Suzanne's mother went to her arms, and wept in her unflinching embrace.

And for the first time, I understood why Emma Moon was loved.

31

West End Central was closed now. The sprawling police station on Savile Row was dark and shuttered and curiously invisible in its after life. As you turned onto Savile Row from the bright lights of the West End, the building no longer felt like it really belonged to that narrow, canyon-like street with its rows of brightly-lit windows of bespoke tailoring.

There were grand plans for West End Central – there are always grand plans for big abandoned buildings in this city – but for now it was ignored by everyone apart from the homeless who had pitched their tent in what was once the main entrance. Eyes in faces I could not see watched me from beyond the flap on their tent, waiting to see if I was trouble.

I turned away and went to the pub that had been West End Central's local, The Windmill in Mill Street, famous for its award-winning pies. West End Central was gone but The Windmill remained popular with lovers of world-class pies and with cops. In fact, any cop who knows London – and pies – will eventually make their way to

The Windmill. I went up to the roof terrace, ordered a steak and mushroom pie, and looked at the lights of Mayfair and beyond while I waited.

London looked like a city made of parks. So green, it was – St James's Park and Green Park to the south, Hyde Park and Kensington Gardens to the west, all of them going on forever.

I knew the waiter who served my prize-winning pie. A big Australian lad who had fallen in love with a local and never made it back to Sydney.

'Shane,' I said. 'I'm looking for a friend of a friend. An AFO called John-Paul Ledoux. Does he ever come in for a pie and a pint?'

Shane looked surprised, then he shook his head and grinned.

'John-Paul and the Beatles are banned, mate,' he said. 'A bit too rowdy for our crowd – and our manager. The Windmill is a classy joint. Last I heard, the Beatles were hanging out up at the Angel. I've got a pal up there at a pub called the Lucky Leper.' Shane looked around, lowered his voice. 'Near where they've got their flat.'

'You know about their flat?'

'Mate, everybody knows about their flat.'

I ate the best steak and mushroom pie in London.

Then I drove to the Angel.

They were not difficult to spot.

There was only one snooker table in the Lucky Leper and John-Paul Ledoux and his friends were dominating it. They were loud, too loud for the pub, but not yet drunk.

John-Paul was a huge, good-looking man, heavy-weight size, younger than I had expected, still the right side of thirty, and he had that arrogance you often find in men who have both considerable bulk and adorably symmetrical features. The fact that he carried a Heckler & Koch sub-machine gun for his job probably did nothing to instil feelings of humility, modesty or low self-esteem.

His friends were less striking. An overweight hulk, even younger and bigger than John-Paul, who responded to the name of Dim. And the other two – Mo and Jim.

Mo – small, shaven-headed, Somalian. Jim – a vicious-looking white boy. It was Dim who came over to me. I had not been aware that they had clocked me staring. But someone – probably my friend Jackson Rose – had trained them well.

'Problem?' Dim said.

Now they were all looking at me. Their smiles fixed. John-Paul held his cue behind his head, tapping the side of the snooker table with his crotch.

'I'm a friend of Jackson Rose,' I said, and I was going to tell them my name when John-Paul Ledoux said it for me.

'Max,' he said. 'Max Wolfe.'

And after that I got my round in, and we all got on famously.

*

Ninety minutes later, John-Paul Ledoux had his arm around my shoulder. He pulled me close, so close that I could smell his Dior Pour Homme.

'This,' he said, squeezing me, addressing Dim, Jim and Mo, 'this is the guy that Jackson always talks about. The friend . . .' Suddenly, shockingly, tears welled up in his big brown eyes. 'The friend who found Jackson when he was sleeping on the streets after he got back from Afghanistan.'

'Top man,' said Mo, beady-eyed and not sounding remotely impressed as he leaned across the table to slot a red in the far corner.

Dim gawped at me like a beast of the fields. Jim laughed stupidly, unsure how to react to John-Paul's unexpected display of emotion. It was Ledoux himself who had invited me to join their evening, and they followed his lead.

'Another round?' I said, feeling the couple of draught Asahi Super Dry that I had already sunk. They had all drunk more than me, apart from Mo, who stuck to Coca-Cola, but only Dim seemed to be feeling it. He rocked on his feet, eyes half-closed, mouth open, as if chewing cud.

'You lot live around here?' I asked, bringing back a tray of four beers and one Coca-Cola from the bar.

Ledoux waved his cue expansively. 'We're all over the place,' he said, before he looked at the others with a sly smile. 'But we've got a flat around the corner where we crash some nights.'

I nodded, sipped my third Asahi Super Dry. I was going to have to slow down. 'What – like a bolthole?'

Jim looked at me sharply. 'Yeah – like that. A bolthole.'

Then he looked at John-Paul and briefly shook his head.

Don't go there.

Don't trust this guy just because he bought a couple of rounds and says he knows Jackson Rose.

I pressed on.

'Good idea to have a place near to work,' I said. 'For those nights it runs late. And for those nights you want to let off a little steam.'

Dim guffawed. 'We do that all right!'

'You should see it,' John-Paul said. 'Have a nightcap.'

Jim, the Essex boy, was not happy.

Mo was staring at me, as if weighing me up for the first time.

But John-Paul Ledoux made the rules.

'It's just around the corner,' he said. 'Finish these and let's go.'

Ledoux led the way. Out of the Lucky Leper into Upper Street and down Essex Road, the Angel behind us now, the multimillion-pound houses of Duncan Terrace making way for blocks of ugly modern flats. Jim and Mo fell in step with me.

'We know who you are,' Jim said, still not really warming to me.

'You're Officer A,' Mo said. 'You were the surveillance officer who parked his car on top of a terrorist who was about to blow himself up.'

'They called you Officer A in court,' Jim said. 'But everybody in the job knew your name.'

'And you won a QPM,' Mo said. 'Queen's Police Medal – as was. When Her Majesty was still with us.'

I glanced behind at Dim, bringing up the stumbling rear.

'Long time ago,' I said.

'Queen's Police Medal,' Jim said. 'Awarded to police officers who have exhibited conspicuous devotion to duty.'

'A medal for heroes,' Mo said.

'You a hero, Max?' asked Jim.

John-Paul Ledoux turned and looked at us, his handsome face split in a grin. They were all a lot drunker than they had seemed in the Lucky Leper.

'This is it,' he said.

It was a top-floor, one-bedroom apartment that had once been a council flat but had been sold by Mrs Thatcher half a lifetime ago. The smell hit you hard. Takeaway food and weed and sweat from multiple bodies. It felt like a student pad on a big budget. Two cracked leather sofas faced each other before a massive flat-screen TV on one wall looming above a crowded drinks trolley. The dishes and glasses were piled high in the sink, items of clothing strewn everywhere, and beyond the door to the bedroom there was a mattress where a bed should be.

There was a kind of fruit bowl by the door. It was full of mobile phones.

'Want me to check my phone?' I smiled.

Ledoux laughed. 'No, you're all right. Those phones . . .' He looked for an explanation. 'Guests,' he said.

I sat on one sofa and Mo and Jim watched me from the other.

'I like what you've done with it,' I said.

Ledoux and Dim carried four cold cans of Red Stripe and an orange juice from the fridge in the tiny kitchen. Ledoux handed one of the beers to me.

'How is Jackson?' he said.

'He's good. I had dinner with him and Nini the other night. They've got a little girl now. Rosie Rose.'

Ledoux chuckled. 'Rosie Rose! Love it.'

Mo and Jim were still staring at me.

I stared back.

'You men got families?' I said.

'Yes,' Ledoux nodded. 'All got families. Apart from Dim, who still lives with his old mum.'

'The only woman who will have me!' Dim said, and they all chortled at that, as they had many times before.

'Then if you've got families at home,' I said, 'what do you do up here?'

Ledoux was still enjoying himself. 'You know what they say, Max. *Why go out for hamburger when you've got steak at home?*'

'Because you get tired of eating steak!' said Dim, and he and Ledoux laughed while the other two, Mo and Jim, just kept staring at me.

'Go on, tell us,' Jim said. 'What you working on?'

I looked at him levelly.

'Suzanne Buksa. She was sleeping on the streets. Someone broke her neck.'

'I thought they already had someone in the bin for that?' Ledoux said, frowning as he flopped down beside me. *Someone in the bin* meaning someone got arrested and is in custody. 'Some old tramp?'

'They did,' I said. 'They do. He was – is – more than some old tramp. He was some old solider. But Suzanne was being harassed by someone flashing a Met warrant card. And that just doesn't fit with the old soldier.'

John-Paul Ledoux stared at his Jamaican beer.

Not smiling so much now.

Dim frowned.

Mo sipped his OJ, his eyes never leaving me.

'Some bloke pretending to be a police officer,' Ledoux said quietly. 'That happens all the time. Doesn't it?'

'But I don't think he was pretending,' I said. 'I think he was the real thing.'

Silence in the room. Only the buzz of the traffic down on the Essex Road and the shrieks from someone watching *I'm a Celebrity . . . Get Me Out of Here!* in the flat below. Thin walls and floors and ceilings. When Ledoux spoke, his voice was thick with emotions that he was struggling to control.

'Nothing to do with us,' he said. 'Mate.'

'OK.'

'We don't know anything about some dead homeless girl,' Dim said.

Jim was, predictably, the first to anger. 'What – you think we want to handle some HIV-positive skank?'

Mo pointed his carton of orange juice at me. 'I don't know what you heard,' he said. 'But you know nothing about us. We know about you, though.'

'We know about that big apartment you've got in Smithfield,' Jim said. 'How does someone on Metropolitan Police wages afford a gaff like that?'

'And why did his career tank after getting that medal?' Jim said, addressing Ledoux, as if he was judge, jury and possibly hangman here. Jim looked back at me with real loathing in his eyes. 'Because he's a dirty copper. A bent copper. And he has the nerve to shine his torch at us!'

Ledoux could not look at me. 'You'd better go now,' he said quietly.

Jim was on his feet.

'Do you think we killed her? That homeless skank? Do you think that's what we do? You dumb, pious bastard! It's *sport* up here. It's just a bit of fun. And we don't kill them. Whatever happens in the apartment, it is not a capital crime.'

'Stop talking,' Ledoux told him, and he shut up immediately.

I was heading for the door.

'Go on, Dirty Harry!' Mo said. 'Get in your Batmobile and fuck off out of it.'

Then I was out of there, but I could hear the furious voices arguing in the flat as I waited for the lift. The lift did not come. Then the door of the flat opened and they were all coming out.

I took the stairs, four floors down to the street.

They came after me. None of us waited for the lift.

I was heading down the Essex Road towards the Angel when they made it to the street.

'We just want a word,' Ledoux shouted, and a bottle shattered on the pavement beside me, the broken glass skidding across the concrete like spilled jewels in the street light. Another bottle sailed past my head. I was trying to walk like a brave man, neither hurrying nor slowing my pace.

But now I ran. And the four of them came after me. And I knew that they were probably not planning to kill me tonight, but that it could easily happen by accident.

A car slid to a halt beside me, its window coming down.

I saw her thin face, the fair hair pulled back in a loose ponytail and those blazing, pale-blue eyes.

'Get in,' Emma Moon said.

32

'You're bleeding.'

A chunk of shattered glass the size of a jagged ice cube was embedded in the fleshy part of my right hand between the thumb and index finger. Blood oozing. No pain yet. I pulled it out and the blood came faster. A bottle smashed against the rear windscreen and we both ducked down. I turned to look back at the four of them. Dim and Mo picking up what they could find and throwing it, although we were already leaving them behind. Jim had given chase but was stopping as Emma Moon put her foot down. And John-Paul Ledoux was standing in the middle of Essex Road like it was his own private fiefdom.

Staring, staring.

'They're not coming after us,' I said.

Emma Moon laughed. 'Oh good. Friends of yours?'

'Work colleagues.'

'Ah.'

'I know they don't look much like cops.'

'Are you kidding? They look exactly like cops to me. Here.'

She pulled off the headband holding her hair in that

loose ponytail and gave it to me. I wrapped it around my hand. The blood was coming fast now and also the start of the pain, that throbbing sting of freshly cut flesh.

We reached the end of Essex Road and she turned right.

'Wait,' I said, looking in the other direction, south to home.

My head was feeling woozy.

'That needs stitches and a tetanus shot,' she said. 'And the nearest Accident and Emergency is at the Whittington Hospital up at Archway. That amount of blood – it's deep. Believe me – I've seen a lot of cuts.'

I did not argue with her. Because I had seen cuts too.

For the first time I wondered what she was doing here. We were a long way from Lord Nevermore's gaff on The Bishop's Avenue.

'I thought you were South London?'

'Seeing my old nan,' she said. 'Newington Green. Lucky for you.'

Lucky for me. I wasn't sure if I believed her. I wasn't convinced her old nan actually existed. But she was relaxed, almost jaunty, and I knew she had saved me from a good hiding, or worse. She was good in a crisis. And glowing. Emma Moon was radiant tonight.

'You don't look ill,' I blurted.

She laughed. 'What? Compared to you?'

'Compared to anyone.'

'I have good days and bad days.' She laughed again. 'Don't you believe me? Do you think I'm faking it, Detective?'

I watched the bright lights of Upper Street flashing past. My head was light from the loss of blood.

And I didn't know what I believed.

I could have flashed my warrant card and jumped the queue. But I didn't. I took a ticket and I sat with Emma Moon in the waiting area of the A&E at the Whittington, staunching the blood with her headband as I waited my turn.

I thought of Scout, home alone. I thought of calling Mrs Murphy to look in on her. But it was past midnight, and it was better all round to just let her sleep. Emma Moon was smiling at me, and I looked into those sharp, pale-blue eyes.

'Thanks,' I said.

'What happened with those guys? Your fellow Metropolitan Police officers? Your work colleagues?'

I shook my head. Bloody hell, my hand hurt now.

'Just a bit of banter that got out of control.'

'Right,' she said, not believing a word of it, crossing her legs. She still had those long dancer's legs. I realised that she would always have them. My head was not where it really needed to be, and I was starting to feel nauseous.

Emma Moon was standing. 'I'll get you some tea and chuck in a few sugars. You look like you need it.'

'Where did you see a lot of cuts?' I said.

She sat down.

'Inside. Where do you think? Not girls cutting each

227

other. Not like you and your pals tonight. They were cutting *themselves*. It happens – my God, it happens all the time, Max. I never understood it. It's not a cry for help. It's a cry for something else. For the pain to stop. For oblivion. Shall I tell you a joke?'

I nodded.

'I have this friend,' she said. 'She is very beautiful, incredibly fit – works out every day – and she reads three books a week – and has great sex in the shower every morning. And yet, and yet – she's always complaining about how much she hates being in prison!'

I smiled weakly. She placed her hands on top of mine, pressed down, her fingers coming away slick with my blood.

'Do you know what that joke is about, Max? It is about counting our blessings, and how hard we find it to count our blessings. Even though counting our blessings is the key to happiness, sanity, survival. And learning to count your blessings is the only thing that will keep you alive in prison. Without that great human skill of learning to count your blessings, you go mad, or they find you dead in your cell, or you lose yourself in the fog of drugs, or you carve chunks out of your own body. In those sixteen years inside, I learned to count my blessings.'

I tried to say something but it came out a bit soft.

She leaned closer.

'I said – but it can't be easy to count your blessings when you are doing time for someone else's crime.'

'Ah, but I loved him, you see. Terry Gatti. My Terry.

At least, he was my Terry back then. Now he is somebody else's Terry. And I was grateful for the great blessing of truly loving another human being. My love for Terry made it all possible. It made prison endurable, and it made sixteen years bearable. It made staying silent something that I never even had to think about. There was never any possibility that I would give up names, or become a witness for the prosecution, or rat anybody out. Because I loved him. That is the greatest mystery story of all, isn't it? The things we will do – and endure – for love.'

The crowds were thinning out.

The bleeding had stopped.

'I think I'm all right now,' I said.

She shook her head. 'You still need it cleaned and stitched up. Want me to call your wife?'

'You don't need to call my wife.'

I looked at her carefully. It felt like we had been stuck in these poses forever. Me hunched over, my left hand pressing down hard on the headband tourniquet. Emma Moon leaning back in the hospital chair, her long legs swinging, her fair hair falling down around her shoulders. Looking like the healthiest person in the hospital.

'They certainly stitched you up, didn't they? Terry and the boys.'

'The world went on without me. So yes – I suppose that's a kind of betrayal. If you were interested – and I admit I was interested – then there they were on some smuggled phone, showing off their lives. Because we

229

can't resist looking at other people's lives these days, can we?' She leaned forward and adjusted my bloodstained tourniquet before leaning back, remembering. 'I didn't have a phone of my own in all those sixteen years,' she said. 'But I had friends who were more cavalier about what they inserted in the various cavities of their body. And over the last, oh, I don't know, it has to be more than ten years, I watched Terry's life without me unfold. The new home. The new wife. *Helen.* The new life. There were glimpses – no more – of them raising a glass on their anniversary in some fancy restaurant, the new swimming pool at night, the lights shimmering under the surface of the water. Not much – Terry was too careful for that – but just enough to rip my heart out, and just enough to make me feel worthless, and just enough to realise that the love of my life was happier without me.'

She was silent as I pressed down on the bloody head-band, even though the bleeding seemed to have stopped now.

'And even that would have been bearable, Max,' she said. 'Looking at Terry's nice life on a smuggled phone. Even that betrayal would have been endurable – *if our David had been allowed to have a life.* If our beautiful, anxious boy had been protected. I would never have regretted loving Terry Gatti – and doing all those years for a crime that he committed – if our boy had not killed himself.'

She adjusted the makeshift tourniquet on my bloody hand.

'There is cruelty in prison,' she said. 'Specific cruelty, casual cruelty and cruelty that is baked into the system. But there is kindness too. Small acts of generosity and thoughtfulness. And somehow the light of that kindness shines with a greater intensity than it ever does on the outside. Towards the end of that hard first year inside, I read a book called *Man's Search For Meaning* by Viktor E. Frankl. And it stayed with me, that book. And so did its central message – *we receive the love we give*. You make friends inside. I imagine university is the same. And the armed forces. And your lot – the police. All these sealed worlds where you make friends to last a lifetime. Friends who will do anything for you. And friends who will hurt anyone who has ever hurt you.'

She smiled brightly.

I must have been staring at her for a long time.

'Max?' she said. 'I think they're calling your name.'

33

I was going up the steps to the big glass entrance to New Scotland Yard the next morning as the uniformed sergeant was coming down. Those steps are wide and there was plenty of room for both of us, even with the uniformed sergeant carrying a lot of meat and muscle on his middle-aged bones. But somehow he managed to clip my right arm with his left elbow.

'Sorry,' he said. 'Sir.'

There is a way of calling someone *sir* that sounds exactly like *shithead*. The police are good at it. I think they teach a class on it at Hendon. I stared after him for a moment and then carried on up the steps and stood in the lobby of that big glass capsule, measuring what had changed.

There were a couple of detectives I knew from the early days at West End Central getting into the lift. I lifted a hand to tell them to hold the door but they didn't hold it and I got a brief glimpse of the furtive, sour expressions on their faces as the door slid shut with me on one side and them on the other.

Pat Whitestone was suddenly beside me, laughing shortly.

'Word spreads fast in this job,' she said, looking at the fresh bandage on my hand but passing no comment.

'Pat—'

She lifted a hand for silence.

'Save it,' she said. 'You're going to have every chance to explain yourself.'

We got into the lift and she shook her head when I pressed the button for our floor.

'We're going to the top,' she said. 'The boss wants a word.' She shook her head and could not bear to look at me. 'You bloody idiot, Max.'

The Commissioner of Police did not really have time for me.

Disturbing new crime statistics had been published that morning about the percentage of burglaries resulting in a prosecution (not many) and shoplifting reaching such epidemic levels that it was not so much a crime any more as a viable career option. Even more disturbing than the crimes that never got anywhere near a courtroom were the crimes that actually did, but then took years – literally years – to be heard, often collapsing before anything resembling justice could be done.

It was all over the news. Social media was frothing at the mouth. So the commissioner, who had a busy day ahead, did not ask Whitestone and me to sit.

He was an unassuming-looking man, bald and bespectacled, but his office and uniform gave him an air of power. There were elaborate epaulettes on the shoulders of his white business shirt – a crown, silver pips and a laurel wreath – and it gave him a vaguely naval air, like some pissed-off admiral.

'This is Wolfe, is it? We've had a complaint about you, lad.'

I glanced at Whitestone. 'The IOPC, sir?'

The Independent Office for Police Conduct investigates serious complaints and allegations of misconduct against the police.

He bristled with irritation. 'A call from a senior AFO. I understand you have been making wild and unsubstantiated allegations about Authorised Firearms Officers.'

'Sir, I have been pursuing a legitimate line of enquiry about the murder of Suzanne Buksa.'

He looked at Whitestone. 'But I thought you had someone in the bin for that one?'

Whitestone's voice was calm and soft. 'We do, sir.'

The commissioner frowned at me. 'So you're investigating that great rarity, Wolfe – a crime that has actually been solved already?'

'May I ask who complained to your office about me, sir?'

'A highly respected senior AFO officer.'

That could be anyone. Almost anyone. Because I knew with all of my heart that it was not Jackson Rose who had reported me.

Jackson might want to kill me for going after some of his shots.

But he would never rat me out.

'I have made no allegations against anyone, sir.'

'These AFOs do an incredible job, Wolfe. Get it right and they get a medal. Get it wrong and they do jail time.'

'Yes, sir.'

'Everyone needs to have trust and confidence in the police, Wolfe. And that trust and confidence is slipping away.'

'Yes, sir. I could not agree more, sir. But I received a tip from a CI that a number of AFOs were abusing their powers of arrest for the purpose of sexual coercion.'

There was silence in the room. When the commissioner spoke again, his voice was measured and calm. 'So when you followed this lead, this important lead in a murder inquiry, I am assuming there was a CAD?'

A Computer Aided Dispatch is created for any planned police operational activity. It is a digital trail so that, if things go wrong, as they sometimes do, we can press a magic button and call for the cavalry.

He was waiting.

'There was no CAD, sir. Because I was not expecting to arrest anyone last night.'

'The CAD is what separates the Met from Third World police forces, Wolfe. It separates us from the cowboys.'

'Yes, sir.'

He looked at a file on the great expanse of his desk. 'You are a bit of a hero, Wolfe. Or at least you were, back in the day. Got a Queen's Police Medal, haven't you? Well, two of the men you were harassing last night have also got QPMs. And in my eyes, and the eyes of the world, they are heroes too.'

'Sir—'

'Do you understand what I do here, Wolfe? I am accountable to the Home Secretary, to the Mayor's Office for Policing and Crime, and I must answer to Londoners and the millions who come to our city from all over the world. But I am also responsible to the men and women of the Metropolitan Police, the officers we send out there every day to protect and serve. They deserve protection too, don't they?'

Whitestone cleared her throat. 'Sir, DS Wolfe has been under immense pressure of late. He knew Suzanne Buksa personally, and her murder hit him hard. The harassment of our AFO colleagues was a misjudgement.' She did not look at me. 'And Max is a single father, sir, and I know there have been problems at home that he has been struggling to cope with.'

'Personal problems, Wolfe? Mental health issues, is it?'

'No, sir. I'm fine. No mental health issues. My family is fine.'

'Max,' Whitestone said. 'None of it is fine.'

'I'll take no further action, Wolfe,' the commissioner said, eager to be shot of us. 'But take some time to reflect on your mistakes, lad, and sort out whatever drama is going on in your personal life. Take a break. I leave that to you to work out, Pat.'

'Sir.'

His eyes gleamed at me from behind his spectacles.

'The entire world is ripping our people to pieces,

Wolfe,' he said. 'They don't need help from one of our own.'

Whitestone and I rode the lift in silence. She shook her head when we got to our floor. 'You've got a temper on you, haven't you, Max?'

'No worse than anybody else.'

'Ah, that's just not true, boy. You've got the kind of fuse that gets a copper promoted, imprisoned or topped. Sometimes all three.'

'I'm all right.'

'You are such a long way from all right, Max. All right is not even on the horizon for you. Go home, Max. Spend time with Scout.'

'Scout's not around much. She's either at school or she's with her mum.'

'You have to work out if this job is still what you want to do. Because I am not sure it is.'

She stepped out of the lift. Apparently I was not going to work today.

'Mental health issues, Pat? Personal problems? Then that's me and everyone else in the Met. You trying to get me kicked out?'

'I'm trying to save your life,' she said, and the lift doors closed.

It was getting on for 10 p.m. when the doorbell rang. Stan looked at me in alarm. The doorbell never rang at night. Scout had her key. DC Bear Groves was on the monitor.

I buzzed him up. He was shaking with nerves.

'You can't tell anyone I came to see you.'

I nodded. I was shocked to be reminded how young he was.

'People are saying you're a rat, Max. They say you are telling tales about our own.'

'What do you think?'

'I think you're right about them,' he said. 'I *know* you're right about them. Those four Firearms Officers. John-Paul Ledoux and his friends. The so-called Beatles. I know what they have done to women. And I know what they're doing.'

I waited.

'I met a girl,' he said. 'A woman. And she was stopped by these bastards. They threatened her with arrest. Some bloody trumped-up charges. And they took her to their flat at the Angel. And you have to get them, Max. *Because this has to stop.*'

I heard Scout's key in the lock and I let out a breath that was pure relief. Bear and I had both turned our heads towards the sound and now looked back at each other.

'Before they kill again,' he said.

34

I was underdressed for the American Bar of the Savoy.

There is a dress code for gentlemen and I did not pass muster. A waiter – well-schooled in turning away scruffy tourists – intercepted young Bear and me at the entrance with a cursory, 'Sorry, sir.'

I showed him my palm and the Metropolitan Police warrant card, and then he was leading us to a corner table.

We settled ourselves and waited for the woman.

'Sorry, I should have warned you,' said Bear – Clark Kent in his Sunday best, immaculate in suit and tie. 'About the dress code. So old-fashioned.'

'No problem,' I said, putting away my warrant card. 'We can go anywhere.'

I looked around the bar. Mostly boys and girls from finance but with a smattering of those high-end Londoners who don't appear to have to work for a living.

'You met her here?' I asked, slightly stunned.

Bear looked embarrassed, his cheeks even pinker than usual. He knew what I was thinking.

What kind of poor Direct Entry Detective straight out

of Hendon meets a woman in the American Bar of the Savoy? And what kind of woman catches his eye across a crowded bar? And what's a young, good-looking lad like you doing with a high-end hooker?

'My father would bring me here when he visited me in London,' Bear said. 'He didn't enjoy the gastropubs of Hendon.'

The waiter brought two beers.

'This is where she hangs out,' he said. 'Kate. Katherine. It's the anglicised version of her real name. Katyusha. I think she admires the Princess of Wales.'

'Don't we all?'

'And she likes the swankier bars of London hotels.' He reeled them off. 'The Rivoli at the Ritz. The Fumoir at Claridges. The Coburg at the Connaught. And the American Bar at the Savoy.'

'OK.'

I stared at him.

He laughed, blushing harder. 'I didn't realise, Max! I'm a simple country boy from Oxfordshire! I thought this beautiful girl was sitting in a bar all by herself and she liked my face.'

'Maybe she did like your face, Bear.'

He had a very nice face, the boy. He radiated youth, and health, and fitness.

'I didn't realise I was going to have to *pay*. Ah, here she is now. Kate! Kate!'

This beautiful young woman approached, unsmiling.

Same age as our Bear – middle twenties – but with a

hard glossy shell that made her seem several lifetimes older than my young colleague. Her clothes were simple, expensive – a white two-piece suit. Tall, striking and wishing she was somewhere else.

'I don't want trouble,' she said, glancing quickly at me and then at Bear. 'I do this only as a favour.'

He squeezed her hand, reassuring, and she touched his face. An act of affection. It seemed real enough to me.

'Katherine?' I said. 'Nobody wants to get you into trouble. This is about making sure that trouble stops. I – we – are investigating the murder of a young woman called Suzanne Buksa. I think it is possible you may have met the men who were responsible for her death.' She stared at me, sizing me up, ready to bolt at any moment. Bear touched her arm. He seemed to really like her and I hoped he had a vague idea of what he was getting into.

'Kate, please tell Max – DS Wolfe – what you told me.'

She squirmed in her chair. A waiter placed a glass of champagne before her. She had not needed to order it.

'Police officers,' she said. 'They were police officers.'

'Tell me about them,' I said.

She shrugged, as if there was nothing much to tell.

'I came out of the Connaught – alone – and I was looking for a black cab in Berkeley Square. A man approached me, showed me his ID.'

I nodded at Bear and he took out his warrant card.

'Did it look like that?'

She nodded. 'It looked exactly like that.' She picked up her champagne flute but did not drink. 'He asked me lots of questions. Who was I? What was I doing? Where was I going? Where had I been? What had I been doing in the Connaught? He acted like he already knew all the answers. People were staring. He told me I was in trouble. And he told me he was arresting me.' She laughed shortly. 'For soliciting. He *handcuffed* me.' She pulled back the pristine sleeves of her business suit. There were livid welts on her wrists. 'See? Even after a month, still the marks.'

'He put you in his car?'

'Yes.'

'What did he look like?'

'Like some kind of Italian guy, or Spanish maybe. Much darker than both of you. Good-looking.'

Ledoux, I thought. *John-Paul Ledoux.*

'And he was alone?'

'He was alone but there were other men at the place he took me to. An apartment.'

'Do you know roughly where it is?'

'I know *exactly* where it is.' She drained her champagne glass and gave me the address of the apartment at the Angel.

'Excuse me,' Bear said, standing up and pushing his way through the correctly dressed crowds.

'It's hard for him,' she said, watching him go. 'He doesn't like to hear it. He likes me.'

She sipped her champagne. Then she drank it straight down.

'You haven't reported any of this to the police?'

She snorted. 'They *are* the police.'

'Another drink?'

She shook her head. 'One is enough.' She leaned forward. 'And you should know – I am here because Bear asked me to see you. But I am not making a statement. I am not going on the record. I am not talking to lawyers, or judges, or more cops. Or any of that.'

'What happened at the apartment?'

'What do you think happened at the apartment? What was going to happen in their apartment from the moment he stopped me in Berkeley Square and told me he was a policeman.'

'Did you get any names?'

'No names.'

'Would you recognise them again?'

'Oh yes.'

'Did they use violence?'

She looked incredulous. 'He used all his power as a policeman to stop me, and put me in that car, and took me where he wanted to take me. Is that violent enough for you?'

'Suzanne Buksa had her neck broken,' I said. 'I understand the horror and enormity of what happened to you, Katyusha. But I am trying to understand if you were ever in fear for your life.'

She looked across the bar, seeking Bear.

He was standing at the bar. He waved gamely and she waved back with an affectionate laugh.

'There was a moment – back at the flat, this horrible

flat at the Angel – when I understood the game they were playing, and when I knew what I had walked into, and what he had tricked me into, and when I knew what I was going to have to do if I was to get out alive.'

'And what was that moment?'

'When one of them put a gun in my mouth,' she said.

35

'I'm not his girlfriend,' Katyusha said as we watched Bear amble off to the tube station, after he had kissed her chastely on the cheek and grinned his big, embarrassed, boy-next-door grin and told me he would see me at work. 'He has to understand that.'

We stood outside the Savoy, watching his large form disappear into the crowds on the Strand.

'You're his boss, right?' she said.

'Yes.'

'Don't think badly of Bear. Because . . . you know.' An embarrassed laugh. 'He paid me.'

'I don't think badly of either of you. Consenting adults and all that. It's when there's a lack of consent that I get upset.'

She stared at me. 'You're a good man.'

'I don't like bullies. I wonder about how good I am.'

She thought for a moment. But only for a moment.

'If you get them for the girl who died – for Suzanne – I'll give you a statement.'

I looked at her. 'You would have to stand up in court.

Some slick defence lawyer would throw things at you. Ugly things.'

She laughed. 'I have had ugly things thrown at me before. I've been out on my own since I was sixteen. I can take it. And it's the right thing to do, isn't it?'

She frowned at the lines of black cabs entering Savoy Court. They were driving on the right-hand side of the road.

'That's wrong, isn't it? The side of the road they drive on?'

'It's a convention from the olden days,' I said. 'In a horse-drawn carriage, the lady would sit behind the driver. So when they arrived at the Savoy, the doorman or the carriage driver could open their door without walking around the carriage if they drove on the right. And Savoy Court is private property. So they can make their own rules.'

She considered me. 'Would you like to take me home?' she said. 'No charge. The girlfriend experience. Special offer. One night only.'

She was a good kid, a brave woman. I liked her. And stunning, of course. And I was lonely. That was the truth. And you get to a point in your life when you think – well, what exactly am I saving it for? *Who* exactly am I saving it for?

But she saw me resisting. 'Oh,' she said. 'Is someone waiting for you?'

I laughed. My turn to be all bashful.

'You never know your luck,' I said.

*

Emma Moon was feeding the homeless.

She was at the far end of the street where I lived, down where Charterhouse Street is mostly derelict, closer to collapse, away from the money and the meat and endless night-time bustle of the market, down where abandoned buildings wait patiently to be turned into fancy apartment blocks, and the homeless gather when the office workers are long gone and the restaurants and bars and cafés are all closed.

She stood behind a small trellis table piled high with pre-wrapped sandwiches and a big metal urn of steaming soup as Luka the shaven-headed maybe-boyfriend supervised the shuffling queue with his blank warden's stare and Roxy curtly handed out sandwiches and Nevermore smiled his unbreakable smile. Emma brushed her unkempt blond hair from her face. She had not seen me. I savoured the moment – watching her when she did not know she was being watched.

A harsh voice hissed in my ear. 'But why are you here?' Summer's eyes blazed at me. This close, her face was painfully thin, the natural-born beauty worn away. 'She doesn't *want* you here,' she told me. 'She was *curious* about you, that's all. *What happened to that scared young copper who put the handcuffs on me?* But she's bored with you already. Because you are just another bent copper on the take.'

I took a step away from her.

'Slumming it, are you?' she sneered. 'Like Little Lord Fauntleroy over there? Like old Boy Nevermore?

Getting your kicks from hanging out with the common people?'

'I live here.'

She pressed her long bony body against me, her emaciated face suddenly lighting up. 'I like it too,' she said. 'Watching Emma when she doesn't know that you are watching her. I like watching her face when she doesn't know that anyone is looking at her. I like—'

'Max!'

Emma was waving to me. They watched me – all of them – Nevermore with his floppy-haired, golly-gosh, rosy-cheeked grin, Summer with her eyes blazing with resentment and the other two, Luka and Roxy, with a kind of blank hostility.

'Want a sandwich?' Emma called. 'They're good!'

I approached her trellis table.

'I'm all right. Got to get back for my daughter.' I glanced at my watch. Just coming up to 9 p.m. One hour to curfew. 'She'll be coming home.'

Emma Moon stared at me. She lightly took my arm in her hand, and gently steered me to one side. They all watched us.

But we were alone. It felt like we were alone.

'What's wrong?' she asked me.

'Nothing, nothing.'

The queue kept moving. The sandwiches were chicken mayo and cheese and tomato. The soup was Irish stew, and the smell made my mouth water.

'It's just – Scout – my daughter – she's been seeing her

mother. And it has been a while since they saw each other. In fact, it has been years since they had any contact.'

'No contact at all?'

I nodded.

'What is she, your ex-wife?' Emma Moon asked. 'One of those people who starts a new family every five years or so? Like a franchise?'

'A bit like that, I guess. But Scout has just established a relationship with her and I don't really know how they're getting on. I don't even know what they do together, or where they go, or what they talk about. All I get to decide is what time Scout has to be home. I would talk it through with my ex-wife – and I know I should. But Scout says they are fine. She wants to work it out between the pair of them. And I guess my ex-wife does too.'

She smiled at me, totally understanding.

'You just want to know that Scout's all right.'

'Yes. That's all.'

Nevermore approached us with his apologetic grin, waggling his eyebrows, about to make a suggestion about the food bank.

'Emma? I wonder—'

'Not now,' she told him, not even looking at him, her eyes never leaving mine.

Nevermore slunk away.

'Go online,' she told me. 'Watch over them that way. They must be taking pictures, right? That's the modern world. If you don't take a picture of it with your phone then it never really happened. Doesn't your daughter have social media accounts?'

I shook my head. 'Scout doesn't do any of that stuff. She's a strange kid. She prefers books.'

'Good for her. Then look for your ex-wife. She'll be taking loads of selfies and posting them online – I guarantee it.' She laughed and stood closer to me. There was that Emma Moon scent of flowers and smoke. 'When I was away – as they say – it wasn't just Terry I watched carry on without me. They were all there! All that showing off for strangers – not my thing, never my thing. But there were all my old friends. And I could not help but follow their progress. Butch proudly posing with his granddaughters. Keith and his strange journey from cocaine-crazed nutjob to yoga mat. Ian – pictures of trains and sunsets with motivational words. And Mick, living the good life in Spain, his smug, sun-dappled posts featuring a lot of food and alcohol – beaded glasses of rosé by the pool, the fish of the day, the bird of the moment. There was always a phone I could borrow. You can get anything in prison. And once I made friends with Luka, it became even easier.'

I glanced at Luka handing a sandwich to a bearded old man and felt a ridiculous stab of jealousy.

'And Terry was there,' she said. 'First Facebook. Then Instagram. Then TikTok. Always a restrained presence on social media. Not all over it, preening in his fabulous life like Mick. But Terry was there often enough for me to get the picture, to get the message. I was out. He had moved on. What a reward for my discretion, for my loyalty, for my love. What arrogance it took for him to be confident that his new life – his new woman – would not make me . . . *tell them everything.*'

She laughed, and she touched my face, as if I inspired some deep affection in her.

'Look online, Max,' Emma Moon advised. 'People complain that it is all fake news. But the real problem is that more often it reveals the bitter truth. Have a look for them online, Max. The truth will make you feel better.'

'Did the truth make you feel better?'

'Not really,' she said. 'It made me want to kill the lot of them.'

36

There is nobody more distant from us than those we once loved.

And so I sat myself at the kitchen island, and I booted up my laptop – but then I hesitated.

Stan eyed me from his basket. *Are you sure about this?*

No, I was far from sure. I did not feel as though I was about to find some cosy reassurance that all was well in the world now that my daughter and her mother had reconnected after all those lost years apart. There was a nameless dread weighing on me, and I thought that perhaps it was simply guilt.

It felt shameful somehow to look at my ex-wife and my daughter enjoying their personal time. Something a stalker would do, peeking at other lives on his little screen. Whatever they did, it was between them, and it could only be healthy and good, and it had nothing to do with me.

Stan watched me with his great bulging eyes. And I closed the laptop. Because I didn't want to know. I preferred not to know.

But then there was the sound of Scout's key in the

lock. I glanced at my watch: 10:15. Fifteen minutes after her carefully negotiated 10 p.m. curfew but not so late that it was worth making a fuss about. She quickly kicked off her DMs because she could not get to her room fast enough.

'You all right, Scout?'

'Fine. Fine. I'm fine.'

'Sleep well.'

'Yes – you too.'

A father and his daughter, as distant and polite and stilted as strangers at a dinner party who have never been formally introduced.

Scout gave Stan a quick, soft pat for old time's sake and he stirred and half-opened his eyes, but she was already gone.

She disappeared into her room, and I heard the noises of that life I could never know. So then I opened up my laptop, and I looked.

You can find anyone these days.

If their name remains the same – that's the crucial element, their name has to be the same – then it is simply a process of elimination.

And Anne had kept her name.

Through it all – her starter marriage to me, in the proper, far-more-successful second marriage in the leafy suburb with the rich guy who came after me and after him, to infinity and beyond, she had kept her name. It was a good name but it is not a particularly rare name so when I had eliminated all the Annes with her family name – a teenage girl in Glasgow, an elderly lady in Newcastle, and all the others who did not quite have the same name – they were the wrong kind of Anne, with a missing *e* – there she was on Instagram. That was always going to be her platform of choice. Where nothing matters more than the visuals, the gorgeous, glossy surface of things.

And at first I thought I had got the wrong Anne again, despite the little blue tick that urged me to believe I had found her.

Because this Anne . . . she lived in New Zealand.

And it was stunning. All of it. New Zealand was stunning, and so was she. Still. Smiling at me from her little byline photograph (which had to be a good ten years old). And still stunning today. She would always be stunning.

New Zealand was there in all its natural jaw-dropping rapture – long white clouds snaking through mountains, the purple majesty of twilight, lakes as still as an ocean of glass.

All of it a mere backdrop for Anne – smiling, bundled up against the weather – and her family.

There was a man – generic good looks, on the macho side, a few bob in his pocket (she definitely had a type) – and a happy tribe of kids. His? Hers? Theirs? Who knew? And frankly – who cared? I only cared about my daughter.

I looked closer. Anne? Is that really you out there?

Because this was the woman who I had spent thousands

of nights sleeping next to, the woman I loved and married and had a child with, the woman who I would have spent my life with if that had ever been a realistic option (it wasn't – we were always going to come apart, the pretend policeman and the pretend model). This Anne who I once knew so well was a total stranger on the other side of the world and – oh, look, her blue-ticked Instagram page had a little slogan at the top. *Living my best life.*

I looked closer. For now I wanted to know everything.

She had lost that catwalk sheen she had in her extreme youth, but come on – there was a beauty that would never be diminished with age. Men would scheme to win her when she was seventy.

But – *Anne in New Zealand?*

How was this even possible? How could I not know?

Because we had been left to get on with it.

As simple – as banal – as that. All those years ago. When she walked out the door to this very apartment for a new life, Scout and I had emphatically been left to get on with it.

And so we did.

I scrolled through Anne's latest life. And I could see the appeal. In all of it. Anne and the new guy – not that new! – were a handsome couple. Was he a holiday romance that she never wanted to end? Some London-based finance guy who had to go home (visa problems, ageing parents)? Who knew? And again – who cared?

The kids looked like happy, healthy, well-adjusted children (wait until the teenage years, Anne, the road gets

bumpier). And New Zealand was – well, it was just ravishing. I had this mad vision where I saw Scout and me
moving there and going out in a kayak on the weekend
(Stan at the bow, like a bulging-eyed figurehead) and
taking grinning selfies in front of a landscape so beautiful
that it looked like it was on some other, far more photo-
genic planet.

I looked inside myself for some pangs of envy but,
honestly, there were none.

Only this deep and abiding sadness.

For my girl. For my Scout.

I wanted to go to her immediately but also – just as
strong, to tell the truth – I didn't want to talk about it.

I was scared and I was sad and I was confused. And
resentment? Bitterness? I could not deny it. I could go,
oh years, without even thinking about what had happened between Anne and me, without even thinking
about her.

Because we had been left to carry on with life, Scout and
I, when she walked away. And we did, we did, we did.

One moment flashed in my mind, as vivid as summer
lightning. Strange that I should think of this now. A
moment – several moments – from Scout's childhood.
Not the big moments of laughter and tears. But moments
that had stuck in my consciousness because they somehow seemed to sum up my beautiful child.

It was when Scout walked into supermarkets. She would
pause, and she would stand there on the spot – waving.
And she would do it in summer, in T-shirts and shorts,

and in winter, bundled up against the London rain and cold. She would do it in school uniform and in mufti, the year she was four and seven and nine.

It had stopped at some point. But it had gone on for years. And when she was a little girl, it always happened.

Walk into a supermarket.

Then stand there – waving.

She was watching herself in the CCTV monitor.

And it always made me smile to see her doing it, and it always grabbed my heart and would not let go. To see my daughter announcing to the world – *My name is Scout Wolfe and I am here.*

I thought of what her mother was missing at those moments, because watching Scout wave at the CCTV camera was worth all the lakes and mountains in the southern hemisphere, and so those moments were bittersweet, even when they made me laugh out loud.

But even the most painful wounds fade with time. They fade to nothing. And so I did not think about Anne – her new man, her new family, her new life.

But I thought about them now.

Now I was looking at that happy family in this perfect world.

Now I had no choice but to think about them.

Now I weighed up all the accounts. And what I concluded was this, the eternal complaint of the parent who stays behind.

Scout should have mattered more to you, I thought.

Scout should have mattered more to you than anything.

Stan sighed in his sleep.

I closed my laptop and let it sink in.

Because now I knew.

Wherever Scout was going in the evening, it was not to spend time with her mother.

37

The holding cells of the Central Criminal Court of England and Wales – commonly referred to as the Old Bailey – are located directly below the courtrooms, so that it felt like Robert McKay was not escorted into the glass-walled dock of Court Two, he just suddenly appeared.

One moment he wasn't there and then the next moment he was, like a magic trick that is greeted with total silence.

He stood in the dock with a uniformed officer on either side of him, blinking in the light of this strange new morning and the gaze of the gawping crowd, all eyes on him, and he looked shockingly young now that he was clean-shaven. But he still had that anaesthetised look in his eyes, he still looked as if part of him had been left in some other time and place as he stared at the bewildering, bewigged, full cast of the criminal justice system.

Suzanne Buksa's mother and sister were in the front row of the public gallery, like the balcony seats in a small theatre, their faces pale and drawn.

I made my way to where DCI Pat Whitestone was sitting with DCs Sita Basu and Bear Groves, who shuffled

along to make space for me. The faces of our two probationers were tight with adrenaline. First murder case, I
thought. In contrast, Whitestone was almost relaxed,
smiling at me like a short-sighted owl as she took off her
spectacles to give them a polish.

'You could have sat this one out,' Pat said. 'It's only
the preliminary hearing.'

'I'm just checking in, Pat. When do you want me back
at work?'

'I don't know, Max – when are you going to stop harassing our own?'

I said nothing.

She lightly touched my arm.

'Max – I understand from our colleagues in the Crown
Prosecution Service that Robert McKay is going to plead
guilty to murder. There's a degree of confusion. He
signed a confession. Then he retracted it. But now he
seems keen on a guilty plea.'

I felt the sickness rising as I stared at the young man in
the dock.

'But he didn't do it. He didn't kill Suzanne.'

'Suzanne had McKay's DNA under her fingernails,
Max. How do you explain that?'

'I can't explain it.'

She was looking at the bandage on my hand.

'Max, what exactly do you think is going to happen if
you start going after cops? Nothing good.'

'Dirty cops, Pat. Cops who give the rest of us a bad
name. Cops that are dragging us all into their sewer.'

'*They didn't do it*. Ledoux and the Beatles. Oh, I know what they are – they are sexual predators, bullies, nasty pieces of work. I don't need you to tell me what they are, Max. But they didn't kill Suzanne Buksa.'

I could not take my eyes off the young man in the dock.

'And neither did Robert McKay,' I said.

She sighed, took off her glasses and gave them a swift polish with her thumb. She put them back on and blinked twice, getting me in focus.

'Then explain this to me, Max – McKay signed a confession admitting he did it.'

'Which he later retracted.'

'And now he says every word is true.'

'We both know you can get anyone to sign anything if you squeeze them hard enough. He's *damaged*. He doesn't know what he's saying.'

'Clearly. That's why his defence are going to go for dim rep. But you know where my sympathies lie, Max? With the girl who had her neck broken.'

Our young folk were watching us.

'Er – sorry – what's dim rep, ma'am?' asked DC Basu.

'Dim rep is diminished responsibility,' Whitestone explained to Sita. 'It is when a defendant argues that, although they broke the law, their mental functions were diminished or impaired at the time of the *actus reus* – guilty act. And because of their unbalanced mental state when the crime was committed, they should not receive the maximum sentence. They want the murder charge reduced to manslaughter. They want McKay to do his time in a high-security psychiatric hospital rather than a prison.'

Sita – always the more curious of our two Direct Entry Detectives – was about to ask a follow-up question when the bailiff said, 'All rise.'

We stood. An older woman in the scarlet robes of a high court judge entered, her shoulder-length wig the colour of old porridge. She settled herself in her seat and peered at the defendant over the top of her rimless glasses. He was asked to confirm his name and address.

Robert Alexander McKay, I thought. No fixed abode.

McKay's voice was strong and clear.

'Guilty, Your Honour,' he said, ignoring the question about his name and address, and in the public gallery, Suzanne's mother cried out with grief, and all eyes turned towards her, and so nobody saw McKay ram his elbow into the face of the officer on his left, but we all heard the grunt of shock and pain, and we all watched as McKay turned, as if in slow motion, and shoved the flattened palm of his hand against the nose of the officer on his left.

McKay looked at the glass dock that surrounded him as if contemplating scaling it, and then decided that this feat could only be done on TV and disappeared back down the rabbit hole to the holding cells.

A siren was already sounding.

'They will have him before he leaves the building,' Whitestone said. 'Still think he's innocent, Max?'

*

The doors of the main entrance to the Old Bailey opposite St George's Court were locked, uniformed officers everywhere, adrenaline pumping, the emergency siren screaming.

Two AFOs were there. And then two more. And then another two. Armed men and women, suited and booted, their firearms held at that 45-degree angle, their faces taut with tension. Without a word, Whitestone and I ran to the back entrance on Warwick Square, where a massive prison transport van was waiting with its engine idling. The doors were already locked.

'What about the entrance to the public gallery?' Whitestone said. 'There's no other way out.'

'Newgate Street,' I said.

'On it,' Bear said, and he followed Sita, who was already on her way.

Whitestone stared at me. 'How else can he get away?'

Newgate Street, I thought.

Warwick Street.

St George's Court.

There was no other exit out of the Central Criminal Court.

Unless you went down.

Beyond the marble halls of the Old Bailey, there is a door marked STAFF ONLY and if you pass through it, and keep going past the offices full of workers staring at their screens and eating their café-bought lunches, you will eventually come to another door, which is unmarked, and if you go through that door you will reach some stairs that are unlit and apparently lead nowhere and have a sign that says NO ACCESS. If you go down those winding stairs in the darkness then you will eventually come to a well-lit boiler room, roaring like the innards of some great ocean liner. But the stairs go down further, to the forgotten bowels of the Central Criminal Court. So you keep going down.

And finally those stairs come to the remains of Newgate prison.

And that is where I went looking for Robert McKay.

Newgate was London's most notorious prison for eight hundred years and the Old Bailey was built on its ruins. Newgate is not conserved or preserved because nobody was ever proud of it, the place where Charles Dickens watched public hangings attended as if they were cup finals.

Tourists can't visit Newgate. But it is still down there, or what remains of it is still down there – a few forgotten corners of that chamber of horrors that are not preserved or conserved. They simply exist, and you can still find them if you know where to look.

And I knew.

I walked down a corridor that was like something from a nightmare. The ceiling and the walls contracted – the ceiling lower, the walls narrower – as you went down it. This was Dead Man's Walk, designed to subdue those about to die, for the condemned man often went fighting mad and fought like demons as they heard the roar of the crowd waiting to see them hang.

Robert McKay stood waiting for me at the end of Dead Man's Walk. He leaned against the crumbling wall of what had once been Newgate's holding cell, the waiting room for public executions. The only light came from what seeped down from the boiler room and – from somewhere – a rumour of daylight. There was a way out of here, but those who knew it had been dead for centuries.

'Robert,' I said. 'I know you did not kill Suzanne.'

His eyes flickered towards me, and there was a light in them that I had never seen before. 'One of *you* did it,' he said. 'A cop.'

'I know,' I said. 'So help me prove it. Tell me what you know. Let's find the bastard together. This is not the way to do it. Please.'

He nodded, took a step towards me. 'You're right,' he said. 'I always seem to take the wrong way.'

Then he drove his fist into my heart.

One punch. Right hand.

And the punch slammed with enormous force against my sternum, the flat bone at the front of the chest where the upper ribs are attached by cartilage just in front of the heart.

I staggered backwards and then I was on the ground, reeling from the trauma of sudden chest compression, pawing helplessly at my heart, feeling like I was dying as Robert McKay scrambled towards that rumour of sunlight.

38

I watched from our big loft window as Scout headed down Grand Avenue, the main entrance to Smithfield, rubbing my heart, still pulsing with shock and pain. It was early in the evening, the city emptying of office workers but hours before the market would start to work through the night. She was a small, lonely figure, her bright yellow Fjällräven backpack slung over one shoulder, and she had told me she was off to see her mother. And when she was at the end of Grand Avenue, I followed her.

I did not have to go far.

There was a strip of shops on the far side, all of them closed for good or for the night. There were lights and music coming from one of them above a window where time and the weather had worn away at words I had looked at a thousand times.

MURPHY & SON
Domestic and Commercial Plumbing
and Heating
'Trustworthy' and 'Reliable'

Scout had her own key. That was a shock. In fact, it was all a shock. I stood on the Grand Avenue watching her take her key out as she went up the steps at the side of the shops and disappeared. I walked down to the square at West Smithfield, my head reeling.

But it was not complicated. It was heartbreakingly banal.

When Scout was meant to be bonding with her long-lost mother, she was going round to the Murphys' flat on the other side of the market.

I walked back to the strip of shops and went up the stairs, hesitating for a moment, wondering if I should let my daughter keep this secret.

And then I rang the bell. Because I needed to understand.

Mrs Murphy opened the door. For a second she looked surprised to see me standing there. But the moment passed, as if she had known that I would turn up here sooner or later. She stood aside and I went in. As always, the tiny flat was busier than Piccadilly Circus at chucking-out time. The TV was tuned to Sky Sports. Somewhere Sinatra was singing for the lonely. Children and animals were everywhere. The trinity of Mikeys were all home. Big Mikey – Mrs Murphy's wafer-thin husband with neat silver hair – was watching the football with a sleeping toddler on his lap. His son Little Mikey – a black-haired heavyweight – was clearing the dinner table with his wife Siobhan. And Baby Mikey, knocking on for ten now, was being read to by Scout from a battered, much-read copy of *Harry Potter and the Philosopher's Stone*. She looked at me and I saw the panic fly for a moment.

But then she turned back to Harry Potter and Baby Mikey.

Mrs Murphy and I watched her grandson and my daughter.

'You didn't tell me,' I said, and keeping the resentment out of my voice was beyond me.

'Scout asked me not to,' she said. 'I couldn't break a promise to my Scout, could I now?'

'This is it? This is what she does? This is what she's been doing?'

'Yes, she mostly reads to the little ones. She likes it. And they like it too.'

'But – I don't understand,' I said. 'I don't get any of it. She told me she was reconnecting with her mum. And her mum lives on the other side of the world.'

'Yes, Scout and I saw that too. New Zealand looks nice, doesn't it?'

Tears came to my eyes. 'Is she crazy?'

'Oh, no. I think of it as the most natural thing in the world.'

'But it's all a fantasy. It's all made-up. It's all a dream. It's not real. It was all in her head.'

Mrs Murphy paused, choosing her words.

'I think she wanted – needed – somewhere to go when things were a bit tricky at home. With you. With her dad. And she wished she had that other place to go to. She really wished it, Max. And the wishing was real – the wishing *wasn't* a fantasy. It was what she wanted more than anything. Even that's not saying it. I will tell you what it was, this thing with her mum. It was a *prayer* – and what is more real than a prayer?'

I watched Scout reading to Baby Mikey. The pair of them laughed together, then turned the page.

'What am I going to do?' I said.

'You are going to do what you have always done,' Mrs Murphy told me. 'You are going to love her. And you are going to do your best to understand. Anne – she's your ex-wife but she's not Scout's ex-mum.'

'Except – she kind of is. Because she's not here for any of it. She's living her best life on Instagram. In New Zealand.'

'But she's always going to be Scout's mother, even if she never sees her. Even if they are strangers. Nothing can stop her being Scout's mum, and that is what our girl is working her way through.'

Our girl.

'I just don't know what to say to her, Mrs Murphy.'

'You don't have to say anything. You two – you'll be fine, I know you will. And we need these hard times – the sad times – the difficult times – so we can cherish the happy times when they come. And they will.'

Mrs Murphy gave my shoulder a shy, quick pat.

Scout looked up at her. 'Your dad's here, Scout,' Mrs Murphy said, and she went to Scout when she saw the quick jolt of panic in my daughter's eyes, and she patted her as light and shy as she had patted me – a touch that said *It's all going to be fine, I promise you* – and then she joined the pair of them on the floor, Scout and Baby Mikey, asking her grandson how he liked the story, and what was old Harry Potter and his pals up to now, and dialling down the drama and confusion and hurt with calm, common sense, and the biggest heart in the world.

And her genius for kindness – don't forget the kindness.

I found my voice. 'Shall we go home, Scout?'

We did not speak on the Grand Avenue, and we did not speak when we went up to our apartment, and we did not speak as we went inside.

But Stan – having woken up and found himself cruelly abandoned and alone – was lying by the front door, pining for company. Scout and I got on our knees and made a fuss of him until his tail was wagging like a windscreen wiper and he was happy again.

Scout headed for her room. I said her name and she turned to face me.

'It's not your fault,' I said. 'Adults mess up their lives and they get to move on while their children pay the bill.'

'Yes,' she said coldly. 'I worked that out already.'

It was not enough. The feeble words I had come up with were not enough. I had another run at it. 'And it's her loss. To miss you growing up – although it is not always a laugh a minute, frankly – is missing something priceless.'

'OK,' she said, thawing just a little.

I should let her go.

There were not going to be warm hugs and soggy kisses to answer all of our problems. She wanted to go to her room. But there was one more thing I had to tell her.

'And I am proud that you're my daughter, Scout. No father could be prouder. No dad could love his daughter more than I love you.'

She nodded, and we turned our faces away so that nobody ever saw the shine of tears.

39

Jackson Rose was down on the street the next evening, ringing my bell as the city began to empty at the end of another working day.

I buzzed him up and was waiting at the door when he arrived. He walked into the loft without saying a word. He was the only person in the world who was close enough to walk into my home without saying a word. Stan came to greet him, tail wagging, and Jackson scratched the dog's head absent-mindedly, staring around the big open space of the loft, as if he was thinking about something else.

'Long day?' I said.

He shook his head. 'Frustrating day. No sign of Robert McKay in this neck of the woods. I have been home. Like to see Rosie before she goes to bed. Then I came out again.'

'How's Rosie Rose doing?'

His handsome face cracked into a smile. 'She's great, Max. She's the best thing that ever happened to me. I never dreamed that something as good as my little girl could ever happen to me. It changes a man – having a daughter. It shouldn't change a man – he should be that way in the first place, I reckon – but it does. I can't explain it. It just – I don't know – *wakes a man up*, I think. Do you know what I mean?'

'Yes,' I said. 'Yes, I do, Jackson.'

He nodded to the closed bedroom door. 'Scout about?'

'She's in her room. Listening to music. Or reading. Or whatever they do with their phones when they are twelve.'

'Scout all right?'

'She's all right.'

'I was thinking,' he said slowly.

I waited.

'We had a complaint about John-Paul Ledoux last year. A female shot. Sexual harassment. She dropped the charges. Left the force.' He shrugged. 'NFA.'

NFA is *No further action.*

'Why don't you tell me about Suzanne,' he said.

We both took a seat at the kitchen island.

'She should never have been on the streets.'

'Nobody should ever be on the streets.'

'She had this stupid rabbit she carried everywhere.'

'A rabbit?'

'A stuffed toy. Not a real rabbit, Jackson.'

'All right. Got it. Not a real rabbit.'

'This rabbit – I thought it was just an affectation. You know, the way you see some street people with dogs just because a dog makes it more likely that people will put their hand in their pocket. But I got to know her a bit, and I changed my mind. This rabbit – Mr Flopsy was his name – was a favourite childhood toy. It gave her comfort. When she was out there. And that's what I think about when I remember Suzanne. This link she had to this happier time. I don't know what put her on the streets. It seems to me that it's a combination of bad luck and bad choices that put you on the streets.'

He raised his eyebrows, said nothing, let me talk.

'But Suzanne was loved. I met her mother and her sister. And she was loved, Jackson. I don't know anything about the wrong men she chose or the wrong drugs she took and the wrong directions she went off in. But I know she was loved. And I know she had a good heart. And I know she should be alive today.'

We sat in silence.

'These guys,' Jackson said at last. 'John-Paul Ledoux and his mates. Mo, Dim and Jim. The bloody Beatles. I hear the way they talk about female shots. Their colleagues. They are not Boy Scouts. I know that. I can see that. If you tell me they are coercing women – it doesn't shock me to the core, to be honest. But *killing* someone? I don't know, Max. I just don't know. Maybe there was a night that their sick little games got out of hand. But – and I don't know if it is because they are my own – I don't know about murder.'

'But we know it happens, Jackson. Don't we? We know that officers in the Metropolitan Police are capable of anything. That doesn't make us all rotten. But recent history tells us it happens.'

'True.'

We sat in silence some more. Then Jackson Rose sighed.

'So when we go after them,' he said, 'are we going to use your car or mine?'

Fred's was not the kind of gym where people stood and stared at the TV.

The gym attracted all sorts – fit old people defying time, brave young people fighting cancer, City boys and girls, those in retirement and those in rehab with their broken limbs and torn muscles and tendons, the white-collar boxers and the aspiring pros. But none of them stood and gawped at the big flat-screen TV, which always seemed tuned to some awful music channel where bikini-clad girls danced on yachts but always with the sound muted because Fred preferred his own playlist.

No, you didn't gawp mindlessly at the TV in Fred's.

But that's what Terry Gatti was doing.

I had come into the gym with a smile on my face. Because Jackson Rose was going to help me find the killer of Suzanne Buksa.

And I was also smiling because Fred's playlist sounded like the one he had dreamed of – only bands who had played the Rainbow. Bob Marley and the Wailers' 'Lively Up Yourself' was segueing into The Clash cover of 'I Fought the Law'.

Fred grinned at me. 'James Brown is up next.'

'James Brown played the Rainbow?'

'In 1973. The same year as Stevie Wonder, Santana,

The Sweet, Eric Clapton, Van Morrison, Roxy Music and Dr John.'

'A very good year.'

Terry Gatti looked as though he had been up all night.

'Was I right?' he said.

We stared at each other.

'Was I right about who killed Suzanne? I told you – we told you, my brother and I – that it was a police officer. I know they have pinned it on some old solider. I know he is going to die for it. Either inside or death by cop. But we both know that he is an innocent man. We both know that the police have done what the police always do – if they can't find the guilty, then they prosecute the innocent.'

'You appreciate the irony, right? You – of all people – demanding justice?'

He gripped my arm. There was a light in his eyes that I had never seen before. It was desperation. And it was fear.

'Was I right?'

I shook him off. 'Looks that way,' I said.

'Then do me one favour.'

Mick Jones's guitar made way for James Brown's funk on the gym's speakers. J B singing about revenge, getting sold out, and the big payback.

'What's that?'

'Come with me. Please.'

We took my old BMW X5 to Chelsea and Westminster Hospital on the Fulham Road.

We went up to the Intensive Care Unit on the fourth floor.

We signed in and I followed Terry Gatti to a room at the end of a wide, white corridor.

Mick Gatti looked closer to death than life.

His eyes were closed but his mouth sagged open. He was full of tubes. The tubes snaked into his mouth and under a thin bed sheet and into his lower body. A catheter drained into a bag that dangled by the bed.

'She's killing us one by one,' Terry Gatti said softly, his eyes never leaving his brother's face. 'You must see it now, Max. Emma Moon is knocking us off one by one. Soon there will only be you and me left.'

You and me?

'*She is taking us down*. And you're on her list too, Max. Can't you see it?'

'What's wrong with your brother?'

'He's in a diabetic coma. Life-threatening.' His eyes welled up and I saw his chin tighten, trying to hold it together. 'So. It's touch and go if he lives or dies.'

'And is he diabetic?'

'First we ever heard of it. This can be stress-related. And she made sure that he had enough stress to kill him. He had a visit from the tax man.'

And I thought – *the money ran out.*

'The taxman is going after your brother?'

'For unpaid taxes going back years. From the years he was in Spain.'

'What's that got to do with Emma?'

277

He sneered at me. 'Emma? Is it Emma now?'

'If the taxman comes after your brother, I don't see how she—'

'Look, I don't know how she does it, all right? Just as I can't explain why Ian stepped off the platform and under a tube train. What was that meant to be? A cry for help? Or why Keith went on the bender that killed him. Or why Butch Lewis's heart suddenly gave out. I can't explain any of it. *But I know it is happening.* Look what she did to my brother!'

'What do you want from me?'

'I want you to believe me. And I want you to stop her.' He indicated the bandage on my right hand. 'You're making the mistake of your life. Emma Moon – she's not your friend, Max. She's not anybody's friend. She's a sociopathic, manipulative minx. You think she's a good person because she sits with you in A&E for hours. You think that makes you special friends? What – you think nobody knows about that? You were *seen*, Max. And now you think you know her? You don't know her at all.'

I stared at the lifeless figure of Mick Gatti. He looked like a man on his deathbed.

'She's doing to you what she does to everyone,' Terry Gatti said.

'And what's that?'

'She's grooming you.'

I shook my head.

'I don't know how you blame any of this on her,' I said. 'Butch Lewis. Ian. Keith. Your brother.'

And I thought – *she scares them to death*.

It was insane. Wasn't it?

I watched him close the door to the ICU room.

'This is between us,' he said.

'OK,' I said. 'So tell me – what was in that safe?'

'You never ask the right question,' Terry Gatti said. 'You ask about who got what – you ask about the safe – but you never ask the one question that really matters.'

'And what's that?'

'Two men died that night. Who killed those two men? The security guard. The gardener. They had families. They had names. Andrew Wojcik, the guard, his wife had just had a baby girl. George Eapia, the good-looking kid from New Zealand. Who murdered them, Max? Who stabbed Andrew Wojcik? Who cracked George Eapia's skull? *Who committed murder that night?* Why do you never ask *that* question, Max?'

'Thieves,' I said. 'Thieves killed those two men. Your little gang of murdering thieving bastards did it.'

'No,' Terry Gatti said. 'Emma Moon killed them.'

Scout was gone when I got home.

The panic flew. Things had been good.

But to come home close to midnight and find her gone – there is a parental terror that is never far away.

I called Mrs Murphy, apologising for the late hour.

But Scout was not there.

I went down to the street. Smithfield was alive with activity, the long convoy of white lorries and vans lined up on the Grand Avenue, the porters full of beans at the start of their long night shift, but beyond the meat market itself, the streets were dark and empty.

And then I saw the lights.

They were all there. Nevermore walking with his hands behind his back, all patrician charm like a Prince Philip tribute band. And the women, tall thin Summer and wild, waif-like Roxy, dispensing sandwiches to the street people with scowling briskness, and the shaven-headed ex-screw, Luka, policing the shambling line of the homeless with his inbuilt aggression.

And at the heart of it, Emma Moon and Scout, all wrapped up sensibly against the bitterly cold night, smiling together as Scout stirred the huge silver soup tureen.

Emma Moon and Scout looked up and saw me at exactly the same moment, and Emma lifted the spoon, as if inviting me to come and have a taste, and the pair of them laughed in perfect harmony.

PART THREE

A triple espresso at the Bar Italia

40

In the morning I woke up with Emma Moon by my side.

It had been a while since I greeted the dawn with someone in my bed and at first it felt like one of those dreams
that come between the end of sleep and fully waking. But
then I sensed rather than felt the warmth of her, and the
length of her dancer's body, and then there was the touch
of skin that felt like an electric shock. She was real.

I lay on my back and stared at the ceiling as she snug-
gled deeper into sleep.

How had we got here?

She had been enchanted by Scout. And I understood
it, because when she was doing something she cared
about, my daughter acted as if there was nothing more
important in the world, and there was a radiance about
her. And so it had been last night, handing out sandwiches and soup to the street people of Smithfield's. And
I was proud of her. Not many twelve-year-olds would
care that much, would think it was important, and would
really try to make a difference in this neighbourhood,
this city, this planet. But Scout did.

Emma Moon was captivated by her, and the feeling

was mutual. Scout came alive in her presence, she shone in a way that I had not seen her shine for a while. When the work was done, and the soup and sandwiches were all gone, and the homeless went off into the night, Scout had invited Emma back to our home and she accepted, announcing that she would make her own way back to Nevermore's house on The Bishop's Avenue, and when her entourage looked unhappy, she simply shrugged and shooed them off.

They obeyed her command.

Nevermore, his patrician's rictus grin never more fixed. Luka the maybe-boyfriend, his great meaty slab of a face creased with surprise. And Summer and Roxy, who looked confused, abandoned and lost without her.

And jealous. They were all jealous. That most of all.

Scout and Emma talked until nearly one while I pottered about in the background, getting Stan off to sleep on his favourite sofa, loading the dishwasher and emptying the washing machine, tending to my household chores, killing time.

'There was a boy,' I heard Emma tell Scout over the hot chocolate my daughter had made for them. 'I met him tonight. His dad kicked him out. He has been spat on, urinated on, and had a drink thrown at him. He has been robbed – this boy who has nothing. They robbed him! And the problem of rough sleeping, Scout – it's only getting worse.'

'There was a girl,' Scout said. 'She slept out on these

streets. And her name was Suzanne. And she was murdered.'

I let them talk.

And then it was nearly one in the morning and I began clearing my throat and looking at my watch – goodness, is that the time? – and Emma said she better get going. I tried to call her a cab while the pair of them gave each other a fierce farewell hug. But there were no cabs.

No problem, Emma smiled. She would sleep on the sofa and let herself out at first light. Fine. Lights out. The big loft settled to its slumbers, and I drifted off, happy to see my daughter so excited, engaged – and happy.

But that still did not explain how Emma Moon had found her way to my bed.

'Your dog really snores,' she said, as if that explained everything.

She rolled on her side to face me, opening her eyes.

'Morning.'

'Morning.'

'She's a wonderful girl, your daughter,' she said. 'Scout.'

How we love those who love our children.

'I should get up,' she said, making no attempt to get up.

She was wearing a T-shirt and pants. I could see the T-shirt and I had felt the pants when her butt accidentally brushed the front of my boxer shorts. I was in my usual jim-jams of short-sleeved white T-shirt and those boxer shorts. She had that sleepy-eyed look, her blond hair all over the place, all over her face.

She did not look unwell. She looked beautiful.

And I remembered what Terry Gatti had said about her.

She killed those two men in the big house.

And I didn't believe him.

But that didn't mean I trusted her. There was a moment when we both could have stayed in bed for longer – but the moment passed.

Then she was up and out of the bed without warning, kicking those long legs into the jeans that she picked up from the floor by the side of the bed, running her fingers through her hair.

Getting ready to go.

She turned and gave me a sleepy, knowing smile that could have meant anything.

I sat up in bed. 'Emma?'

We stared at each other.

'What do you want to know?' she said.

'Are you really dying?'

Her smile faded. 'Do you think I would lie about something like that?'

'I don't know.'

'Remission,' she said.

I nodded into the long silence.

'Those two men who died the night they took the safe. The security guard and the gardener.'

'Andrew and George. What about them?'

'Andrew and George? You sound like you knew them.'

'Oh, I did know them. I knew Andrew Wojcik, the security guy, and I knew the gardener, George Eapia, even better.'

'You *knew* them? What does that mean? How the hell did you know them?'

She turned her back, tightened her belt, forced her hair into some kind of order.

She's doing what she does with everyone, Terry Gatti had told me. *She's grooming you.*

I got out of bed. We stood there staring at each other, the rumpled bed between us. And suddenly everything was clear.

'That's how the Gatti brothers and the rest of them got inside that house,' I said. 'Those two dead men – they were your lovers.'

'They were *my friends*. At least, I considered George – the gardener – my friend. Andrew – the security guy – let's say we were just starting to get to know each other. Nobody was meant to die. I will regret their deaths for the rest of my life.'

'Terry Gatti says you were the one who killed them.'

She smiled sadly. 'The truth is – *they killed each other.* George – the gardener – wasn't meant to be there that day. There was . . . an altercation. Andrew Wojcik was former Special Forces. George Eapia was a new age New Zealander who loved his gardens. It was a bit of an unequal fight. But George had a knife.'

'What did they fight about?' I said, my stomach sinking because I already knew the answer. 'They argued about you, didn't they? Because – what? They were both in love with you.'

She raised her eyebrows. 'I think George was trying to protect me from Andrew's advances. Sexual jealousy more than love.'

'What happened?'

'So many questions, Detective!'

I took a breath. How could there not be questions now?

'So you befriended the gardener – George – and knowing him was your introduction to the security guy? That got you into the house? You went to the house pretending to be looking for your gardener friend – knowing it was his day off? Is that how it worked?'

'Is that how you would have done it? Not bad, Sherlock. In fact – very close. I went to the big house looking for my gardener friend but he was not there. And he was not there until the moment he turned up without warning and it all kicked off. It was a neat plan that never included anyone ever getting hurt – get into the property, distract and then subdue the security guy, nobody gets harmed, everyone gets rich – but then it all went wrong. Especially for me. George Eapia and Andrew Wojcik got into a horrible fight. And they were not the only ones who lost their life that night.'

Then she came around the bed and placed a soft, chaste kiss on my closed lips.

And I wanted her to stay. I wanted her to get back into bed with me. Despite everything.

'I have done nothing wrong,' she said. 'I stupidly slept

with one man – a good-looking New Zealander who I actually fancied anyway – and acted like I might sleep with another – a big Pole who was not a bad guy – because the man I adored, Terry Gatti, told me that it was necessary to set us free for life. And I was young and I was stupid and I did bad things because I was in love with a bad man. I regret all of it. But I'm innocent, Max,' she said. 'I'm guilty of loving the wrong man – but that's all. You know that, don't you?'

She let herself out.

Emma Moon was long gone by the time Scout got up.

I tried to remember the last time I had seen my daughter so happy.

She sat at the kitchen island scrolling through her laptop. I got a glance of the screen as I fixed her Weetabix and sliced banana.

Shelter. St Mungo's. Centrepoint. Charities for the homeless.

'Dad, do you think there's an age limit for volunteers?'

Dad?

'I am pretty sure there will be an age limit.'

'How old?'

'Eighteen – I'm guessing.'

'Oh, well. Then I can just help Emma until I'm eighteen, can't I?'

I managed a smile. But I could not help feeling good too. You are only ever as happy as your unhappiest child, they say, and they are dead right.

And today my girl was flying.

Scout bolted her Weetabix, slammed her laptop shut, hefted her bright yellow Fjällräven backpack, and went off to school with a secret grin that she probably didn't even know was there.

When I took Stan out for his morning walk, Terry Gatti was waiting for me across the street.

'Good night, Max?' he said.

I stared at him.

'Have you been standing here all night?'

'No – I was at the hospital all night with my brother. Until he died. Until Mick died. Why do people die just before the dawn? It's a mystery. But my brother is dead. He never came out of that coma. And she killed him. But I saw her leave this morning with that little secret smile on her face. So I know what you have been doing. The pair of you up there shagging like rabbits while my brother was dying. And you are too stupid to see that you and me are the only two left on Emma's list.'

I felt no compulsion to tell him that nothing had happened.

Or maybe I had it all wrong. Perhaps something *had* happened. Maybe she had her claws in me now and I was happy for them to be there.

'What would she do if she wanted to destroy you?' Terry Gatti asked. 'What is the *one thing* she would do? I'll tell you, shall I? She would befriend you – and your daughter. She would get you to want her. She would get you to do what I know you've been doing up there all night. Emma Moon has a genius for grooming suckers. You stupid copper! Do you really think you're that irresistible to women? Do you really think you're such a chick-magnet, Max?'

I shrugged. 'It sometimes crosses my mind.'

There was something in his manner – some ancient jealousy – that reminded me of the rest of them. Of Lord Nevermore, the doting benefactor, and Luka, the sort-of boyfriend, and Summer and Roxy, the fawning friends from the jail years.

They all looked the same when Emma Moon walked away.

'Well, you're not!' Gatti said. 'All Emma wants is to see you on your knees. All she wants is to ruin you.'

'Why do you hate her? She did your time for you, pal. All those years, Terry. She stuck by you. She kept her mouth shut.'

'Maybe she had good reasons to keep her mouth shut. Yes, she did the time. Credit where it's due. But now she's killing us. One by one.'

I took a breath.

'This tax inspector who came to see your brother – do you have a name? A business card?'

He thought about it. 'He gave Mick a card. I don't know if he chucked it. It would be unlike my brother to put it somewhere safe. It might be with his belongings at the hospital.'

'What about CCTV footage? You have cameras at

your house, right? You must have a few images of the guy. I want a name. I want to see what he looks like.'

Gatti smiled without warmth. 'You're going to help us now, are you? Going to have a quiet word with the Revenue, are you? Because you owe us? Because we handed you John-Paul Ledoux and the Beatles on a plate, even if the Met are too stupid to see it. Because you feel guilty about my brother?'

I nodded. Let him believe what he wanted to believe.

'Just get whatever you have across to me, will you? I want to know – why did the tax man come for your brother now?'

Stan gave me his *but-what-about-me?* look. He was keen to get going. And me too.

Terry Gatti watched us walk away.

'She's playing you, sucker!' he called as Stan paused by a lamppost, sniffing delicately before lifting a hind leg.

41

At some point in the evening, the young woman had become separated from her friends. She came out of the club and stood on the neon-lit side street, staring around uncertainly, unsure about her next move. Her face was flushed and she shivered in the night air.

The meat market area had once been full of clubs. Most of them had gone now, another thing that had not survived the pandemic, but this one in a quiet street just off the Barbican had somehow kept going. The music boomed behind her. A bouncer yawned and stared at his phone. The young woman looked for the friends who were all long gone.

Then the man stepped out of the shadows and approached her with something in his right hand. He was large, both tall and hefty, and he loomed over the young woman.

'I know him,' I said softly. 'He's the youngest one. Dim they call him.'

'Yeah, and I know him too,' Jackson Rose said.

We stood across the street, watching them: Dim

showing her his warrant card, the girl suddenly apprehensive, the bouncer waking up, half-heartedly intervening and then losing all interest when he understood this was a police matter.

Then Dim was leading the young woman away.

Jackson cursed. 'It's like something out of a David Attenborough wildlife documentary. Get separated from the herd and the predators have you for breakfast.'

We crossed the street, Jackson already ahead of me. Dim had taken his prey a hundred metres further down the road, away from prying eyes. The young woman was facing a wall, fighting back tears as Dim prepared to search her.

'You've been a very naughty girl,' Dim said. 'Let's see if you've got anything very naughty concealed about your person.'

'Let her go,' Jackson said, not raising his voice.

Dim and the girl stared at him.

'Go now,' I told her, stuffing two twenties into her hand, then pointing west. 'There will be cabs on the Farringdon Road. Go home!'

Dim no longer had his warrant card in his hand. He was holding a small, cellophane-wrapped packet of white powder all ready to be found on his victim. He slipped it into his pocket.

'Jackson – mate!' He beamed.

'So that's how it works,' I said, and his big dopey grin faded when he saw me. 'You don't just flash the warrant card. You plant some – what is it? Coke? Talcum powder? – and you have them under arrest and back at the flat in the Angel before they know what's happening.'

'Jackson – mate – what's *he* doing here?'

'He wants a word, Dim.'

The girl was still standing there, uncertain if she was under arrest or not.

'You've got your cab fare,' I told her. 'Please go now.' And she went.

'A word?' Dim said. 'I don't know about a word right now, Jackson.' He looked at his watch. 'I'm still on shift.'

With an apologetic cringe, he made to walk away.

Jackson placed a palm on his chest and gently stopped him.

Then he looked at me. 'Where we going to take him?' he said.

'I know a place,' I said.

I parked the old BMW X5 on a backstreet in Mayfair.

The three of us walked down the sloping entrance to an underground car park, Dim walking between the pair of us, Jackson with an arm around Dim's shoulder.

'What's this all about then, Jackson, mate?'

Jackson laughed. 'Ah, Dim – you already know what it's about.' And to me. 'You still got the key?'

'Oh yes.'

There was a metal door by the side of the underground car park. The key struggled with rust – it had been a while – but finally opened with a metallic clang. We went inside.

It was pitch-black, the air thick with dust. I hit the switch and the underground car park was flooded with yellow strip lighting.

'Do you know what this place was, Dim?' I said. 'The place that was above this car park? You'll laugh.'

Dim looked around at the great empty cavern. 'Was it – I don't know – was it a pub?'

'A pub? Good guess. Because the pubs all closed down, didn't they? No – you know what this place was, back in the day? When we were – those of us in the job – a bit more visible in the community than we are today. It was *a police station.*'

West End Central, Savile Row. My police station.

I found a chair in the one-man security cabin by the entrance and wheeled it across the car park.

'I really should be getting back, mate,' Dim was saying to Jackson.

'Sit down and shut your cakehole,' I told him.

Jackson placed his hand against the bigger, younger man's chest and gave him an encouraging shove.

Dim sat down.

'We're not going to tie you up,' Jackson said. 'Do you know why?'

Dim shook his scared, meaty head. I enjoyed seeing him scared. I loved it. 'Because we don't need to tie you up,' Jackson continued. 'Because you are going to do exactly as you're told. All yours, Max.'

I looked down at Dim.

'You stop women with your warrant card and then you

plant drugs – real or fake – on them and then you place them under arrest to make them come to your flat in the Angel. That kid tonight – I saw it all. The warrant card is scary enough. But the planted drugs – that's clever. Nasty. Vicious. But clever. It made her more terrified than she already was. And this is my question – did you pull that stunt on Suzanne Buksa?'

'Who? What's the name again?'

'*Suzanne Buksa.*'

I showed him my phone.

It was the photograph we had used at that dismal press conference. Suzanne when she was smiling, happy, optimistic, healthy and home.

'She was murdered,' I said. 'A cop – or cops – had been harassing her for some time. Ring any bells?'

He looked briefly at my phone and looked away. 'I never saw her before in my life.' His slow-witted brain groped for excuses. 'That girl tonight – I thought she might have been dealing in there, Jackson.'

I shook my head.

'We watched you at work, Dim. We know exactly what you thought. Arrest her, scare her witless and take her back to the Angel. Are John-Paul Ledoux and your other mates waiting there? Is that the way it works, Dim?'

'No comment.'

Jackson stepped forward and slapped him across the face.

'Jackson – mate!'

'You make my life harder,' Jackson told him.

'What?'

'You heard. It is tough enough already for shots. And you – your kind – make it harder. You make it – impossible.' He sighed with feeling. 'What the law does is so hard,' Jackson said. 'Protecting all the good people from all the darkness out there. And what *we* do – the police with guns – is even harder. Because every cop goes to work not knowing if he's going to come home alive. But us – me and you, Dim! – we don't know if we are going to be on a murder charge at the end of the day.'

Jackson slapped him across the other cheek. There were tears in Dim's eyes. Shock more than pain. And humiliation.

'It's so hard and you and your kind make it harder, Dim boy. Because you give the world a good reason to hate us.'

Then Jackson grabbed him by the scruff of the neck and shook him.

'I've never seen her before!' Dim said. 'John-Paul is the one who likes it rough. Why don't you give him a slap?'

'Maybe I will!' Jackson said. 'Maybe I'll slap the lot of you!'

I laid a restraining hand on Jackson's shoulder. He stepped back, took a breath.

'You ever have a night when it got out of hand?' I asked Dim. 'You ever have a night where you fake-arrested some scared girl and took her back to the flat and then it all went wrong? You ever have a night like that, Dim?'

'Do you think we kill them? Do you think that's what

we do? It's just the lads letting off steam! It's *sport*. It just a bit of fun. And we don't *kill* them. Whatever happens in the flat, it is not a capital crime. We don't murder anyone.'

'Did it go wrong with Suzanne Buksa?' I said. 'Did you arrest her and take her home and then it all went wrong? Is that what happened? Tell me.'

He hung his head and shook it. He would not look at us.

I looked at Jackson and he shrugged. We helped Dim out of the chair. We led him towards the exit door.

'This chat is strictly between us,' Jackson said. 'If you talk to anyone about tonight, you're in trouble. Got it, Dim?'

'Got it, Jackson, mate. But, Jackson — mate — we're not murderers. We're just ordinary coppers who like a laugh.'

'Get out of my sight,' Jackson said.

We let Dim out of the car park and he immediately broke into a run.

We closed the door and stood in the musty darkness of West End Central's abandoned car park.

'Well, that was a waste of time,' Jackson said.

'No, it really wasn't a waste of time, Jackson. Because we witnessed a serving officer in the Metropolitan Police using his warrant card to stop, detain and arrest a young woman. We saw him prepare to plant drugs — or what looked like drugs — on her person. We saw the whole rotten game. It's *happening*, Jackson. It's real.'

'And the first thing he is going to do is call John-Paul Ledoux and the rest of them.'

'Of course he will.'

'And then they will come after us.'

'Then we better be ready for them.'

'We should have beaten it out of him.'

'And what would have been the point of that, Jackson?'

'The point? The point is we would have a confession!'

'Yes – a confession that we'd beaten out of him!'

We fumed in silence. Jackson seemed suddenly exhausted.

'I was always harder than you, Max,' he said.

It was not true. I was always harder. But Jackson Rose was always wilder.

'I'm going home to Rosie,' he said, heading for the car park exit. 'I'm going home to my daughter.'

42

Our Direct Entry Detectives, DC Bear Groves and DC Sita Basu, were growing into the job. The boss and I were not great believers in the Direct Entry scheme, always ready to raise a wry eyebrow at the theory that further education was a far better foundation for modern detective work than rolling around in a gutter with drunks on a Friday night while wearing a scratchy, cardboard-like uniform that was designed in the nineteenth century.

But today I caught Pat Whitestone's eye as we both watched Bear and Sita at their workstations – and we shared a conspiratorial smile, like proud parents after good A-level results had come in.

Bear and Sita had overcome all the big firsts of the job in Homicide and Major Crime Command. Their first murder victim. Their first arrest for murder. Their first murder case. And now their first manhunt, as the search for Robert McKay continued.

My initial impression of the pair was that Bear was tougher but Sita was smarter. But it was Bear who had been overcome with emotion when we sat in the Smith-field's pub the night we found Suzanne Buksa's broken body. And it was Sita who reacted more quickly when McKay did his runner from the Old Bailey, running towards danger without hesitation and without being asked. They were both smart enough and brave enough to make it.

Sita was on a more even emotional keel, less likely to be overwhelmed by the ruin that one human being can inflict on another human being. But they worked well apart and well together – the privately educated rugby player and the daughter of hard-working, self-employed immigrants. Pat and I liked them. We would always, I guessed, remain suspicious of the Direct Entry system – and sceptical of the theory that policing could be learned in the classroom rather than the street – but we had both been pleasantly surprised by our new recruits. They didn't whine. They were not afraid to ask. And they dealt with whatever got thrown at them.

When the stuff came through from Terry Gatti, I forwarded it to Bear. There wasn't much.

A screenshot of a business card from an inspector of His Majesty's Revenue & Customs. Three snatch shots of the taxman taken from the door camera at Terry Gatti's home showing a portly, middle-aged man in a suit and tie toting a wafer-thin briefcase.

And a name – Brian Beath, it said on the card.

Bear looked up from his workstation.

'I want to talk to this guy at the Revenue,' I told Bear. 'I want to know if they had a tip-off about Mick Gatti's finances. I want to know – why did they investigate him now?' Why not ten years ago when it was all cocaine and paella and party night on the Costa del Sol?'

Bear nodded and went to work.

Then I joined Whitestone at her workstation where Sita was looking over her shoulder at the five photos I had taken across the street from the Barbican club.

Dim holding out his warrant card to the young woman.

The young woman protesting that she had done nothing wrong.

Her head turned away as she pleaded for help from the bored bouncer.

Dim leading her away.

And Dim starting his body search, the girl against the wall, his hands on her hips behind her, just before Jackson and I interrupted him.

I said nothing.

The five images said it all.

'What happened to the girl?' Whitestone said.

'I gave her cab fare and sent her home.'

Whitestone pulled a face. 'A statement would have been good.'

'We need more than that if we are going to take them all down. This guy – Dim – he is just part of it. We want John-Paul Ledoux. And we want the rest of them. Don't we?'

Whitestone thought about it. None of it was easy. We would be going after our own, and all of her instincts told her to protect our own.

'This' – she indicated the images of Dim and the woman,

303

her face twisting with contempt – 'is nowhere near enough for a murder conviction. You understand that, right? And none of what you saw means that one of them – or all of them – killed Suzanne. And we had Robert McKay pleading guilty to that murder before he absconded.'

'Except we know – we *know*, Pat – that Suzanne had been harassed by a man flashing a Metropolitan Police warrant card.'

'And this . . .' She took a breath, released it with a sad shake of the head, her eyes never leaving the screen. 'We can't let this stand. It doesn't matter who they are.'

'If we are going to get all of them, then we need to get inside the flat at the Angel,' I said. 'After we let them take someone home. Then kick their door down and go in with the cavalry.'

'Too dangerous,' Whitestone said. 'We would be putting a member of the public in potentially mortal danger. No, the only way to do it would be to set a trap and wait for them to take the bait. And for that – we need a real live young woman.'

And she looked at DC Sita Basu. Her pretty, serious face was still staring at the images on the screen. Sita looked too young, too inexperienced, too *new* for what Whitestone was contemplating.

'I don't know, Pat,' I said.

'If we want them,' Whitestone said. 'Then this is what it takes.'

MURDER FOR BUSY PEOPLE

DC Basu was still staring at the images of Dim apprehending the woman.

'I'm not scared of these bastards,' Sita said quietly.

'Max?' Bear called.

I went over to his workstation.

'Nobody of that name – Brian Beath – works at HMRC. I also ran a facial recognition programme on the Revenue's database of staff. Nationwide. No joy. So this guy – Brian Beath – he's a fake tax inspector?'

'Looks like it. Good work, Bear.'

'It's a unique name. *Brian Beath*. What kind of name is that, do you reckon?'

I thought about it. 'It's the kind of name you don't make up. The business card may be bogus. But my guess is that's his real name.'

'Want me to try running it through the PNC?'

The Police National Computer. A database of criminal records on anyone ever convicted, cautioned or even given a warning by the law. If you have ever brushed up against the police, then you are on the PNC and you will remain there for the rest of your life.

I thought about it some more. 'Try the PNC, Bear,' I stared at the snatched shots of Brian Beath on the Gatti doorstep. 'And then try Equity,' I said.

'Equity?'

'Yes – you know. The actor's union.'

43

The CCTV footage from the Rivoli Mini Mart showed Robert McKay doing what looked like his weekly shop.

'Is that him?' Whitestone said.

The camera caught a large man at that weird high angle of CCTV. His beard had started to grow back but the face was clear and the bulk of the man was unmistakable. He was filling two carrier bags with bread, cheese and big bottles of water. And an X-ACTO knife, also known as an exacto, a utility or craft knife. An old scar from years ago, just under my ribs on the right side of my torso, began to throb in recognition of that craft knife.

'It's him,' I said.

We watched McKay count out a fistful of coins in payment.

'Shop owner recognised him from the news,' DC Basu said. 'Watched him leave the shop, cross Whitechapel Road and apparently enter St Mary's tube station. He was so certain it was McKay, he even took a photograph.'

The CCTV footage was replaced by a single still image of Robert McKay, a carrier bag of shopping in each hand, heading into a façade of glazed red terrace, the branded architecture of the London Underground of one hundred years ago.

ST MARY'S WHITECHAPEL ROAD STATION

'There's a time and date stamp on the CCTV,' Whitestone said. The still image was replaced by footage of McKay paying for his groceries at the Rivoli Mini Mart.

'Ninety minutes ago,' I said.

'So he got on the tube ninety minutes ago and he could be anywhere by now,' Bear said.

'Unlikely,' I said. 'That station has been closed since 1938.'

When we arrived in the BMW X5, Met vehicles already filled the street.

Response cars, blue lights pulsing. Two wagons full of uniforms who had already disembarked and were unspooling blue-and-white crime scene tape at both ends of the street. An ambulance. Digital radios chattered like birdsong.

The shots were arriving. Two cars full of Authorised Firearms Officers. Black vests over white shirts and black tie, the curiously formal look undercut by the black baseball caps. They all carried sidearms, the black, flat-nosed Glocks strapped low on their thighs, and Sig Sauer MCX assault rifles, the Black Mamba, strapped across their shoulder and held at that 45-degree angle the shots adopted when they were waiting for the action to start.

Jackson Rose was in the first car.

John-Paul Ledoux and the Beatles were in the second. They all gathered around Jackson, waiting for instructions. They did not look at me.

'McKay will fight them,' I said. 'And they'll kill him. He will fight them and he will give them no choice but to kill him. That's what is going to happen here.'

'Leave it to them, Max,' Whitestone said, but I was already on my way, and I heard her swear behind me.

St Mary's Whitechapel Road has been closed for nearly a century but there is a door that remains open, a nondescript grey door to the right of the station that is used for engineering access and as an emergency exit.

Whitestone had come after me. She grabbed my arm.

'This guy has already killed once,' she said.

'We both know that's not true,' I said, and I opened the grey door.

'Don't they ever lock that bloody door?' she said, and I heard her curse my name again as I took the green-tiled stairwell down into the darkness.

Down at track level, St Mary's was still remarkably intact but the eight-foot-high brick walls that had been erected in the Blitz to protect sheltering Londoners from passing trains have never been removed. The high brick walls on every side made it feel like a maze.

'You can get lost down here,' Robert McKay said from behind me.

He looked as though he had not slept since I had last

seen him in the bowels of the Old Bailey. He had a hand-made cheese sandwich in one hand and the craft knife in the other.

'This is not the way,' I said. 'If you wave that thing at them, they'll kill you now.'

'A cheese sandwich?'

'Listen to me, Robert. I know you didn't kill Suzanne.'

'She was my friend.'

'I know she was your friend. But they found your skin under her fingernails. You understand what that looks like, don't you?'

'My skin was under her nails because we argued. Because I tried to stop her going with that man. I held her arms to save her life. I tried to stop her getting in that car with that policeman.'

'Then you have to explain it all. You have to say it in court. They might even believe you. But that is the only chance you have. And you can't sign anything they put in front of you. Now – put down that knife, finish your cheese sandwich and come with me. It's not too late.'

But then, all at once, it was too late.

'*Stop! Armed police! Stand still! Show me your hands!*'

'*Armed police!*'

'*Armed police!*'

'*Armed police!*'

'*Drop the weapon! Drop the weapon!*'

'*Drop the weapon and show me your hands! Armed police!*'

Robert McKay did not drop the weapon. He did not even drop his cheese sandwich. But he ran. Although not before I caught the stung look in his eyes as his gaze met mine.

As if I had betrayed him.

But then he was suddenly gone, his large body squirming with astonishing speed through a gap in one of the high-screen brick walls and perhaps a dozen shots were rushing past me in pursuit.

But one held back.

'How do you think this is going to work, Max?' John-Paul Ledoux asked me, grinning his charming man smile. 'Do you think we're plotting to put a bullet in your brain? Do you think we are that crass?' He put his handsome face close to mine. 'Of course not. Because what would happen if you accidentally on purpose caught a bullet? The same thing that happens every time we pull the trigger on some lowlife drug dealer or murdering terrorist. Suspension. Inquiry. Investigation. Murder or manslaughter charge. Dismissal or jail time. No thanks! So we're not going to slot you, Max. But that doesn't mean you get to watch your kid grow up.'

There were screaming voices from what felt like far away.

'*Armed police!*'

'*Raise your hands!*'

'*On your knees!*'

'*Do it now!*'

The voices were not getting further away. They had found him. And it sounded very much like Robert McKay was cornered.

'Here is the way it is going to work,' Ledoux continued. '*We will not have your back just at that moment when you really, really need us to have your back.* We let you walk into the room where the bad man is waiting with a weapon. And we let HIM do the job for us. We thought it was going to be today! We all clocked you running off to play the hero. Let him go, we thought. Let that psycho squaddie stick his knife down Max Wolfe's throat. But it did not happen today. So it will happen on some other day. There's always another day. And your little girl – I guess she will go into care, right? And we all know what happens to little girls who go into care.'

I had my hand around his throat. I wanted to tear his face off. He pushed me away with the butt of his Black Mamba.

Then he laughed at me.

'I am going to see you locked up,' I said. 'You and your stinking friends. I am going to make sure I live that long, Ledoux.'

And then we heard the shot, the single shot that seemed to rend the air, to tear the air apart, to go on and on, a shot fired in anger and terror and with unerring precision.

'*Shot fired!*'

'*Shot fired!*'

'*Shot fired!*'

The radio crackled on Ledoux's shoulder.

He laughed.

'Shot fired by SFO Jackson Rose,' he said. 'Sounds like your old pal got trigger happy.'

44

'But you told me to wear my own clothes,' DC Sita Basu said to DCI Pat Whitestone.

Sita was wearing a modest trouser suit with some kind of scarf tied round her neck. She did not look like she was going dancing. She looked like she was returning her library books. Whitestone and I considered her like doubtful parents just before prom night. Bear smiled encouragement from his workstation.

'I think you look nice, Sita.'

'But she doesn't look like she's going clubbing,' Whitestone said. 'She looks like the girl next door.' She turned to me.

'Perhaps that's what they like,' I said. 'John-Paul Ledoux and the Beatles.'

Sita looked hurt. 'You said—'

Whitestone raised a hand. 'Sita, you look fine. Natural. I like it. This was always going to be a long shot. And if it does happen, then remember – Code A as soon you get inside. Don't wait, OK? We just need them to stop you, arrest you and take you back to the Angel. Just press send on Code A to tell us you are inside.'

'And we will come running,' I said.

'You'll be wearing a covert listening device so it will all be on tape,' Whitestone said. Sita nodded but did not look reassured.

'We'll be there long before they find the wire you're wearing,' I said.

In truth, I hoped it did not work. I hoped that it would be a quiet night at the clubs, and our young Direct Entry Detective would have something interesting to put on her CV. But I hoped that we would not find John-Paul Ledoux and the Beatles tonight.

And above all, I hoped that they would not find Sita Basu.

From the dark side of the street, we watched Sita go into XOYO in Shoreditch and thirty minutes later we watched her come out alone, standing outside the club examining her phone, as if separated from her imaginary friends.

Nothing.

And then the same routine at Egg London in King's Cross, and again at The Beams in Stratford.

She went into the club, she had a glass of something non-alcoholic, and then came outside, and she stood alone. The clubs all seemed to be in former warehouses, and refineries, and abandoned industrial space.

Young people dancing in a ghost city.

'We could try south of the river,' Bear said in the back seat of the BMW X5. 'The Electric Brixton. The Ministry of Sound.'

313

'Everything we know about them suggests they always stay north of the river,' I said. 'They want to be close to the flat at the Angel.'

And then I saw them.

Two of them.

John-Paul Ledoux himself. And the one called Mo. One moment they were not there and then suddenly there they were, looming gigantic on either side of Sita Basu, crowding in on her space, warrant cards flashing.

The bouncer stepped forward and he quickly backed off when he saw their warrant cards.

It took a minute. No more. Their authority worked that fast.

We watched Ledoux and Mo lead Sita away into the shadows beyond the bright façade of the club.

'This is Delta 1,' Whitestone said into the wireless radio microphone on her lapel. Her voice was unnaturally calm. 'We have positive visual ID and contact – repeat, *contact* – with two of the targets and we are proceeding to the grab zone now, over.'

My ear was suddenly full of digital chatter, all of it in the exaggerated calm that professionals use at moments of extreme tension, like a doctor who has discovered a tumour the size of a grapefruit or a pilot with all his engines on fire.

Nothing at all to worry about! Everything is going to be just fine!

And I looked for Sita Basu with the two men in the shadows. But she was already gone.

*

The lights were on in the top-floor, one-bedroom flat at the Angel.

We parked the BMW outside a row of lock-ups across the way.

I could see one uniformed police officer crouching behind a long line of recycling bins, suggesting there were a dozen more of them back there. There was a team of AFOs a street away, and an ambulance. I had expected some degree of hostility, or at least reluctance, from the Firearms Officers, but they gave no indication one way or the other that they were concerned about going after their own. Their team leader was a woman.

And we waited. The plan was to get the Code A from Sita and then go in fast and hard with the uniforms hiding behind the recycling bins. The shots with their firearms were a last resort. Then we waited some more.

'Perhaps we missed them,' Bear said. 'Perhaps they are already inside.'

'We didn't miss them,' I said, but I wondered if they had searched Sita and found the wire, and I wondered what would happen to her then. 'Just wait.'

It is just over six miles from The Beams in Stratford to the Angel.

I had just done it with my blues-and-twos on. Ledoux and his friend could not afford to be in that kind of a rush with Sita in the car.

'Here they come,' Whitestone said.

We watched Ledoux park in a disabled bay and get out of his car. Mo was in the back seat with Sita. The two men took her arms and led her into the block. I already had my hand on the door.

'Wait until we know she's inside,' Whitestone said sharply. 'Wait for that Code A.'

So we waited some more, and now the waiting was harder. The lights were burning in that top-floor flat. And nothing happened. The three of us – Whitestone, Bear, me – stared at our phones. We were all waiting for the Code A text message to tell us she was inside.

And it didn't come.

And I remembered my night at the flat. I remembered the fruit bowl by the door.

I remembered it full of mobile phones.

I got out of the BMW X5.

'Max,' Whitestone said. '*Wait.*'

'She's never going to call.'

'I said *wait!* If she's not inside—'

'She's inside right now. But she doesn't have her phone. First thing they do is they take the woman's phone away. She is never going to call that Code A in, Pat.'

I walked over to the recycling bins. A dozen young faces looked up at me. One of the uniforms had a heavily scarred, bright-red battering ram, also known as the big red key, the Nigel and the bosher.

I took it from him and headed for the block of flats.

The big red key weighed 16 kilos. I was feeling it in my arms when I got to the lift. I could see Whitestone and Bear and the pack of young uniforms following me as I took the lift to the top floor. There were voices on the stairwell. Whitestone and Bear were coming out of the other lift.

I walked to the front door of the top-floor flat, swung the battering ram back, and then brought it forward, aiming it at the lock.

It was a good door, reinforced with a London Bar, a solid stainless steel bar that fits over the frame and lock. It would have taken all night to kick that door down.

But the big red key opened it first try.

Then we were inside.

The Essex boy, the one called Jim, was just inside the door. He stared at me uncomprehending as I let the big red key drop on his feet, breaking a toe or two. He doubled up, screaming.

It was a small space and the smell hit you hard. Weed and bodies and yesterday's Deliveroo. I remembered the worn cracked leather sofas facing each other and the massive flat-screen TV on one wall looming over everything, and the crowded drinks trolley. But the living room was empty.

I went to the bedroom.

Sita was on the mattress with three men leaning above her.

John-Paul Ledoux. Mo. Dim.

Ledoux stared at me and was the first to understand what was happening.

'Oh you little bitch,' he said, and raised his hand to strike her but she swung her right foot up between his legs and it stopped him in mid-strike, and by then I had my hands on him and as I heard the voices screaming orders behind me, I thought, *A formal arrest will always be accompanied by physically taking control.*

The uniforms were everywhere in that little flat.

They were shouting their arrival, designed to embolden themselves and put the fear into our targets. I looked down at Sita on the mattress, tiny and pretty and demure, and her shoulder bare where one of them had torn at her clothing, and I nodded at her, because she had done so well, and I saw she was in great pain and holding her shoulder, which seemed to be at some unnatural angle – 'I think I hurt something,' she said – and then I was slamming Ledoux's face against the bedroom wall as I pulled his arms up behind his back.

'You killed Suzanne Buksa.'

'Who the fuck is Suzanne Buksa when she's at home?'

'You do not have to say anything,' I said, and slammed his head into the wall.

'We didn't kill whatever her name was!' he said, his words muffled by having his mouth partially pressed against the wall. 'You dumb bastard, Wolfe. We were never interested in homeless waifs, or some drug-ridden skank.' He looked over his shoulder at Sita, standing now, straightening her torn clothes, and he laughed. 'We like them *clean*. That's what made it fun. Getting them all dirty.'

Bear pulled him away from me, spun him around and punched him full in the face. Ledoux reeled backwards. Bear kept punching.

Whitestone was shouting in Bear's face.

'You,' Whitestone told him, 'you need to calm down now!'

Bear stared at Sita, his face white with shock. The noise in there was deafening. The uniforms had the other three on the ground. Only Ledoux himself was still standing.

He spat out half a tooth.

'They're already coming forward,' Pat Whitestone told Ledoux. 'The women you arrested. The women you brought here. They are coming forward, making their statements, and there will be more of them, and they will tell their stories and you will all go down.'

'But not for murder,' John-Paul Ledoux said, looking at me with the one eye that was still open. 'And Jackson Rose knows it.'

45

Twenty-four hours later Jackson Rose was sitting at the counter in the Bar Italia on Frith Street staring at the big portrait of Rocky Marciano.

I sat next to him and a triple espresso appeared in front of me as if by magic.

I thanked the waiter with my eyes.

'In most places a picture like that would be to give the place some authentic vibes,' Jackson said, nodding at Rocky. 'But Marciano loved this place, didn't he? It was the only place in London where he could eat proper Italian food and get real Italian coffee.'

I sipped my triple espresso. On the big screen, Roma were playing AC Milan. It was still early. Too late for the dancing kids, too early for the office workers.

'What happened down there, Jackson?'

Jackson licked his lips. There was a faraway look in his eyes. I had never seen him looking so lost.

'I think Robert McKay wanted to die. I think he was ready to die. We had him backed into one of those bricked-up corners down there – the walls they put up in the Blitz and never took down?' He was living it again.

'And he had that craft knife in his hands. And he wasn't responding to our efforts to subdue and control. And in the end he just smiled and came at me with the knife and pulled his hand back and showed every intention of very much wanting to plant it in my heart.' We sat in a long silence, the eternal buzz of Soho drifting into the Bar Italia. 'So I shot him.'

'And what happens now?'

'Now we follow strict procedural guidelines. Now they take my life and stuff it down the toilet.'

I knew it was a bit more complicated than that – but not much more.

Discharging his firearm and taking a life meant that my friend Jackson Rose would now be investigated to determine if he acted within the law. A Post Incident Manager – usually an inspector or above – would be in charge of an investigation. A Police Federation representative would have already been appointed to support Jackson. Before they even went off duty, written statements would have been taken by all the officers who witnessed the incident and they would be submitted to the Independent Office for Police Conduct within seven days.

Jackson had immediately been removed from all operational duty.

He would not work again until he was cleared of any wrongdoing.

His firearms would have been handed to an exhibits officer in a controlled forensic environment. A lawyer had been appointed to represent him. He would be offered counselling. He could expect to be interviewed again and again and again in the coming days.

All the officers at the scene would have immediately seen a doctor.

They would have been instructed to telephone their family to say they were unharmed, because any fatal shooting incident becomes instant headline news. Forty-eight hours later, all those officers present would have had to undertake a hearing test after being exposed to a live gunshot to see if they had suffered lasting damage.

They would then submit more detailed statements for the investigators. They would also be offered counselling for their mental health.

The lead investigator of the IOPC would have been introduced to all the officers involved.

And as the shooting had resulted in a fatality, there would be an inquest.

And only after the inquest had been concluded would Jackson discover if he was able to return to duty or if he was going to jail.

Even if he was found to be innocent, Jackson's return to duty would be at the discretion of his senior commander.

'I can't sleep, Max. I don't know when I will be able to sleep again.'

I softly patted his back.

'Listen, you did your duty. You did the job they trained you for. That's all. That's it. You had no choice. McKay was a threat to your life. He was given every warning. You told him to put his blade down and he refused. You are not going to be prosecuted. You are not going to be sent to jail. You did your job.'

'You know what our instructions are when we discharge our weapons? Do you know the very first thing we are asked to do when we have shot a terrorist or someone with a knife in his hand? Do you know what *the very first thing* we have to do is, Max?'

'You have to give immediate first aid to the person who has been shot.'

He nodded. 'And that's what I did. I was on the ground with Robert McKay, the blood everywhere already, and I was trying to see if I could save him when I heard the voice of AFO Darren Jenkins.'

'Who is AFO Darren Jenkins?'

'That's our pal Dim. And he said – "But he was putting down the knife, sir!" That's what we get for bringing in the Beatles.'

'The other shots saw what happened, didn't they? You're not going down because of what some sex offender with a grudge says.'

He took a deep breath, his eyes drifting from Rocky Marciano to me.

'I know I will be cleared. I know I am not going down for unlawfully taking a life. And I am sorry that Robert McKay is dead, but I know that he gave me no choice. And I know that nobody is going to believe a word that any of John-Paul Ledoux's mates say about me. But here's the thing, Max – what they put you through for discharging your firearm is *so bloody hard*. And that's when you get it right. Imagine what it is like if you get it wrong. And what happens to my family if I ever get it wrong, Max? What happens to Nini and Rosie if I make a mistake and I get done for murder?'

We sat in silence. There was nothing I could say to him to make what he was going through now any easier. We both knew that in the end he would be cleared of any wrongdoing and allowed to go back to his job. What had changed was that Jackson Rose was no longer certain if carrying a firearm for the Met was a job he wanted.

'Jackson?'

'What?'

'I want to thank you for helping me. I could not have done it without you. Ledoux and his friends are going to be put away for a long time. Every day new victims are coming forward. There are multiple offences of sexual assault, false imprisonment, coercive and controlling behaviour. And rape.'

'But not murder,' he said. 'All those offences, all those horrible crimes – but not murder.'

'Ledoux says you know they did not kill Suzanne Buksa. He says you have known it all along . . .'

Jackson stared at Rocky Marciano.

'Ledoux and the others – they are AFOs, Max. Authorised Firearms Officers. Grunts. They all want to become *SFOs*. Specialist Firearms Officers. More status, better pay. More training, more skilled. Better uniforms. And I checked the records, Max. The night that Suzanne Buksa was murdered, all four of them were at the Judgement Range.'

The Judgement Range is in Gravesend, Kent. It is where Firearms Officers go to hone their craft, to perfect their skills and to attempt to upgrade their career.

'What are you saying, Jackson?'

'John-Paul Ledoux and his friends – they are scumbags. They are the worst of us. They are the kind that give us all a bad name. But their alibi is rock solid. They didn't kill Suzanne, Max.'

I felt my stomach fall away.

'And whoever did is still out there,' he said.

46

'*Our revels now are ended,*' said Brian Beath from behind a great grey beard and a flowing wig. '*These our actors, as I foretold you, were all spirits – and are melted into air, into thin air.*'

Brian Beath was a good actor. Even I could see that.

I stood at the back on the thin crowd in Bedford Square watching an open-air performance of *The Tempest* – tourists coming and going to the British Museum, office workers with takeaway coffee in their hands – and I was mesmerised by his performance.

He looked like Gandalf on that little makeshift stage but he sounded like the word of God. Everything that came out of his mouth seemed to matter.

'*We are such stuff as dreams are made on, and our little life is rounded with a sleep.*'

That was the best bit. I can't pretend I understood every word. And yet – somehow – the deeper meaning shone through.

The show's over.

Life is done.

You've had your fun.

Everything ends.

There was no real backstage area, just a screen offering token privacy to actors changing costumes dangerously close to a busy bicycle lane, and that was where I found him, gingerly tugging at the adhesive tape that held his bushy beard in place.

'Mr Beath? I'm a big fan. That was . . . really good.'

He pulled off his beard and, yes, it was really him from the Gatti brothers CCTV camera.

He flicked me a look. 'Thank you, dear boy.'

He frowned at the small pot he was dabbing with a cotton swab. 'Who's been at my cleansing-oil again? Miranda, you little tart, is it you?'

Miranda denied everything. Brian Beath turned back to me.

'Do you have a pen?'

'What?'

'For the autograph?'

I smiled apologetically. 'I really just wanted to talk to you about your work.'

A brisk nod. 'Prospero's speech is misunderstood,' he said. 'These are words of consolation, reassurance. Nothing lasts – but that is exactly why life is so sweet! That very transience.' He pulled off his wig and his bald head flashed in the sunlight.

'And there was that other thing I loved you in,' I said.

We both thought about it.

'I was the stand-in Falstaff at the RSC last summer. Were you at Stratford?'

'That's not it.'

'Oh God – you're talking about something on the bloody telly! Look, dear boy, we all have to pay the mortgage. Sometimes you have to do a crisp commercial or *Emmerdale*.'

'No – it was the one where you played a tax inspector. Remember that one?'

He was suddenly wary.

'No, no, no. You're mistaken. That wasn't me.'

'You *pretended* to be a tax inspector. It was a career-defining performance.'

He was suddenly affronted. 'You're not a fan at all! I don't have to talk to you. Whoever you are.'

I showed him my warrant card, which stopped him breathing for a few seconds. 'Oh, but you really do, Mr Beath. You really do have to talk to me. In fact, talking to me is the only thing that is going to work for you now.'

'I don't want any trouble,' he said.

'Talking to me makes your troubles go away.'

He looked around, and then wanted to get it all over with.

'I thought it was possibly a prank. You know – one of those pranks with an undeniable cruelty at their heart. But then most pranks are like that, aren't they? There's always that element of sadism. And then I understood that it was not even an unfunny prank. The money was too good.'

'How much?'

He looked furtive. He put the cleansing pot down and then picked it up again.

'Five,' he said.

'Five hundred quid?'

'Five thousand.'

'Nice work if you can get it. And what did you have to do for your five thousand pounds?'

'That man – those men – those two brothers. I didn't realise who they were when I took the job. If I had, I would have definitely given them a wide berth, darling.'

'But that was why the money was so good, Mr Beath. What were you told to do?'

'Convince one of them – Mr Michael Gatti – that he was under investigation by His Majesty's Revenue and Customs. That was *it*. They gave me a business card with my name on and I was told to improvise once I was through the door. Love a bit of improv, of course. And it all went very smoothly. They believed me.'

He could not resist the warm glow of professional pride.

'Yes, I saw it. Or at least a few stills. And of course Mick Gatti believed you. Because you're a good actor. Maybe too good. Mick Gatti is dead, do you know that?'

His face went white under the make-up that remained.

'That wasn't the plan! She told me – *put the fear of God in him. You're an actor – you can do that, can't you?* She

329

was very clear — the idea was to *terrorise* him, to make him feel that he was under investigation for his years in Spain. But I never . . .'

'Who hired you?'

'The woman. Approached me — here in Bedford Square — just as you have. Talked to me about *The Tempest* and Shakespeare. An educated woman. A woman of letters. She never gave me her name.'

I laughed at him.

'It's true! She groomed me. She gave me the job. And she gave me the money, five thousand in crisp red fifties, and the business card. And she sent me to work. But I never—'

'Blonde? Leggy — like a dancer? Forties? A smoker?'

He shook his head. 'Ten years younger. Non-smoker, as far as I could tell. But tall, painfully thin — like a catwalk model. As pulchritudinous as that. But possibly no stranger to recreational drugs.'

Summer. Of course — Emma Moon would get one of her underlings to do her dirty work.

'It was two hours of work. The length of the shortest play. *Macbeth*, I mean — we call it the shortest play. That's all — Inspector, is it? Is that what I call you, sir? Please tell me the correct term of address, sir. I want to cooperate. It was just one hundred and twenty minutes in a lifetime of work!'

'It was a great performance, Mr Beath,' I said. 'You scared the life out of him.'

*

330

I called Pat Whitestone.

And I thought of Butch Lewis, his heart giving up on the Heath, lying in the grass as if napping, the great black and tan head of the Rottweiler watching over him.

And I thought of Ian Doherty, walking away from his latest motivational homily – *Enjoy every sandwich!* – and stepping under the oncoming tube train.

And I thought of Keith Jones, rolling up his yoga mat for the last time and returning to old ways that would destroy him.

And I thought of Mick Gatti, terrorised into a coma that he would never wake from because the money had run out, and the tax man was at his door, asking all those difficult questions.

'It's true, Pat,' I told Whitestone. 'Emma Moon is scaring them to death. And I think I know how she does it.'

47

I drove the BMW X5 through the open gates of the big house on The Bishop's Avenue and there Summer was, sitting alone on the wide front steps, as if waiting for us to arrive.

She got up, turned and fled round the side of the house.

'I understand how Emma Moon does it now,' I said as we came up the drive. 'I can't explain all of it, but I understand how it is done. I can't explain why Butch Lewis had his heart give out on Hampstead Heath. But I know that Emma Moon orchestrated it. And I don't know why Keith Jones went on the coke-and-crack bender that killed him. But I know she encouraged it. And I couldn't tell you why Ian Doherty stepped off that platform and under a tube train. But I reckon he had his reasons, and I think she gave them to him. But hiring an actor to torment Mick Gatti to his death proves it – *Emma Moon makes your ultimate nightmare real*. That's what she does, Pat. That's how she kills them. With Mick Gatti it was money – or living his life without money. She played on his terror – his abject terror – of total financial ruin.'

'Room 101,' Bear said from the back seat. '*1984*.'

For once I got the literary reference.

'Yes, I read that book at school too. George Orwell would have understood. Room 101 was the place where you met your worst fear. The room where you were broken beyond repair by the thing you dreaded most.'

'But can we prove any of that?' Bear said.

He was sitting alone in the back seat. DC Sita Basu was getting physio for torn muscles.

'We don't have to prove all of it,' Whitestone said. There was a sworn and notified affidavit from Brian Beath on her lap. She patted it with something like affection. 'Because we already have enough.'

I pulled up in front of the big house and we got out. Whitestone looked at me.

'And do you think you were on her list?'

I shrugged, shook my head. It didn't matter now.

'What's your worst fear, Max?' Whitestone said. 'What's in your Room 101?'

'Beats me, Pat.'

But I thought – *Scout.*

I saw my daughter's face before me, more real than the open door of the big house.

Losing Scout. Failing as Scout's father. Scout in harm's way.

I knew what was waiting for me in my Room 101.

They were all in the library. Almost all of them. Summer was missing.

But Emma Moon was at a heavy oak desk, gazing into

her laptop, Nevermore standing at her shoulder, whispering encouragement. Roxy and Luka, reclining in armchairs, gormlessly staring at their phones.

'Emma Moon?' I said. 'I am going to need you to come with us. We have reason to believe that you have violated your release under licence.'

Nevermore's jaw dropped.

'This is absurd! How has Emma ever violated the terms of her release? What are you arresting her for? What is her *crime*?'

'Harassment,' Whitestone said. 'Malicious communication intended to encourage or assist serious self-harm. That carries a five-year jail term right there.'

'Harassment of whom?'

'The late Mick Gatti,' Whitestone said. 'That's fucking whom. Where's Summer?'

'No idea,' Emma Moon said. 'Summer's using again. And when she's on her poison, Summer comes and goes.' She looked up at me. 'Max, what's all this about?'

Whitestone laughed shortly. *Max!*

'You are directly responsible for the death of Mick Gatti,' I said. 'We have a sworn affidavit from the man you hired to harass him. DCI Whitestone mentioned malicious communication. Personally, I think you would be lucky to get away so lightly. I think you are looking at voluntary manslaughter or involuntary manslaughter. The CPS can take their pick. But that's worth two to ten years right there.'

'This is absurd!' Nevermore thundered.

'And she is *on licence*,' I said, rounding on him. 'Do you know what that means, to be out on licence?'

'Possibly better than you,' he sneered.

I reminded them anyway. 'That means technically you are still serving the sentence that was handed to you – but after serving half of your fixed term you are out and about as long as you adhere to certain conditions. Being released on licence is the chance to reintegrate into the community, prevent reoffending and rebuild family ties. Hounding people to their graves is not adhering to the conditions of your release.'

'People?' she smiled. 'I've killed more than one?'

I took out my handcuffs.

'Is that really necessary?' Nevermore said.

'Let him do it,' Emma Moon said, holding her hands out to me, still shining that knowing smile at me, as if we shared a secret. 'Let the big man do it again.'

The bureaucracy of police custody.

Like checking into the hotel from hell.

Emma Moon had done it before. Details, details. Time of arrest. Offence under investigation.

'Call it malicious communication for now,' Whitestone said. 'It will do for a start.'

Whitestone and I escorted Emma Moon to the interview room.

This was the time for her to give it some no comment, this was the time to wait for her lawyer to turn up, this was the time to steal a few hours to think about her best move.

335

But Emma Moon was not interested.

'You are declining your right to free legal advice from this police station's duty solicitor,' I said. 'Is that correct?'

She nodded and smiled at me. 'Why do I need a brief? I haven't done anything wrong, Max.'

'You need a brief because you were released under licence and now you are on your way back to jail to serve another sixteen years,' Whitestone said sharply, not enjoying her familiarity with me, and not finding it so funny anymore.

'You can change your mind at any time about legal advice,' I continued. 'You can also instruct us to contact your own solicitor. But we have the right to question you about the crime you are suspected of without a legal representative present. As custody officers, we are not allowed to disclose to anyone over the phone that you are under arrest and in custody. However, you have a right to contact a notified person, meaning you have the right to nominate someone likely to have an interest in your welfare. Do you want to call Nevermore? Roxy? Luka?'

'I'm curious,' Emma said, looking from me to Whitestone and back again. 'What exactly do you think I've done?'

'We know you got your cut-price Kate Moss to hire Brian Beath,' Whitestone said.

She shook her head. 'And who exactly is Brian Beath when he's at home?'

'He's an actor,' I said.

'OK. An actor. Right.'

'He posed as a tax inspector with the late Mick Gatti,' I said.

'Scared him witless,' Whitestone said. 'Scared him into the coma that killed him. Scared him to death.'

'And what's that got to do with me?'

'We told you already,' I said. 'Summer hired him on your behalf.'

'Play it dumb if you want,' Whitestone said. 'We don't need your confession. We have our sworn affidavit from Mr Beath, who is willing to testify. Frankly, Mr Beath is willing to do anything we ask him to do if it keeps him out of trouble. And it's *enough*, Emma. That is already enough to send you back to HMP Bronzefield for the rest of your sentence.'

'But again – what do you think I've *done*?'

'You put people in the same space as their worst night-mare,' I said. 'You put them in their own private hell and then you chuck away the key.'

She shook her head. 'This is crazy,' she said.

'Mick Gatti,' I said. 'You took him apart with the thing that terrified him the most. Bankruptcy. Poverty. The tax man on his back. And it was *enough* – what you did was enough to put him in a coma, and enough to kill him.'

She shook her head. 'Why would I want Mick Gatti dead?'

'Because you did the hard time while they got on with their lives,' I said. 'Because you protected them and they never protected you. Because your son died. David died.

You wanted Mick Gatti dead for the same reason you wanted all of them dead.'

All of us dead, I thought. Because I knew with total certainty now that I was on that list too. And she had already worked out the one thing in this world that frightened me. The only thing that really frightened me. That something would happen to Scout.

'But you are not arresting me for the death of Keith Jones, are you? Or Ian Doherty? Or Butch Lewis?'

'Look at it this way,' Whitestone said reasonably. 'You got out – and all these men started dying. That's some coincidence, isn't it?'

'But how did I kill Ian Doherty? He stepped in front of a tube train. What am I meant to have done? Persuaded him that he was better off dead?'

'Something like that,' Whitestone said. 'Malicious communication. Why don't *you* tell *us* what you said to him to make him step off that platform?'

'And Butch died of a heart attack.'

'Cardiac arrest,' I said.

'Whatever.'

'Yeah – *whatever*,' Whitestone said. 'Tell his wife – *whatever*. Tell those grandchildren who loved him – *whatever*. You're all heart, aren't you?'

'And Keith,' Emma said. 'The Nutjob they called him, not without reason – stuck a gram of God-knows-what up his hooter and into his veins. How did I arrange that? I must be some kind of criminal mastermind! And I'm *not*, Max, you know I'm not.'

'We don't have to explain any of it,' Whitestone said. 'Not to you, not to the judge. But it doesn't matter. Because we already have you bang to rights for hiring an actor to harass Mick Gatti to his grave. And stop calling him Max, will you?'

'What was my motive?'

'Revenge,' I said.

'If that's true – if I somehow arranged for the death of Mick – and for the deaths of all those men – then you should be very afraid of me.' Looking straight at me now. 'Shouldn't you, Max? I must be a very dangerous woman. You should be very afraid.'

'He doesn't need to be afraid of you,' Whitestone said. 'Because you're going to be a little old lady when you finally totter out of jail.'

'You think I wanted them to die because of what they did to me?' Emma Moon asked. 'Look, I hoped they would have unhappy lives. I hoped that they would suffer, Max. I prayed to God that they would suffer as I have suffered. The kind of suffering where you feel you would tear your skin off just to stop it all for just one second. You give me too much credit. I'm not that smart. And I am not a killer. It takes a lot to take another human life and I don't have it in me. I just don't. Do you really think that dying is the worst thing that can happen to you? What soft little lives you must have lived! Try burying a child. Try living a life locked up. Being alive and tormented for every living moment – ah, that's a lot harder! I never wanted to kill them, Max. Not even my ex-husband.

Certainly not poor old Butch with his dodgy ticker. And not the others. I just wanted them to live their rotten lives and to feel a touch of the pain that I felt in that cell, mourning my son. That's not much to ask, is it? After sixteen years inside. After losing the best years of my life, after protecting people who abused me. I never wanted them dead, not any of them. I wanted them to suffer. The deaths of those men – this actor I am meant to have hired – it had nothing to do with me!'

Emma Moon was a good liar. But I was sick of all her lies.

'And I know you're not dying,' I said.

48

Scout was not at home.

I knew it the moment I walked through the door. That old parental radar detected that she was not where she should be on a school night so close to our agreed curfew hour of 10 p.m. Stan watched me from his favourite sofa as I walked through the great wide-open space of our loft, listening for signs of life and then standing outside her closed bedroom door, before finally saying her name, already knowing there would be no reply.

I found her on the other side of the Grand Avenue, the quiet side of Smithfield, where the streets run down to the river, standing alone on the strip of pubs and bars and cafés, shuttered for the night.

The place where Emma Moon had fed the homeless.

'I guess nobody is coming tonight,' Scout said.

'Scout,' I said. 'Emma went back to prison.'

My daughter's face clouded with that infinite irritation that a child can summon up so easily for a slow-witted parent.

'I *know*,' she said. 'Because she was allowed one phone call. And she made it to me.'

We stared at the empty street.

'I just thought maybe the others would keep doing her work,' she said. Then she looked at me. 'Silly really. Emma was the one who made it happen. And without her . . .'

'I know you liked her. And I know she liked you.'

'That's OK,' Scout said, shaking her head, and then we were walking home, crossing the Grand Avenue where the cars and vans and lorries were beginning their long night shift, heading for home until Scout stopped at one of those narrow side streets that fill the area. I recognised it too. There had once been a skip on this street but it was gone now.

'This is where Suzanne died, isn't it?' Scout said.

'This is where we found her,' I said, as gently as I could.

Scout stared into the shadows. It had so recently been a crime scene but now it wasn't, and it had that spring-cleaned look of a place that had been picked clean for evidence.

'Not one single flower,' Scout said, an observation made without rancour or bitterness or any emotion that I could detect. 'People lay flowers, don't they? When someone dies. I saw it online – the flowers that were left out for Princess Diana when she died. People do it all the time, leave flowers for the dead. But not for Suzanne. Not one flower.'

'We can lay some flowers for Suzanne,' I suggested, expecting an immediate dismissal, scorn for a dumb idea that was too little too late.

But Scout brightened. 'Can we?'

'Sure.'

'But where do you buy flowers at this time of night?'

'I know a place,' I said.

We drove to New Covent Garden Flower Market, which is so far from Covent Garden that we parked under the silhouette of Battersea Power Station. And we stepped into a world of flowers.

Scout had grown up looking at Smithfield, and immediately grasped the concept of a market devoted to fruit, vegetables and flowers, and immediately recognised the loud, frazzled men and women going about their business.

We wandered aisles piled high with every kind of flower, like a couple of tourists, and the scent was overwhelming.

Scout turned to face me.

'But isn't it just wholesale?' she said.

'I'll talk to someone. We'll get some flowers for Suzanne.'

But what I really wanted to say to my daughter was – *it will be all right.*

Later we drove home through the empty midnight streets with the back seat of the old BMW X5 piled high with sunflowers – I found a trader willing to cut us a deal, but they are wholesalers in the end, and so we bought far more than was necessary for our purpose – and we carried them in our arms to the strangely clean backstreet where I had found the body of Suzanne Buksa. We stood there for a long minute, the sunflowers spilling over themselves, piled on top of each other, and I searched my mind for words that might be appropriate but really, placing the flowers had been enough.

That was what Scout wanted to do.

'We can go home now,' she said after a bit, and that is what we did.

She did not mention Suzanne. She did not mention Emma Moon.

Like every child of divorced parents, she was no stranger to a sense of loss. The feeling of people slipping out of her life was not a new experience.

My daughter was getting used to losing people.

Terry Gatti had been calling.

I had had enough of him, and I didn't return his calls, and deleted his voice messages without listening to them. But as Scout brushed her teeth and prepared for bed, strangely calm after our midnight excursion to that secret city of flowers, the phone vibrated again and I picked up just to tell him to get lost, once and forever.

'There's only us left, Max,' he said. 'You and me. We are the only ones on her list who are left alive. They're all dead now apart from you and me. And it's not over. You think it's over because Emma is back inside? It's not over while you and me are still breathing.'

'Listen, pal—'

'No, you listen to me, Max,' he said. 'You asked me once what was in that safe.'

'You mean the safe that allowed you and your brother

to retire? The safe that you nicked? The safe that cost two men their lives and Emma Moon the best years of her life?'

'Yeah, that's the one. And I didn't tell you because of course that would have been an admission that I was there that night. But I am ready to show you now. I *want* to show you. I want to show you tonight.'

There was silence on the line.

Scout appeared in the doorway of her bedroom, child-like in her pyjamas, raising her hand in salute.

I raised my hand and she disappeared into her bedroom.

'Come round here now,' Terry Gatti said. 'And I will show you what we have all been dying for.'

49

There was the smell of a man newly living alone in Terry Gatti's big Essex mansion, the scent of lager and curry and weed and dishes in the sink and windows that had been closed for far too long.

He was not quite drunk but he was getting there. Wild-eyed and desperate in his soiled polo shirt and shorts, barefoot and dapper no more, suddenly in a life that he had never imagined for himself.

'She's left me. Helen. My wife. Gone back to her parents. Nobody else involved, if you can believe that.'

I couldn't. There is always someone else involved. But I didn't give a damn about Terry Gatti's broken heart.

'What was in that safe?'

He laughed shortly. 'Riches beyond imagination.' He checked the street in either direction – there was nothing stirring out there, just affluent suburbia after its bedtime – and quickly closed the door behind me. 'There was what you would expect. Cash in assorted currencies. Some nice pieces of jewellery. Tiffany, Cartier, de Beers. Watches. Panerai, Hublot, Rolex.'

He touched his wrist in remembrance of Rolex past. There was nothing there tonight.

'And that haul kept you in the lap of luxury for nearly twenty years?'

He shook his head. 'No – that paid the lads.'

'Then what else was in the safe?'

I watched him lick his lips. 'It's best if I show you.'

We wandered deep into his home to an office overlooking the back garden. Huge floor-to-ceiling windows, the large but neglected garden illuminated beyond. A swimming pool that could use a good clean shimmering with a blue that belonged in the Caribbean. Next to it was some kind of hot tub, bubbling away, sending steam into the chilled night air. At the far end of the swimming pool, a stone Buddha stared impassively at the raggedy garden.

Terry Gatti was at the desk, removing a chain from around his neck.

On the chain was a key.

He opened the desk and took something out.

'Come and see.'

It was a Polaroid.

I stared at it, and suddenly I understood.

'Blackmail,' I said. 'You didn't know this photograph was in the safe. But when you found it, you realised it was your pension plan, your meal ticket for life. And you've been blackmailing the owner for sixteen years.'

'The house was owned by an old English family. They

owned the contents of the safe. The Ukrainian who was living there was just a tenant. What was in the safe never belonged to him. None of it did. This photograph – it belonged to the son.'

'And who was the son?'

The glass wall broke like a bomb going off.

Terry Gatti and I had stepped back in shock and we were staring at the large stone Buddha that had shattered the glass. Shards of glass were still falling as Luka Brady stepped inside the room.

He grinned at both of us, his bald head gleaming with sweat.

Nevermore came in after him, stepping daintily over the broken glass, and then looking at me with a sigh.

'Well, this is awkward,' he said, his face flushed red. He nodded to Luka.

The shaven-headed lump was taking something out of his leather jacket.

It looked like a blue handgun with a bright yellow cartridge.

A Taser X3.

He aimed it at my face.

And it went tick-tick-tick when he pulled the trigger.

I writhed on the floor and the pain did not stop, the pain went on and on and it was the only thing I knew, that paralysing pain, the only thing I could think about, and my muscles were all in spasm, my spine arching as if it wanted to snap, and I thrashed in agony as if desperate to abandon my own body, and someone was screaming and screaming, and I realised it was me.

Fifty thousand volts of power had invaded my central nervous system.

A galaxy of black and white stars burned and blazed before my eyes.

Men were talking and, remarkably, they all sounded almost reasonable.

'I never wanted it to end this way, Boy.' This from Terry Gatti.

'Then you should have come off the payroll years ago, shouldn't you?' Nevermore in response, peevish and snappy.

And when the stars began to die and my vision began to clear, I looked up and saw Nevermore with the Polaroid in his hand, staring at it in total disbelief.

'Is this it, Terence? Is this *really* it? You're not holding out on me, are you?'

'That's it,' Gatti gasped.

He was in his office chair now, and Luka was concentrating on wrapping him in duct tape. His mouth was already half covered.

'My oh my,' Nevermore was saying.

Then he was looking down at me, waving the Polaroid. 'Have you seen this?'

I was incapable of answering. My body could not stop shaking. There was drool on my chin. I told myself that the pain would pass. I tried very hard to believe it.

'Terence,' Nevermore said, 'may I ask why you were

showing this image to a detective in the Metropolitan Police?'

I closed my eyes. I wondered if I was going to die tonight. I wondered what Scout would think when she woke and found me gone. I wondered what she would think when she knew I was gone forever. I wondered how it would be for her, growing up without me. Tears came to my eyes. I wanted to go home.

But Daniel 'Boy' Nevermore wanted to explain.

'The house was indeed owned by my family. The Ukrainian living there didn't actually have a pot to piss in. Friend of my father's. I supervised the house. I was the only one with access to the safe. Along with some family trinkets and petty cash, I stored an image in the safe. A Polaroid.' His laugh was like a bark. 'Is this *really* the same Polaroid, Terence? I wonder! Because that's what the Gatti brothers have been blackmailing me with for the last half a lifetime. *This bloody Polaroid.* Mr Gatti here – and his late brother – wanted the paydays to keep coming. I explained that the money had done what money always does in the end – the money had run out. But he wouldn't listen – would you?'

Luka slapped Terry around the head.

'But my trust fund is empty. My father's investments have not gone as planned. *I could not pay any more.* Mr Gatti and the other Mr Gatti would not listen to reason. They threatened to place the Polaroid in the public domain. The money was gone but the blackmail continued. Luka and I planned to collect the image tonight. And here we all are.'

'You killed those men,' I managed. 'You killed all those men . . .'

'To show greedy Mr Gatti here that I was serious. Although' – he shared a secret smile with Luka – 'I didn't actually kill anyone.'

'You scared them to death,' I said.

He enjoyed that.

'Oh please! *They scared themselves to death.* It's an age of anxiety – didn't you notice? I didn't *kill* them, I did not need to. I just gave them the means to kill themselves. I gave them permission to die. I gave them a reason to end it all. I made death seem like a good move. It's perfectly true that the sudden release of extreme stress hormones causes the left ventricle of the heart to become temporarily weakened and struggle to pump blood. The medical term is stress cardiomyopathy or takotsubo syndrome. It's what happens when someone experiences severe emotional or physical stress. It's also known as broken-heart syndrome. I didn't kill anyone, you stupid policeman. I broke their spirit! I took away their reason to live! *I showed them why death was preferable to life.*'

He reeled them off.

'Butch Lewis – all Luka here had to do was to show Mr Lewis some images of his lovely little granddaughters being picked up at the school gate by Luka himself – holding hands with the oldest girl. A pretty young thing.'

The shaven-headed goon shyly chuckled at the memory, stepping back to admire the duct tape that was now wrapped around the arms, shoulders and terrified face of Terry Gatti.

'Butch's delicate old ticker took a turn for the worst,' Nevermore said. 'Ian Doherty – for all his artistic pretensions – had images on his computer that would have got him locked up for a long, long time. When he knew we had a few thousand of those incriminating images, he took the easy way out and stepped under the Northern line. Keith – the yoga teacher formerly known as The Nutjob – he was the easiest. A few grams of rough-cut amphetamine sulphate through his letterbox and all thoughts of the sun salute and downward-facing dog went out of his head. You see – I did not kill *any* of them. There is no need for all that unpleasantness. All you need to do is to give someone a good reason to kill themselves. All you need is to break their hearts.'

'It wouldn't have worked with me,' Terry Gatti tearfully sneered.

'Because you don't have a heart, Terence!' Nevermore said. 'You let the woman you allegedly loved – the woman you had a child with – do sixteen years in prison for you and your brother and all your light-fingered chums. You can't break the heart of a man who hasn't got one.'

'But – why?' I said. 'Those men had done nothing to you. Those payments you've been making over the years – the rest of them didn't see a penny of it, did they? Only the Gattis.'

'I wanted my photograph back!' Nevermore roared with a furious petulance, almost stamping his foot. 'And

I needed to show Terence here that I was deadly serious. And he didn't believe me. Or his greed – his pea-brained South London greed – would not let him believe me. But he was scared. I could see that. He could feel it coming. He thought you could protect him, Detective. That's how thick he is.'

'My brother . . .'

'Oh, your thuggish brother was the easiest of the lot. Hire some old thespian fart to play the taxman!'

My vision was clearing now. 'You got Emma to get Summer to hire that actor,' I said.

He looked offended. 'I did *not* need help from Emma Moon. Half a gram of heroin and young Summer will do pretty much anything that anyone asks her to do.'

Luka Brady was considering Terry Gatti and me with a professional eye.

'So are we doing both of them?' he asked.

Nevermore nodded. 'Oh yes.'

'Killing a cop?' Luka said. 'Hashtag – just saying, chief.'

'Killing a *dirty* cop,' Nevermore said. 'Killing a *bent* copper who lives in a swish apartment that no ordinary policeman could ever afford.'

'My parents died,' I muttered to myself. My head was woozy beyond belief. They all called me a dirty cop because they thought that life was simple and straightforward and easily understood when all the twists and turns of all our lives are beyond knowing. 'My grandmother brought me up,' I mumbled. 'She left me everything. I remembered my dad saying – you will never lose money on London property . . . not dirty . . . not bent . . .'

'What's the dirty cop saying?' Nevermore asked.

'I think he's begging for his life,' Luka said. 'They all do that in the end.'

'Emma,' I said. 'Emma Moon . . .'

'That bitch!' Terry howled from inside the duct tape that now half-covered his face.

But he was wrong. 'She had nothing to do with it,' I said, understanding at last. 'They were setting her up. Letting her take the blame for all those murders. Setting up Emma to take the fall for Nevermore as he tried to keep his dirty little secret – that pathetic Polaroid! – from daylight.'

Luka stared down at me furiously. 'Worried about your girlfriend, are you?' he asked, and kicked me hard in the ribs.

I groaned and rolled on my side. My body flooded with shame to think of Emma Moon back in HMP Bronzefield. Twice now she'd done time for the crimes of the men in her life. And twice I had helped to put her behind bars.

'You said Emma had a list,' I told Gatti. 'A kill list. She never had a list.'

Luka ruffled Gatti's thick black hair. 'Guilty conscience, Tel?' he said.

Nevermore was staring at the Polaroid.

'I was the one with the list, Constable,' he said, not looking at me. 'And on my list there were two things. I wanted the demands for money to stop. My trust fund was depleted – but try explaining that to a couple of crooks from Catford! And I wanted my photograph back. Those were the two things on my list! The Gatti brothers and their chums had had their money's worth out of me and my family. I tried to make them see reason – to make them understand that it had to end. But the criminal class don't know how to quit while they are ahead. So here we are now.'

He shook his head at the photograph.

'*And all for this,*' he sighed, looking down at me. 'All that human suffering – all that money! – hardly seems worth it, does it? Oh well – at least the demands for money are going to stop. At least the threat to put this photograph online will end right here. Isn't that correct, Terence?'

Luka casually placed the muzzle of the Taser against Terry Gatti's neck and shot him.

Gatti screamed and writhed and the yellow and blue Taser X3 went tick-tick-tick.

'Do you want to take them upstairs and do them in one of the bedrooms?' Luka said.

Nevermore grimaced with distaste. 'The garden, I think. The swimming pool. Let's take Terence for a midnight dip. Give the policeman your clever Taser there and get his fingerprints all over it. Then take him upstairs and wrap a belt around his neck. This is the narrative – *bent detective kills criminal and then himself.* I think that will cover it, to be honest. Nobody will mourn these two.'

'A business deal that went wrong,' Brady said, grinning slyly. 'Perhaps a lover's tiff. I like it.'

'What a lurid mind you have, Luka. Just get on with it, will you?'

Brady began dragging Terry over the shards of broken glass and out into his garden.

Nevermore was looking down at me with amused contempt. 'This isn't awkward, after all, is it? This is perfect . . .' He held out his hand. 'Let's watch, shall we?'

I lay there, gurgling up at him, the pain now a dull and insistent throb, but still everywhere, in my legs and arms and behind my eyes, and it had paralysed me, made the smallest movement agony.

'May I help you?'

He had his hands around my waist and I thought at first he was going to attempt to lift me, but he was removing the leather belt from my jeans. When he had it off he pulled it tight so it made a small noose, and this he placed over my head and around my neck. Then he pulled.

'Get up,' he ordered, with just a flicker of impatience, and then I was on my knees, and walking on my knees because my legs would not lift me. He gave a sharp, insistent tug and somehow I was more or less up on my feet, stumbling after him, over the carpet of broken glass and into the garden, the pain still blurring everything. 'Good boy,' he said.

Luka already had Terry Gatti upside down in the hot tub, holding his head under the bubbling water, gripping him by the thighs as Terry thrashed and writhed and fought for his life.

Nevermore watched with interest, holding the belt around my neck loosely, as if I was a good dog who would not stray far from the porch.

I swayed and staggered on my feet beside him, my vision coming and going, smeared with the black and white stars and then suddenly clear, and it was in one of those moments of clarity that I saw DCI Pat Whitestone's face appear in the bushes at the end of the garden.

I blinked and she was gone.

Terry Gatti had stopped moving.

Luka pulled him out of the tub. Terry Gatti's handsome face was now the colour of boiled meat. It was over that quickly. Luka was dragging the body to the swimming pool. I felt a tug on the belt around my neck.

'Your turn to die,' Nevermore smiled.

And then suddenly there were armed officers everywhere.

Coming out of the bushes, their faces covered in black balaclavas to inspire terror, the barrels of their Heckler & Koch sub-machine guns glinting in the garden lights, screaming their commands that were designed to be obeyed instantly.

Get on the ground now! Do it now! Now! Now! Now!

Nevermore and Luka dropped to their knees and their bellies and I saw the flicker of pure terror on the face of Nevermore as one of the shots placed the barrel of a handgun – one of those weird, flat-nosed Glocks – into his ear.

Then Pat Whitestone was there, and Bear and Sita, all

of them in PASGT ballistic helmets and Kevlar body armour.

'Come here,' Pat said, and she removed the belt from around my neck as Sita and Bear held me up, then gently led me through the smashed window and into the office. They eased me into the chair.

The Polaroid was on the desk.

'Summer came into the station after Emma Moon was sent back to Bronzefield,' Pat was saying. 'Confessed everything. Floods of tears. Still strung out on smack.'

Bear rolled his eyes. 'Barely coherent.'

'In a very bad way,' Sita said.

'Summer told us that it was Nevermore who got her to hire the actor to hound Mick Gatti. And told us she was the one who had photographed Luka picking up Butch Lewis's granddaughters from their school. And provided Keith Jones with the drugs that killed him. And sent the child pornography to Ian Doherty that encouraged him to jump under a train.'

'A busy girl, our Summer,' Bear grimaced. 'And a hopeless junkie.'

Whitestone shot him a look and he grinned with embarrassment.

Young Bear still had a lot to learn.

'And Summer told us that it was Nevermore all along who had the beef with the Gattis,' she said. 'But she didn't know why.'

I nodded at the Polaroid on the desk.

'There's the why.'

Whitestone picked up the photograph, Bear and Sita on either side of her.

Bear laughed and shook his head.

'I don't understand,' Sita said.

Pat Whitestone showed me the Polaroid. 'This is it?'

I nodded. 'That is it.'

There was nothing on it.

Whatever image the Polaroid had once contained had been drained of colour and contour until there was nothing left, nothing at all beyond a glossy square of black. A white-framed square of nothing.

We all stared at the faded Polaroid, wondering what moment it had once captured.

'I imagine it once contained an image of a sexual nature,' I said. 'And whatever it was, it would have been enough for Nevermore to be disowned by his father. There was a lot of booty in that safe they stole – but the Polaroid was the real treasure, the Polaroid was the pot of gold for the Gatti brothers. That's what the Gattis have been using to blackmail Nevermore over the last sixteen years. And they never got around to telling him that somewhere between then and now, the image had just melted away.'

'Nevermore wanted something back that didn't even exist anymore,' Sita said.

Whitestone glanced towards the garden.

'And so he murdered the lot of them,' she said.

50

A visit from Scout's mother.

I know, I know. It was out of the blue – quite literally.

Anne – her name is Anne – Scout's mum, my ex-wife – called in the middle of the two long-haul flights it takes to get from Auckland, New Zealand, to London, Heathrow.

'Max? Are you there? I am at Chek Lap Kok. I can't talk for long; our flight is boarding.'

Her voice was the same – Northern England with a touch of class, as though she had spent long years around money down south – but I had no clue where she was, or what she was talking about, or why she was calling. Metallic Cantonese and Mandarin announcements were in the air where she was calling from.

Scout was watching from the sofa with Stan. My face must have worn an expression she could not read. An expression from long ago, or perhaps one that was completely new.

'Chek Lap Kok,' Anne was saying. 'It's Hong Kong's airport.' And then she was turning away from the phone, addressing a child or – it was not impossible – perhaps her husband. 'No, can you *stop* – can you *just stop*?'

I waited. There didn't seem like anything else to do.

'Lachlan's father is dying,' she said.

'Who?'

'Lachlan, Max – *my husband*. We are trying – *just stop it, will you?* – to get back in time.' Her voice snagged on something, a ragged emotion for someone I would never know in some other life. 'He's in a home – well, it's a hospice now – just outside of London.' The long moment of silence. 'And I wanted to see Scout,' she said.

How to explain our relationship? To me, our family felt totally unique – as though nobody had ever screwed it all up quite as badly as Anne and I did – but it was, I knew in my heart, shockingly ordinary.

When she left us when Scout was four, I know that Anne wanted to do the right thing, and she wanted to be a good mum – despite, you know, the new life that was beginning – but it did not work out that way. Life got in the way of all the good intentions. That's not unique. That's the human cliché. Contact between Scout and her mother was sporadic and then – somewhere between then and now, a good few years ago – it became non-existent.

'Max?' Anne said.

I shook myself out of my reverie. 'Of course,' I said. 'Call when you get in. Come around when you want.'

'The same place?'

I looked out at the great expanse of our loft. The great sweeping skyline beyond the window, my daughter's face wide-eyed and serious in the foreground. The boiler was wheezing like an old man with emphysema. It wasn't going to last much longer.

'Yes,' I said. 'We're still in Smithfield. The same place.'

'I should have called,' she said, her voice – I couldn't get over it – totally unchanged! And our lives totally unrecognisable. 'I know I should have called.'

I didn't know if she meant she could have called before she left Auckland, or if she could have called in all those years when there was no contact at all, not a word, and she was going through the dramas of the heart that always, always seemed to follow this beautiful woman around.

And she was beautiful, Anne – and she *is* beautiful – and she is one of those women who turned heads when she was scarcely out of childhood and she will turn heads when she is seventy.

That's the first thing I loved about her – the way she looked.

And isn't that a flimsy foundation to build your life and your family upon?

'It's fine,' I said. 'It's all fine. Please come when you can.'

And when she was gone I gave Scout the gist of it.

A dying parent – Lachlan's father. Scout and I had never met Lachlan, of course, we only really knew the guy who came along after me.

And I told her about the dash across the planet, and the curse of the grown-up children with ageing parents.

And Anne's wish to see Scout – a mother's wish to see her child.

'Where is she now? My mum?'

'In Hong Kong. Changing flights. It's about twelve hours, I think. From there to here.'

Half a world away.

And in the end it really wasn't complicated. And I suppose we could have distrusted Anne's motives. We could – both of us, either of us, Scout and I – have reflected on a guilty conscience, and an absent parent offering far too little, far too late, and trying to make up lost ground.

But without ever discussing it, Scout and I decided that we would see Anne's visit as something else.

We would see it as an expression of love.

They turned up late the next day.

Anne – radiant even now, with all those years gone, bleary with the fog of major jet lag – changed but unchanged.

And Lachlan – one of those finance guys that takes care of himself, his eyes raw with tears of mourning, and his chin trembling with the promise that they – his tears – could start again at any moment.

And three children – two boys and a girl – one of hers and one of his and one of theirs, I guessed at first sight, but that didn't feel quite right. Some distant bell was ringing, telling me the boys were hers and the little girl was theirs. I didn't like to ask and, to be honest, I didn't care that much. All of them were a few years younger than Scout, all of them lovely-looking kids, all of them in glasses, like a flock of beautiful, baby owls.

And my Scout – she had brushed her hair and washed her face but the clothes she wore were the clothes she always wore outside of school uniform – T-shirt and jeans and white trainers battered grey by these city streets.

The great reunion of Scout and her mother was almost formal.

I felt it too. The need to present ourselves well.

See? We survived without you.

Anne hugged Scout and kissed her head and cooed about her beauty and how she was all grown up and how good it was to see her. And Scout smiled politely, like the late queen in the presence of an over-familiar, over-friendly head of some Commonwealth country.

For some reason I did not understand, our visitors had their suitcases with them. They must have briefly checked into one hotel and were now set to check into another. *AKL – HKG – LHR* said the stickers. A small child draped itself on one, gawping at Scout.

'How's your father?' I asked Lachlan, and his face crumpled and he began to sob.

'We didn't make it in time,' Anne said. And then, sharply, 'Lachlan, darling?'

He gasped for air.

'Sorry,' he said, smiling at his dumbfounded children.

'Twenty-four hours and fifty minutes,' Anne said, and it took me a moment to realise she was talking about their flight, and perhaps trying to explain why everyone's nerves were a little ragged.

But I looked at Lachlan with some sympathy. It's hard to have a parent die.

Mrs Murphy was in the kitchen – '*This* I have to see,' she growled when told of Anne's visit – preparing coffee for the adults and juice for the children and biscuits for all – and Mrs Murphy was the only one who seemed to find the visit a bit of a farce.

For Scout and me it felt – what? It felt like our life was catching up with us.

It felt necessary. It felt *normal*. It felt nice. And even if it was all slightly stilted – Scout and her mum sat on the sofa making conversation – 'Have you come far?' the Queen used to ask, and I thought Scout might use the line now – and anti-climactic – Anne pointed out that her children were Scout's half-brothers and half-sister and my daughter clearly just didn't feel it – and even if it was all a bit weird – Lachlan could not really stop crying about the dad whose death he missed – I was glad the visit had happened, and I could tell that Scout was glad too. It put loss – all those lost years, all that lost feeling – into some kind of perspective.

And Stan saved the day when he stirred himself from where he had been napping in a quiet corner of Scout's bedroom – something he did more and more as he got older – and wandered into the loft, prompting squeals of euphoric disbelief from Anne and Lachlan's kids.

'Mama! Look at his big eyes!'

'Bulbous eyes are typical of the breed,' Scout said, addressing the company with a heartbreaking formality.

I looked at my daughter with love and pride. Whatever had happened in the past, Scout and I were people from another time now. It was hard – impossible – to hold any grudges against this nice, pretty lady from New Zealand who was trying so hard. This was our life – our home, our city, our dog. It was not her life.

'What a handsome chap,' Anne said, admiring Stan, and that made me smile because Anne was not remotely a dog person.

Stan batted his eyelashes at her, seeing straight through her. And Stan became the focus of all our attention from the moment he appeared and as her children stroked and loved him, Anne and I shared a look that I knew we would both remember.

Because I understood and she understood too that we had reached the state of grace that all old lovers finally reach, if they are lucky.

Anne and I no longer had the power to hurt each other.

And that was a good thing. And Scout seeing her mum was an even better thing. And even if she never actually took up the invitation to come down to New Zealand and stay, it was good to be asked.

And that was the visit. It was not momentous. It was normal. It was even – that word again – nice. And there are worse things in this world.

I had waited for a wave of emotion to overwhelm me. It never came.

They eventually departed – the youngest child starting to grizzle, the older two delirious with jet lag – and they went with hugs and kisses and promises and invitations. But the only tears were shed by Lachlan for his dead father, so those tears had nothing to do with us. Those tears were not our problem.

Scout and I were both a little stunned.

We smiled at each other, happy and relieved.

What just happened?

Only Mrs Murphy remained unmoved, unimpressed and unforgiving.

Only Mrs Murphy – who had retreated to the kitchen, furiously stuffing the cups and plates into the dishwasher, talking to herself – had watched all of the proceedings, even Stan's show-stopping guest appearance, with a stony face and an angry heart for all that had been abandoned in the long, long ago. Mrs Murphy only met Scout and me after Anne had gone, and she knew the load that my daughter – like all the children of divorced parents – had been asked to carry.

So Mrs Murphy was polite, attentive, friendly with those jet-lagged, dog-loving children and their parents. But she did not forgive and she would never forget.

'New Zealand, is it?' Mrs Murphy could be heard muttering to herself in the days to come. 'I never heard of such a thing!'

And that was an expression of love too.

51

When our visitors from New Zealand were gone, Scout and I put on Stan's collar and lead and walked down to check on the flowers that we had left for Suzanne.

We were worried they may have been stolen.

Instead, they were covered – lost somewhere among a great snowdrift of other flowers that had grown around them, as if by magic.

The sunflowers that we had bought in the night market had stirred some collective memory of the young homeless woman who had once lived on these streets, clutching her childhood stuffed toy, who was now gone forever.

The narrow turning where I had found Suzanne's body – more of an alley than a side street – was jammed full of flowers, stretching from one end to the other, and as we watched, a ruddy-faced porter in a blood-smeared white coat placed his own small bouquet.

He caught my eye as he turned away.

'Nice kid,' he said. 'Bloody shame.'

'People remember her,' Scout said, turning her face up to me. 'They remember Suzanne.'

Stan sniffed the ground tentatively, the first sign that

he was looking for a suitable toilet venue. It would not be here.

'Be respectful, Stan,' Scout told him. 'We'd better walk him.' She hesitated. 'I'm fine doing it by myself. If you want to stay here for a bit.'

'Do you have poo bags? Senior Treats? Wipes for your hands?'

She rolled her eyes. *Daaaaaaad!* Of course she had all of these things. She had grown up with a dog and she knew the drill.

When Scout and Stan had gone, I stood there for the longest while, watching the flowers pile up, watching the porters from the market and the locals – young couples, mostly, either childless or with a babe in arms, not yet moved away from the city – bring their flowers and pay their respects and be alone with their thoughts of Suzanne.

Not crowds, never crowds, but a steady trickle of humanity, remembering Suzanne Buksa.

Then DCI Pat Whitestone appeared. She was carrying some flowers of her own that looked as though they had been picked from her garden. I watched her place them with the rest.

'I heard about this,' she said. 'We should have done it from the start.'

'Scout's idea.'

'You can be proud of that girl.'

'I am.' I inhaled. The scent of the flowers was overwhelming in this confined space. 'We saw Scout's mum,' I said. 'She came around with her new family.'

Whitestone raised her eyebrows. 'Goodness. And why now?'

'They were in town because the guy – Anne's husband, Lachlan – had an elderly parent who was on their last legs.'

'And how was it?'

'It felt normal, Pat.'

'There's nothing weirder than normality.'

'But it went OK. I'm glad Scout saw her. I guess – going forward – the two of them have to work it out for themselves. And they will.'

We stood looking at the flowers in silence.

'I can't stop believing that I failed Suzanne Buksa,' I said. 'I could have saved her if I had listened a bit harder, cared a bit more, and not been so wrapped up in my own world.'

'You did your best for her, Max.'

'And a lot of good my best did her.'

Whitestone shook her head.

'Some murderers get away with it. That's a sad fact. And they don't tell you about all those unsolved murders on the TV and in the films because it's not a good story. But we have a 90 per cent success rate. That's not bad, Max. It's a lot better than the statistics for burglary, assault, rape, name it. But there are – what? – three thousand homicides in this country every year? So that means there are hundreds that never get solved. And it looks like Suzanne, sadly, is going to be one of them. But we do our best because that's all we can do.' She slapped my back, trying to snap me out of it. 'Now come on. We're celebrating. The kids graduate today.'

We went back to the flat and waited for Scout and Stan to return and when they were home safe and sound and had both been fed, Whitestone and I drove to an Italian restaurant on Frith Street where the party had started hours ago.

Their six months' probation was finally over and a dozen Direct Entry Detectives were knocking back grappa shots, fresh-faced kids who had all had one or two too many, and were being watched over by a few of their smiling bosses, like indulgent parents.

The Direct Entry scheme has a lot of dropouts. So these young men and women had a good reason to celebrate, and they had earned the right to tell their war stories about the mind-numbing bureaucracy of policing, and the venality of the criminal class, and the wary indifference – or open hostility – of the general public, and the quiet demise of anything resembling a normal social life and the life-sucking demands of what they had learned to call – *the job.*

Whitestone ordered Prosecco for the table and the pair of us clinked glasses, proud of Sita and Bear, our two Direct Entry graduates.

We toasted their new careers.

And then the restaurant was closing, the other senior detectives all gone and only me and Pat Whitestone were left with our young graduates, and we were all out on the street, Pat and I standing to one side as the other kids shared their hugs and goodbyes and headed for the last tube.

It was that moment when you have to decide if the night is over or if the night is just getting started.

'You live around here, don't you, Bear?' said Sita.

And so the four of us went back to Bear's place.

Bear had a one-bedroom flat above a dance studio in Covent Garden.

There was a laptop left open on the coffee table.

Bear moved swiftly to snap it shut.

Sita and Whitestone shared a laugh at that.

'What were you looking at on there, Bear?' I said.

'Sorry for the mess,' he said, blushing.

'So this is where you bring the ladies, Bear?' Whitestone said, looking around the small but wonderfully located flat.

'This is where the magic happens!' Sita laughed.

'It's nice and central,' Bear insisted. 'I can walk to work. My father needed some convincing before he would stand as guarantor.'

Sita – who shared a council flat with three other girls out on the borders of the East End–Essex badlands – sighed with envy. 'How the other half lives, eh?' she said.

'You should see the view from the rooftop terrace,' Bear said. 'You can see clear across the river.'

Sita was impressed. 'He's got a rooftop terrace!'

'Only a small rooftop terrace,' he smiled, his handsome face creasing with domestic pride. 'Come on, I'll show you.'

Bear grabbed four cans of Red Stripe from the fridge and we headed up to the roof.

And he was right. The view was spectacular. The city stretched away to the river and beyond, some of the great landmarks of London – the Savoy, the Shard, the London Eye – lit up as if just for us. The city glittered like a box of jewels emptied by some careless god. It had a strangely calming effect on the evening.

We stared at the lights and sipped our Red Stripe.

'Well done,' Whitestone said. 'To both of you. It's not easy to do what you've done – to come from university to the job.' She raised a can. 'So – good luck for the future.'

We touched cans of Red Stripe, drank them in silence and stared at all the lights.

'I should hit the road,' Whitestone said, finishing her drink.

'Me too,' said Sita.

I noticed Bear had slipped his arm around her waist. She looked uncomfortable.

'Nightcap?' he grinned.

'Go on then,' Whitestone said.

'I'll get them,' I said, and I went back down to get more beer.

Bear's fridge was comically geared to the single life.

There was a half-eaten pepperoni pizza, a bottle of champagne for some special night and a large container containing some pond-like pink liquid that had to be a protein shake of some kind, brewed to increase muscle mass and improve recovery. I needed both hands to remove it so I could reach the four-pack of Red Stripe at the back. The lid of the muscle-man shake was not screwed on properly and some pink gunk sloshed all over the floor.

I took out the four-pack of Red Stripe, screwed the top on the protein shake and looked around for something to clean up the mess I had made on the kitchen floor.

I began opening drawers.

Bear was not big on housekeeping.

But I finally found an unopened roll of kitchen towel and when I took it out, that is when I saw it.

A child's stuffed toy.

At first I could not understand what I was looking at.

It looked curiously donkey-like. But it was meant to be a rabbit.

The last time I had seen it was when Suzanne Buksa had clutched it – Mr Flopsy – to her thin chest and told me that she was being harassed by a policeman. I had looked for it, and I had thought I saw it in the mouth of a young fox, and I had still looked for it, and in the end I had given up looking for it, and I had believed that I would never see it again. I had, in truth, almost forgotten the battered stuffed toy that Suzanne Buksa carried with her everywhere.

And here it was.

I took Suzanne's stuffed rabbit out and stared at it.

'Found you,' I said.

I went back to the roof.

Bear was standing between Sita and Whitestone, his back against the railing while they faced him, laughing at something he had said. Bear was smiling, that big easy smile, and the smile seemed to falter for a moment and then recover when he saw what I was holding.

'Now you have to explain this to me,' I said.

'What?' Whitestone said. 'What is it?'

But he knew. He shook his head.

'I found it near the scene,' he said. 'I took it. I don't know why. A souvenir. Stupid of me. It was the night I came to your flat. Remember? I should have turned it in – I know I should have – but it was our first case, and we had worked so hard . . .'

He was turning to Sita for support.

Sita was staring at what I was holding.

Whitestone was stepping away from him.

Bear tried to laugh it off. 'It's just a souvenir, Max!' Bear said. 'It's just a keepsake, *sir*. You don't really think I had anything to do with that girl's murder, do you?'

I gave Whitestone the stuffed toy. She held up a palm, stopping me. She reached into her pocket, took out a pair of thin blue latex gloves, put them on. And then she took it.

I faced him. 'The killer had a warrant card,' I said. 'That's what Suzanne told us from the start. He had harassed her for weeks. Stalked her, bullied her, used her. And killed her. And Pat here thought that it was a fake warrant card. And I thought it was John-Paul Ledoux and his mates. And we were both dead wrong.'

'Look, this is ridiculous—'

I held up my hand for silence. 'What happens now is that you are going to be arrested and you will have a visually recorded interview,' I said. 'And it will not be done by us.'

'But I can explain it *to you*, I want to explain it *to you*. There is no need to get anyone else involved! Look, did you know she was on the game? Suzanne – do you really think that butter wouldn't melt? It's just not true, Max. She was a little slut—'

'Enough,' Whitestone growled, and he was silent.

I had taken out my phone. No Wi-Fi signal. I cursed.

'I am going downstairs to call this in,' I told Whitestone, and she nodded, and when Bear moved forward she placed a restraining hand on his chest, very lightly. It was enough to control him. He glared down at her, unhappy with the way this was going.

I paused. 'You two all right with him?' I said.

'Go,' Whitestone said, her eyes never leaving Bear.

'You are under arrest,' Sita said. 'You do not have to say anything . . .'

I bolted down to the flat.

Still no signal.

I looked around for a landline but of course there was none. And as I went down to the street, I thought of the prostitute Bear had accidentally hired, and his casual contempt for Summer that Whitestone had slapped him down for from the start, and the laptop that he had so quickly closed when we bowled in tonight.

And I thought of Suzanne Buksa. And the policeman who had showed her his warrant card, and told her to get into his car.

I arrived down on the street.

Crowds of revellers and tourists, coming out of the bars and theatres and restaurants, and finally a full signal on my phone. I phoned Metcall for immediate assistance and the First Contact operator gave me an ETA of five minutes, but by the time I rung off I could already hear our sirens.

And that was when I heard the first scream.

Detective Constable Bear Groves died falling the four storeys from the rooftop terrace of his flat to a street in Covent Garden so crowded with pleasure seekers that it was a miracle he was the only person to die.

And I talked to them, to DCI Whitestone and DC Basu, when they were still up on the rooftop terrace, Pat kneeling by the side of Sita as she sat on the ground, clearly in a great deal of pain, clutching what turned out to be a shattered collarbone.

They both insisted that Bear had tried to make a run for it, and they had fought him, and he had beaten them off and then attempted to escape across the neighbouring rooftop, when he slipped and fell.

It was possible, I thought that night, and I still think so today. It may even have been what actually happened.

It is certainly what DCI Whitestone and DC Basu told the coroner at the inquest, and the investigation by the Directorate for Professional Standards, and the press, the bloggers, and all the true crime podcasters.

And that's what they told me.

'The bastard fell, Max. End of story.'

But only the women really knew.

52

DC Sita Basu was sitting up in the ICU of the Chelsea and Westminster Hospital, her right arm in a sling, blue hospital smock, smiling shyly at the young people who surrounded her bed.

The mood was jolly.

I knew a few of their faces from that Italian restaurant in Soho. They were other Direct Entry Detectives from the same batch as Sita – and Bear. They looked at me as I knocked on the open door, their laughter and chatter subsiding in the presence of a senior officer. I wasn't one of them. They soon made their excuses and left me alone with Sita, promising to return soon.

She grinned at me, woozy from her medication.

'How's it going, Sita?'

She looked at her hands. 'They are cold all the time. Feel.'

She held out her hands to me and I took them in mine. They did feel unnaturally cold. And I knew this was not good news with a shattered collarbone.

'The doctors say it happens when you get broken bone in blood vessels,' she said. 'They're checking it out.'

I was still holding her cold hands.

'You'll be fine,' I said. 'You're young and you're strong. Give it time and physiotherapy.'

She nodded, withdrawing her hands.

I took a seat by the side of her bed as she leaned back on the pillow, sighing with the pain. I looked out of the window. From the ICU, you could see clear across West London from up here.

'There's something I want to tell you,' she whispered.

I thought she was back on the roof, up there with White-stone and Bear, and then the struggle, and then Bear was gone, and then there was only Whitestone and her.

'Sita, you don't have to tell me anything.'

'It's not about Bear.'

'OK.'

'But I want to tell you this one thing.'

'Go ahead.'

'I don't know if this is for me,' she whispered. '*The job.* I don't know if the job is for me. Not because of Bear. Not because of what happened on the roof. But I have been thinking about it for a while. A lot of the Direct Entry Detectives drop out before the two-year probation is up. Most of them, maybe.'

'I know they do. But you stuck it out. And you've done so well.'

'But before I came to the Murder Investigation Team, I was on a lot of domestics. They put most of the Direct Entry lot on domestics.'

'I know. Because nobody wants to work domestics.'

'And this man – this young man who lived next door to the woman who was abused by her partner – he spat on me.'

'He spat on you?'

'Because I'm police. Just for being police. And it made me think then – and I think still – that this is not for me.'

'I get it,' I said. 'But I think you're wrong. I think you were made for this job. I think you're tough, and I think you're smart, and I think you're kind, and I know you are exactly what we need right now. Listen to me, Sita – we got Bear Groves because of you.'

'That's not true, Max.'

'But it is, Sita. He wanted you to stay for a nightcap. He wanted you to stay for the night. And that's why I was rattling around his kitchen. That's why I found the proof he killed Suzanne. And John-Paul Ledoux and his mates are going to be sent away for the next twenty years. They were a grooming gang, Sita, the Met's very own grooming gang, and we cracked them because you put yourself in harm's way.'

She leaned back on her pillow, closing her eyes.

'And I'll tell you something about the creep who spat on you, Sita.'

I looked out of the window, across all those streets and all those lives, and I heard her breathing heavy with the medication and the pain.

'When someone's kicking his front door down in the middle of the night, that creep will call you – or someone just like you. And if someone robs him in the street, or

beats him up, or pulls a knife, then he will come running
to you, begging for help. And if ever he needs someone
to stand in front of everything and everyone he loves, he
will expect you to do it.'

I thought of my friend Jackson Rose. The inquiry
into the death of Robert McKay had concluded he had
been lawfully killed because he posed a lethal threat to
life. Jackson had returned to active duty but I knew he
would think about Robert McKay for the rest of his
days, and I knew he would continue to wonder if he
should find another job before this one tore his young
family apart.

'The job can wear you out,' I said. 'I can't deny it. But
you are the best of us, Sita – you and Jackson Rose. *The
best of us.* You guard people who you will never know
while they sleep. You put your life on the line every time
you go to work. You are good, and you are brave, and
every day you stand between the innocent, and the decent,
and all the rotten stuff that's out there. And that will
always be true, Sita.'

But by now DC Sita Basu was sleeping.

The ICU at the Chelsea and Westminster is on the top
floor and I started down the stairs to the street, the ground
floor far below as busy as a railway station, and I watched
as Summer came through the main door.

She paused, removing her dark glasses, studying the
hospital guide. Then she entered a lift.

A man and woman were arriving at the ICU. Middle-aged, Asian, bearing flowers and fruit, and frantic with worry about their daughter.

Sita's parents.

I watched them disappear into the I C U.

Two floors below, Summer came out of the lift.

A porter was passing.

'Excuse me,' I said. 'What's down on the second floor?'

'Cancer's on the second floor,' he said.

Emma Moon was in a room on the second floor.

Roxy was sitting on her bed. Summer was in a chair, her eyes red from crying, but everything apparently forgiven.

Emma was paler than I had ever seen her. Thinner than I remembered.

And she was amused to see me.

'I told you I was ill,' she smiled.

I stood by her bed.

'Did you change your mind about treatment?'

She laughed. 'I'm stage 4, Max. The stage 4 kind. The end-of-the-road kind. N S C L C – non-small cell lung cancer. It's far too late to change my mind about any-thing! They make me comfortable in here. That's no small thing.'

'There's nobody sitting outside your room,' I said.

I meant a warden or a policeman.

'Because I'm a free woman! Your boss – that D C I Whitestone – and the governor of H M P Bronzefield – they sorted it out between them. Turns out that I didn't offend under licence after all. That was all a dreadful misunderstanding – wasn't it?'

I nodded. 'I'm sorry,' I said. 'It wasn't you. It was never you. And I'm sorry for ever believing that it was you.'

I saw Roxy and Summer exchange a scowling look but Emma Moon seemed almost carefree, liberated from all the petty grudges of the past in this room on the second floor of the Chelsea and Westminster.

'It was the men,' I said. 'It was always between the men. Between Nevermore and Terry Gatti.'

'The big men,' she said. 'I didn't even know there was a photograph in that safe. Nobody ever told me anything.'

'The Gattis had been blackmailing Nevermore for years. But – like every blackmailer in history – they didn't know when to quit. And Nevermore wanted Terry to stop asking for money. It was as banal as that. That's why they all died. Butch Lewis. Ian Doherty. Keith Jones. Mick Gatti. And Terry. Nevermore was trying to show them he was serious. But in the end Terry couldn't give him the Polaroid he wanted. Because it did not even exist anymore.'

'Were you there? At the end? With Terry?'

I nodded.

'How did it happen?'

'Luka drowned him in his jacuzzi.'

Silence in the room as Emma took that in.

'It's how he would have wanted to go,' she said, and it got a laugh from Summer and Roxy, but I sensed the surge of real grief in Emma Moon, some distant echo from the ruins of the love of her life. Some secret part of her had never stopped loving the man she did sixteen years inside for, and I felt it again – that totally inappropriate blast of jealousy.

'Nevermore was hiding behind you,' I said. 'He was always hiding behind you. He just wanted what they found in that safe. A photograph of him that didn't even exist. A Polaroid that had faded to nothing. And he needed them to stop asking him for money.'

'None of it matters much anymore,' she said, visibly fading even as I watched. The news of Terry's death, I thought. The finality of bereavement.

'But I think you are wrong, Max. I think Nevermore cared about me once. This young woman – not unattractive, in my day – who did sixteen years because she would not rat on the man she loved. I think he admired that. And I think he cared about the self-harming, human waste in our prisons. Locking up people who maybe could do with a helping hand. He cared about it all. It's just he cared a bit more about his father cutting him off because of some photograph of some party where he had one too many.'

'One to many of what?' Summer asked, and Roxy grinned and they sniggered in perfect harmony once more. But Summer's face twitched with the nervous tic of the addict.

And I looked at Emma Moon's long, fair, ailing form

and I thought – *you were what you appeared to be.* You were good, and you were kind, and I never believed it. But it was far too late to say any of that.

She tried to make it easier for me.

'Thank you for coming,' she said. 'I appreciate it. Because I doubt if we will see each other again.'

I felt a surge of helpless despair. 'Is there really no hope?'

I didn't even know what I meant.

For you, for me, for us.

'They're still saying that chemotherapy and radio-therapy and the immunotherapy drugs are an option. Pemetrexed, cisplatin and docetaxel. But I think I am going to give it all a miss. Because I think it's the right thing to do. I know it would be different if my son was still alive. Then I would cling to life, even when life wasn't worth clinging to any more. But without David – well, you understand. You're a parent yourself.'

I should have let her go on the night we met in the big house and then I should have gone after the guilty, I thought now, but did not have the words to say. I should have believed that the cruelty she had seen in her life had made her believe in kindness above all else.

And I should have taken her in my arms on the night we shared a bed.

But I had done none of these things, and now the chance to do any of them was gone forever.

Summer and Roxy, the fallen supermodel and the feral waif, watched her like anxious children hovering over a feverish parent, and I wondered what their lives would be like without Emma Moon.

She softly exhaled, closed her eyes and sank back into the pillow, as if this was the end. 'Enough,' she said, suddenly very tired. 'It's time to go home to your daughter now.'

And that is what I did.

53

Old dogs rise late, as if to conserve their energy for the days that remain.

And so it was that the sun was already up and shining like the first day of summer when Scout and Stan and I crossed that wide open field on Hampstead Heath that runs down to the ponds where the wild swimmers splash.

Small white butterflies hovered above the wild flowers. Hunting them had been the great summer joy of Stan's earlier years but today he just stared at them, as if trying to remember why he had ever wanted them.

Our dog was old now, and not simply getting old, and perhaps that was one reason why Scout had once again begun to join Stan and me on our weekend walks.

We did not talk about it, the way that the time was running out, but I think both of us had realised that we understood all the important things we needed to understand without ever talking about them.

Scout watched Stan staring at the white butterflies and I watched them both, remembering the first trip that the three of us had ever made to the vet's surgery, to get puppy Stan the vaccinations that he needed as his visa out into the world.

There had been a man, and his daughter, and their dog in front of us at the vet's.

The man, the daughter and the dog were all ten years older than us – a dog's lifetime, more or less – and the man had carried their elderly pet into the vet's surgery, and his teenage daughter had followed him, and when they came out maybe twenty minutes later, they no longer had the dog with them, only his lead and his collar, and they were both in the muffled tears of newly minted grief. I had thought about that man and his daughter and their dog over the years – that family who were ending their journey with their dog just as we were starting out on our journey. And I had talked about them with Scout.

'*Do you remember that first trip to the vet . . . ?*'

Because of course the sight of them – and their death in the family – had felt like a prophesy. We steel ourselves for the blows that have yet to fall. How do you think it ends? Grief is the price we pay for love.

Scout's laughter was a reminder that we were not there yet.

Stan had snapped out of his butterfly reverie and had ambled off in his bandy-legged gait, heading down to the ponds where the ducks held a constant fascination for him, and the swans were to be avoided at all costs. Scout went after him, the pair heading down to the ponds where the wild swimmers were bobbing, and I followed.

'*Do you remember . . . ?*'

Scout had been so young on that evening when we took Stan to the vet for the first time, when we watched that family broken by the death of their old dog, but she had not been quite young enough to believe in the promise of the Rainbow Bridge – the mythical place on the other side of this life where old dogs wait until they are one day reunited with their owners. Dog heaven, essentially.

It was a lovely idea, but even when she was still agnostic about Father Christmas, Scout struggled to believe in the Rainbow Bridge and so did I, that place where 'your hands again caress the beloved head'.

Although – here's the funny thing – as I got older I came to believe that the reassuring, consoling promise of being reunited at the Rainbow Bridge was no more improbable than the beliefs of every major religion that mankind has ever believed in.

'*Do you remember . . . ?*'

Rainbow Bridge, I thought, as Scout and Stan halted at the ponds, the water turned to molten gold by the dazzling sunshine – why not? And if not exactly the Rainbow Bridge, then something – anything – just like it. I wanted to believe.

Because you can't own a dog, and watch their heartbreakingly brief life unfurl, without understanding – really understanding, deep down in your blood and your bones – that everything ends. And you can't watch your child grow up without knowing exactly the same hard truth.

The years to come will fly – for all of us – faster and faster and faster.

I know they will – and Stan will be gone and one day I will be gone too.

It's true, Scout.

Here is the eternal parental heartache, and the one thing you never get over.

I want to be there for you forever, and I know that I will not be there for you forever.

But if there is anything at all on the other side – if there is something that resembles the Rainbow Bridge that my daughter and I both tried so hard to believe in – then that is where I will be waiting for you, Scout, and I hope I will have to wait for a hundred years.

I can sense the time accelerating already, and our time together running out.

And, my darling daughter, I am less certain about everything in this wide world as I get older, and that's why I now hold out the crazy hope that there is some kind of Rainbow Bridge beyond this life.

That place where we meet again, and love remains, and will never die.

And if it exists – long shot! – then that is where you will find me waiting.

Then watch me run to you.